THE PROMISE BOX

This Large Print Book carries the
Seal of Approval of N.A.V.H.

THE PROMISE BOX

TRICIA GOYER

THORNDIKE PRESS
A part of Gale, Cengage Learning

Detroit • New York • San Francisco • New Haven, Conn • Waterville, Maine • London

GALE
CENGAGE Learning®

LIBRARY OF CONGRESS CATALOGING-IN-PUBLICATION DATA

Goyer, Tricia.
  The promise box / by Tricia Goyer. — Large print edition.
    pages ; cm. — (Thorndike Press large print Christian romance) (Seven brides for seven bachelors series ; #2)
  ISBN-13: 978-1-4104-6075-2 (hardcover)
  ISBN-10: 1-4104-6075-4 (hardcover)
  1. Amish—Fiction. 2. Montana—Fiction. 3. Large type books. I. Title.
PS3607.O94P76 2013b
813'.6—dc23   2013020390

Published in 2013 by arrangement with The Zondervan Corporation LLC

Dedicated to Linda Martin
Your handwritten notes through the years
have been a special treasure! Thank you
for your love and encouragement, Mom.

In returning and rest shall ye be saved; in quietness and in confidence [trust] shall be your strength.

~ISAIAH 30:15

GLOSSARY

ach — an exclamation
appeditlich — delicious
bensel — silly child
blappermaul — blabber mouth
brieder — brothers
bruder — brother
brutzing — pouting
boppli — baby
danki — thank you
dat — dad
dawdi house — grandparents' house
demut — humility
guder mariye — good morning
gut — good
in lieb — in love
ja — yes
kapp — head covering
kinder — child
kinner — children
maut — hired girl
mem — mom

ne — no

oma — grandma

opa — grandpa

Ordnung — unwritten set of rules and regulations that guide everyday Amish life. Meaning "order" or "discipline"

Rumspringa — running around. A time when Amish youth are encouraged to experiment and explore.

wonnernaus — a polite way of saying "none of your business"

wunderbaar — wonderful

CHAPTER 1

Lydia Wyse shook rain from her red curls, wishing she could as easily shake memories of the last time she'd seen Mem's lowered *kapp* and bowed head, praying for her daughter's return. Return not only to West Kootenai, Montana, but to the Amish. Lydia was returning all right, but not in the way Mem had wished. Tomorrow was Mem's funeral, and during the nine hours of driving — from Seattle to Montana — each minute had brought her closer to home. To heartache.

Lydia had stopped for gas in Eureka, about an hour from her parents' house, and rain now drenched her long curls. Soaked, standing in line to pay, she spotted a few Amish women climbing from a white van and hurrying into the grocery store attached to the gas station. Seeing them, a twinge of familiarity — of longing — filled her heart, but she stuffed the emotions down.

"Are those Amish from West Kootenai?" she asked the gas station attendant who took her cash.

He shrugged. "Don't know. Just Amish. Not really sure where they're from."

"Just Amish."

She walked out of the gas station and got back on the road, thinking about the phrase. All her life she'd wanted to be anything but "just Amish." Even when she wore the same type of dress, the same type of *kapp* as the other girls, she'd felt different. When she was sixteen, she'd discovered why.

The rain stopped its patter on the windshield. Lydia cracked the window, letting the cool, pine-scented breeze filter in, spreading a spray of curls across her cheek. She pressed harder against the gas pedal, wishing she could leave the memories behind. But she could never outrun the dark clouds of her past, no matter how hard she tried.

Picking up speed, her yellow Volkswagen Beetle snaked along the narrow country road. As she grew closer to West Kootenai, tall mountain peaks pierced the thinning clouds, rays of sunlight splitting the firmament.

Her mother's death hadn't come as a surprise. What *had* surprised her was the faint excitement at seeing those women in their *kapp*s and Plain dress. How could being raised Amish seem so familiar, yet foreign? Painful.

She'd never be "just Amish." Mem, her adoptive mother, had finally disclosed that when she'd turned sixteen. Lydia should never have been born. How horrible that her birth-mother had been traumatized twice — first by her conception and second from her birth. Since knowing the truth, Lydia had been running, searching for who she was apart from the Amish community. After all, her birth father was anything but Amish.

Running until now. Her mother's funeral had forced her to return. Return to her parents' home. Return to the quiet Amish community where her parents had found healing after Lydia walked away from their lifestyle and beliefs.

Alongside the road, black-and-white cows dotted a field, bright green from summer sun and rain. A few lifted their heads when she passed, as if surprised by the sight of her red hair through the window.

Rain always gave her a fuzzy silhouette. With one hand Lydia held a death grip on the steering wheel and with the other she pushed the mass of curls back from her face for the hundredth time that day, wishing she'd had enough foresight to grab a hair band. That had been the only good thing about wearing a *kapp* during her growing-up years. She could pin her hair up with a dozen pins, tuck it under the starched white head covering, and forget about it.

A *kapp.* One thing that wasn't so bad about being Amish. That and the fact she'd had plenty of time to daydream stories as she mucked stalls, hung clothes on the line, and stitched perfect designs on dishcloths.

If only life was so simple. She'd told herself she wouldn't look back — and she rarely did. But now she had no choice. Like a hook caught into her heart, the truth of who she was, how she'd been raised, reeled her in.

Truth. She could only run from it for so long.

Gideon Hooley approached the gelding with easy steps. The horse didn't cast one look, but from his perked ears Blue knew he was not alone in the pasture. The horse's brown coat shimmered in the sunlight, muscles rippling as he took one step forward. Tense. At any moment he could turn, chase Gideon down, and trample him. Gideon had seen it before. But something deep down in his gut

14

told him Blue was different, no matter what others said.

"Untamable" was how Dave Carash described him. The *Englisch* man blamed it on the fact he'd had to pull the foal after the mother died in labor. "Poor thing was without oxygen and as blue as the Montana sky," Dave had said, and the name had stuck. The problem was the *Englisch* man worked hard to provide for his family and hadn't given enough time to the temperamental creature.

Gideon had seen it before. Horse owners often had better intentions than time and skill, and sometimes Gideon felt that instead of helping people with horse problems he was actually helping horses with people problems.

He took another step forward. "Beautiful day, isn't it, Blue?" He walked a wide circle to approach Blue straight on. Many horses were nearsighted. Things far off scared them. They needed to see them up close to trust them. But letting anyone come close was hard. Gideon understood.

The horse tossed his head.

Gideon removed his brimmed hat and turned it over in his hands, letting the sun warm the top of his head. Mr. Carash had hired him to train Blue, but today was an introduction of sorts. Gideon hadn't come with a rope or bridle. He'd come with a soft voice and an even softer hand.

"I heard some guys tried to chase you down." Gideon chuckled. "Would have liked to see that." He smiled, eyeing the bay with its long neck; fine, clean throatlatch; and deep, sloping shoulders. The gelding watched him, curious.

Intelligent eyes. With the right training he'll be a fine horse.

"Must be hard when you feel threatened." Gideon's throat tightened even as he said those words, and he glanced to his right and looked at the distant hills. "When yer scared fer your life, I understand. There were things I went through as a kid that scared me too."

His gut cinched, and his mother's words came back to him. *"Out of all the places to visit . . . why'd ja want to return to Montana? It's a* schrecklich *place."*

"Scary for a little boy, ja, *but I'm a grown man now,"* he had told her.

"Still . . . do you not mind what happened?"

"Getting lost, being scared, ja. *How could I forget?"* Even as an adult he still dreamed about that night in the woods alone. And his parents had never let him forget it was his disobedience that had gotten him into

so much trouble.

"That's not the only matter." Mem's voice had lowered, and she'd settled into the kitchen chair, preparing to launch into a story.

His dat strode in with quickened steps, startling them both. *"Leave it no mind, Lovina. It wonders me why you need to bring it up."*

"Gideon needs to know the truth at some time," she mumbled under her breath.

"Not that *truth."* The words fell from Dat's lips like horseshoes from a hook. Flat. Hard.

From the look in Dat's eyes that day, Gideon had known he wouldn't get his father to speak a word of it. Mem either. Fine. He didn't need to hear their story. Something had happened in West Kootenai, Montana — more than just getting lost on the mountain when he was four. No one spoke of it, but the hidden truth had haunted his growing-up years.

Gideon glanced at the skittish horse again. Sympathy caused his heart to ache. This horse was afraid of a heavy hand. Gideon, on the other hand, feared the truth would rope him up and cause him harm — not to his body but to his heart.

He continued forward until he stood by the gelding's side. The wild grasses blew in

17

the breeze, feathering against his ankles. With a slow, steady movement he reached up and stroked the horse's neck. "There you go, boy. Nothing's gonna hurt you. You're a strong boy. Smart too."

This morning he'd gone to the West Kootenai Kraft and Grocery and had a large stack of pancakes, chatting it up with some of the other Amish bachelors. But he'd wanted to be here instead, with this horse. Even as a kid he found safety and companionship with horses more than people. Mem said that would change when he met the right woman. He'd believe that when he saw it.

Gideon had come back to Montana with his cousin Caleb to hunt. They'd arrived two months ago in April to be eligible for a resident hunting license in November. When hunting season rolled around and he headed up into the hills for sport, adventure, and provision, he could forget the past. But until the cold winds blew in and the season of hunting started, Gideon sought truth.

Do I really want to know?

CHAPTER 2

It had been a long drive from Seattle. The dreary weather had matched Lydia's dour thoughts. Everyone, she supposed, ached when they lost their mother. Maybe her ache was greater knowing Mem had felt a death at Lydia's leaving. Yes, they'd seen each other almost once a year, but it was hard connecting with a woman so opposite her. Or maybe, like her boss, Bonnie, had said, Lydia had focused on their differences so she wouldn't feel so guilty about leaving.

There were many times Lydia had wished she'd kept her mouth shut about her Amish parents and where she'd come from, but Bonnie was one of those curious types who sought people's stories like a schoolboy sought change under a couch cushion when he heard the ice cream truck. And as she'd handed Bonnie the keys to her studio apartment so Bonnie could water her five houseplants while she was gone, Lydia hadn't missed her boss's slightly cocked eyebrow and narrow gaze. The look said, "A story's going to come out of this."

Could Bonnie be right? The Amish community she journeyed toward consisted of twenty families who lived among the *Englisch* in a small mountain community only a few miles from the Canadian border. With only one store and not even a post office, going there was like voyaging back thirty years to a place where neighbors counted on each other, loggers felled tall trees by hand, and children caught fish in mountain streams with long sticks and twine.

And then there were the bachelors.

She'd been back only one other time during late spring, and the small community had been buzzing with the presence of almost thirty Amish bachelors. As her mother had explained, a group of young men arrived every spring to live and work for six months to obtain their residence license so they could legally hunt in the fall. Six months to scope the mountains for game. Six months to live in the crosshairs of young women who hoped a bachelor would return home with not only an eight-point buck, but her as a bride.

The country music station Lydia had picked up played a mournful love song, and she reached over and flipped off the noise. Foolishness. All of it.

The road straightened for a spell, and Lydia glanced at the pile of spiral-bound manuscripts sitting on the passenger's seat. She edited nonfiction books and the occasional romance novel — not that Lydia knew a thing about that in real life. Bonnie called her old-fashioned. Bonnie meant her work style, but Lydia knew it was more than that. She had a television and a microwave and drove a car, but one thing Lydia hadn't gotten used to was working on a computer. When giving her an editing project, Bonnie was gracious enough to print and bind the manuscripts. And after Lydia was done, Bonnie hired someone to enter all her work into the computer.

"For anyone else, Lydia, I wouldn't do it. But you're good. Really good. You see words differently than others. You gather them like wildflowers and arrange them like a bouquet on the page."

It was a kind compliment, but it didn't satisfy. Lydia enjoyed editing, but what she really wanted to do was write a book. She wrote little things for their company newsletter, but she waited for "the" book idea like a rooster watched for the first light of dawn. It hadn't come, but it was out there . . . right over the horizon. And maybe returning to West Kootenai would spur an idea. After all, how many other book editors traveled to the mountains of Montana to bury their Amish mother?

Mother. The word had caused more confusion than peace over the years. Ada Mae Wyse was the mother who'd taught her Scriptures on her knee, but the woman who birthed her haunted Lydia's thoughts. Lydia's conception — a secret she hadn't told a soul since first hearing Ada Mae's explanation of her birth — would make a tragic story, all right, but not one she'd write about. Not now. Not ever.

The bridge over Lake Koocanusa glistened in the misty rain. Her vehicle was the only one crossing the wide expanse, and she glanced for the briefest second at the shimmering blue water below. When her parents had first moved to the area there'd been an accident on the lake, and an Amish woman had drowned. A shiver ran up Lydia's spine thinking about it. She bit her lip, tightened her hands around the steering wheel, and focused her eyes to the road as a hollow ache filled her stomach. It pressed against her organs and lungs, making it hard to breathe. Tragedy struck the *Englisch* and Amish alike. She should know that. Her life wouldn't be here if it weren't for tragedy.

Make that *tragedies.*

She squared her shoulders and prepared for the jarring where the smooth pavement of the bridge ended and the road turned to dirt and gravel. None of the roads from here on out were paved.

She climbed the mountain at a steady rise for the next fifteen minutes. Finally the road flattened out.

Almost there.

After another few minutes of driving, homes began to dot the roadway. It was easy to tell which were Amish. They were simply built, and all had white curtains in the windows; anything with color or pattern would be deemed too proud in their eyes.

A small log schoolhouse sat in the distance. A warmth filled her chest as she thought about her favorite teacher in Ohio, Miss Yoder. She'd only taught for three years before getting married and starting a family. But Lydia's memories included field trips to the cheese factories in Sugarcreek, softball games with neighbor schools near the end of the school year, and sleepovers with the other girls at Miss Yoder's house. They talked about places Miss Yoder had traveled, visiting family. It had been the first time Lydia considered life beyond her small community.

Lydia's cell phone rang, causing her to jump. She hadn't had cell service for most of the last few hours — it had been spotty after leaving Kalispell.

As a habit, Lydia pulled to the side of the road before answering.

"Hello?"

"Lydia, it's Bonnie."

Lydia smiled. Her boss said the same thing every time she called. She'd worked with Bonnie for the last two years. She knew her number, her voice.

Lydia put her car into Park and turned it off. "Hey, Bonnie, did the Murphy project get to the printers?"

"Yes, just an hour ago. I thought you'd want to know."

Lydia tapped her fingers on the steering wheel. In her peripheral vision a horse galloped in the fenced pasture. That wasn't something one saw every day in Seattle.

"I'm excited." Lydia pulled her attention back to the phone call. "It's a great story. I couldn't imagine trying to home educate three sets of twins."

"Didn't you go to a school like that?" Bonnie asked.

"Like what?"

"A small Amish school with just a few kids."

"We had twenty scholars, and it seemed a lot to me, especially being an only child."

"An only child in an Amish home. Seems like an interesting book, don't you think?"

Lydia sighed, grabbed her camera from the front seat, and stepped out of the car. There was a large pothole filled with water right outside the driver's door. She hopped over it and then juggled everything as she removed and placed her lens cap on the hood, turning around to where the sun bathed the high mountain peaks with golden light.

To write about her family would bring up her adoption, and then someone might become curious about her birth. No, that couldn't happen.

Lydia tucked her cell phone between her shoulder and jaw and focused the camera on the mountains, snapping a shot. "Nothing about my life is typical Amish."

"Except for the fact you like to cook, which seems completely Amish to me."

"Yes, there's that."

"Which is why I'm calling. I think you should write a book about being Amish."

"Um, except for the fact that I left the community, remember?" Lydia's eyes swept the field. They fixed on a structure at the far end of the pasture. She gasped. Then, with a sad smile, she lifted her camera and pointed it toward the simple Amish homestead, snapping a shot. She'd never realized that her parents' home could be seen from the main road.

"I'm serious, Lydia. Amish books are selling like crazy. I've had three distributors ask me if we had any Amish in our lineup."

"You didn't tell them we did . . . *did you*?"

Bonnie offered a nervous chuckle. "I said there was something we were considering. How hard would it be to just become Amish again and write about it? You grew up that way."

Lydia moaned. "You don't know what you're asking — what that would entail."

"Yes, but it's a part of you. Your heritage, your cooking. The way you only pay with cash. Gee, just look at your apartment. I'm certain I could go in there with one small box and pack up all your personal items and your five houseplants and rent it to a college student who'd feel quite at home in its dormlike setting."

"Bonnie —"

"Which I totally could do if you decided to stay longer —"

"Listen, I'm not going to 'just become

Amish again' to get a book contract. It's not just a lifestyle; there's spiritual meaning too." Lydia shrugged, watching the movement of her shadow. "And even if I wanted to go back, I'm not even sure God would take me."

Lydia expected a lecture. Instead Bonnie released a low sigh.

"Well, then talk to Him about it, won't you? I never guarantee anything until it's in writing, but by the eagerness of our distributors I'm as close to making a guarantee as I can be."

"I'll think about it . . . but don't get your hopes up." Yet even as she said the words, Lydia's heart galloped, just like the horse in the field. She glanced through the windshield at the manuscripts in the passenger's seat and imagined a cover with her name on it. She pictured choosing a random city, flying there, and walking into a bookstore to find her book — *her book* — on the shelf. Mem had told her that her life was a gift, that God didn't make mistakes. Lydia bit her lip, warmth filling her chest. Maybe following her dream and listening to Bonnie's advice would prove Mem to be right.

"I don't know what happened to you — what made you run. I'm not sure I'll ever know. But any given moment you have the chance to redeem your story, Lydia. There's something God's going to do with you in Montana. I can feel it."

Lydia sighed. She'd gotten used to Bonnie talking about God. While Lydia believed in Him, she had a hard time believing God was concerned about her life, her problems.

A small group of sparrows fluttered through the pasture's grass. Out of nowhere a thought — a Scripture verse she'd learned in school — filtered through her mind: *"Are not two sparrows sold for a farthing? and one of them shall not fall on the ground without your Father."*

She was about to tell Bonnie to drop the idea when a stirring fluttered in her heart as soft and light as her curls bouncing on the breeze.

Do I care for you?

I care for the sparrows, don't I?

The words weren't audible, but they pierced Lydia's heart.

She looked around at the pasture, the trees, and the small Amish homestead in the distance. The warmth expanding in her chest was her first draw to "home" since leaving. *Finding Home.* It was the first twinge that a book — a real book — resonated inside her.

Lowering the camera with her right hand,

Lydia took the phone from the crook of her neck with her left and pressed it more tightly to her ear. Her fingers trembled. The breeze picked up, carrying the scent of wild roses on its tail feathers.

"Maybe I will write down what returning home means to me, but don't count on me seeking publication. There are just too —" She blew out a breath. "There are some things I can write only for myself."

A car sped up the road, then jerked to the side and parked unexpectedly. Blue reared up. Gideon jumped back and raised his arms up as protection from Blue's hooves in case the horse turned. He didn't. Instead Blue took off across the field, galloping at full stride.

Gideon grabbed his hat and tossed it to the ground. "*Lecherich!* Ridiculous!" He eyed the yellow car, knowing it had to be a tourist. Sure enough, a ball of red hair with a heart-shaped face and slim figure climbed out of the car. He watched as with one smooth motion she took out her camera and snapped photos, first of the mountains and then of one of the Amish homesteads.

Tourist.

No one in the area drove as such. No one would intrude by taking photos of a place without asking. Angry tension tightened his shoulders. First, that he'd have to start over with Blue, warming the horse up to him again. Second, that he'd have to educate another *Englisch* woman about what respect meant. What privacy meant.

Growing up in Bird-in-Hand, Pennsylvania, he'd seen tour buses of folks armed with cameras. He'd been followed by cars, with passengers taking photos. His buggy had been hit before because a driver veered too close to get a good shot.

Gideon took two steps forward and swooped up his hat from the ground, brushing it off. Good thing he was around to talk to the woman — young children walked these roads during the long summer days. He'd hate to see anything happen because she was trying to get a good photo of "primitive" people to take back and show her friends.

Gideon shook his head as he strode her direction. Frustration dammed up in his throat, and his heartbeat quickened. Some folks didn't have a lick of sense.

Lydia looked through the viewfinder of her camera. Her throat grew raw. Laundry fluttered on the clothesline behind her parents' place, evidence of her mother's work. She guessed it had been hanging a couple of days. Dat most likely hadn't even noticed it in his grief.

She turned away. Bonnie was relating a story about her mother's funeral. How come people always did that? As soon as you lost someone, friends were compelled to describe their own family member's passing. It didn't help, except to make Lydia realize even more that no one walked this earth without loss, without pain.

"Ma'am." A male voice.

Lydia jumped. She spun around and watched the man who strode toward her. Dark hair peeked out from under a brimmed hat, along with the deepest brown eyes she'd ever seen.

The lump in her throat grew larger as the wind rustled his dark hair. A hero walking toward her in long strides. Had she wandered onto a movie set?

She shook her head. She was grieving, not blind.

"Listen, Bonnie, I'll call you right back." Without waiting for a response, she hung up her cell phone and stepped forward, blowing out a breath. A red curl brushed against her cheek, and she ran her fingers through her hair, trying to tame it.

The man hopped the fence and stood

before her. Lydia tilted her head and offered a smile, willing her beating heart to calm. He was handsome, yes, but most likely taken. All great guys were. Besides, she hadn't come to West Kootenai for romance.

"Ma'am. You should put that camera away." His voice was firm.

Her smile fell. "Excuse me?"

"I saw you taking photographs of that Amish home over there, and I think you should put your camera away."

Her mouth dropped open.

He took another step forward, eyes fixed on hers.

"Sir, I don't know who you think you are . . ." She took a step back and gritted her teeth. "Maybe you should introduce yourself, and maybe you should have asked me about who I am. Perhaps I have every right to take a photograph of that Amish home. Did you ever consider that?"

She took another step backward toward the driver's side door.

He stilled, his narrowed gaze widening. "Ma'am . . . wait." His voice softened and he stretched a hand toward her.

She'd heard about men like this. Switching from dominance to passivity as a way to get one's guard down. Was this really about the camera, or something else? She glanced to her right, then her left. Not another soul in sight. No one to hear her scream . . .

Her lips tightened and she raised a flattened palm toward him. "You're right. I'm sorry. I'll be on my way." She took another step back.

"Ma'am —" He lunged toward her. "— you're gonna —"

Her foot sank into the forgotten puddle. As her ankle twisted, Lydia's body fell sideways, no longer under her control. She released the camera as she reached back to catch herself. The bite of gravel dug into her hand, stinging, but it slowed her fall as she tumbled sideways almost as if in slow motion. Her arm, side, and hip sank into the gravel of the road. A splash, and cold water from the puddle chilled her foot and lower leg.

The man was instantly beside her, kneeling. His mouth downturned, he placed a hand on the top of his head. "Ma'am, are you okay?"

He reached for her ankle, unhindered by the water and mud. His touch was warm. She jerked her foot away.

"I was going to say 'Other than my bruised pride' I'm fine, but it's awfully cliché." She straightened. "But I suppose that's where clichés come from — they're used because they work."

The rumble of a chuckle started deep in his throat. "Then I suppose I shouldn't tell you to 'look on the bright side.' "

" 'The bright side' meaning all I have is a wet foot and damp clothes? And you think that's funny?"

He grinned.

Lydia wiped the splattering of mud from the bridge of her nose and eyelid and shot him a glare.

"Is this how your mother taught you to treat a lady?"

"Mem taught me many things, and respecting all God's people is one thing fer sure." Another chuckle bubbled up. "But I'm certain if she was standing here, even my mem would have a hard time not laughing. Or should I say, she'd 'back me up.' "

"Funny or not, you should be ashamed of yourself for just standing there — worse than tossing around overworked and uninspiring clichés and not helping me up."

"*Ja,* of course." He reached a hand to her, his grip warm, strong. With a soft tug he pulled her gently to her feet, allowing Lydia to catch her balance so she wouldn't have to scramble or fall into him, thus protecting her insult from further injury.

As soon as she was able, she pulled her hand away. Surely the fluttering of her heart was due to the fall. The last thing she needed was to be attracted to a Montana mountain man. "You should have just said there was a puddle." She narrowed her gaze and raised her voice. "You should have known better."

He dropped her hand like it was a poisonous snake, and when she focused on his eyes the humor was gone. They'd darkened under lowered lashes. Sadness? Shame?

The man stepped back. He held her camera in his other hand.

"You saved it." Her words were no more than a whisper.

"I figured you could clean up, but I didn't want your camera busted." He looked down at it with curiosity.

In amazement, Lydia looked around her. The man's hat sat at the edge of the mud puddle. He must have dropped it lunging for her camera. Her gut tightened.

It was an Amish hat.

She studied him more closely, not knowing how she could have missed the clues — the simple pants and handmade shirt, the suspenders and the long hair over his ears. If the wind stopped rustling it up, she guessed his hair was cut straight across his forehead too. It was those deep, dark eyes and the striking features that had caused her to miss the fact he was one of the Amish bachelors.

The humor in his eyes was long gone. Her heart sank and grew cold as if it too had been dunked in the muddy puddle. It was obvious something she'd said had cut deep. But what?

Lydia shook her leg. Mud dripped off the hem of her slacks. "It weren't —" She stopped, surprised at how quickly she'd slipped into Amish speech. "I mean, it wasn't your fault. Uh . . ."

"Gideon. My name is Gideon."

A strong name. A hero's name.

She offered a small smile. "My name is Lydia."

He handed the camera back, and she opened the door and placed it inside her car. "It wasn't your fault, Gideon. Thank you for saving my camera. I'm headed to the, uh, Wyse place. Can you remind me which way to go?"

His eyes moved over her and lingered on her hair as if imagining a *kapp,* then he cleared his throat.

"*Ja,* I know the place. It's . . ." He fumbled his words.

What had gotten into him? But he turned

36

away and pointed to the house across the pasture before she had a chance to read the story his eyes revealed.

Gideon's mem had told him that someday there'd be a woman who looked so good in the face it would give him a *bauch* ache and cause his heart to beat double. Gideon placed a hand over his stomach, noticing it did ache. But he was certain this Lydia was just opposite the type of woman Mem had in mind.

She brushed her thick, red hair back from her face with her free hand. Her cell phone was still in her grip.

"Do you mind telling me how to get there?" she said again.

A truck drove by, its wheels bouncing in the mud puddles on the road, sending sprays of mud in all directions. The woman stepped closer to him so as not to get splattered. Within arm's reach. She smelled of vanilla and cinnamon — like his favorite cinnamon roll.

"The Wyse place? That's the one you were jest taking photos of." He pointed. "Can't you see it's right there?"

"I can see it, but I'm trying to remember which turnoff to take. I know there are several up that way. I don't want to go knocking on doors and be a *bodderation* to find the right one."

"Wait . . . you speak Pennsylvania Dutch?"

"*Ja*. Yes. Does it matter? It's my dat, you see. Mr. Wyse is my father."

Lydia. *Lydie*. He should have known. This woman's reputation proceeded her. He'd only been in West Kootenai a day or so when one of the Amish women in town shared the fate of the older Amish couple. *"Poor Mr. and Mrs. Wyse. Only one kinder and she's gone to the ways of the world."*

Then, just yesterday, he'd heard from his cousin that Mrs. Wyse had passed. Wanting to offer his help, Gideon had stopped by and found Mr. Wyse cutting out wood for the coffin. Even though they hadn't shared more than small talk before then, Gideon couldn't leave the man to do the task alone. And even though Mr. Wyse had refused the help of a few other men who offered, he allowed Gideon to stay. Maybe because Gideon hadn't asked if he could . . . he'd just walked to the sawhorses and set to work. No one should be alone at a time like that.

As they worked, instead of speaking of the deceased, the older man had spoken of a daughter who liked to read, who baked the best apple pies, and who had eyes as green as the pasture grass. Gideon had pictured an old maid back in Ohio — nothing like this.

He studied the woman's eyes — just as pretty as her dat had mentioned — then cleared his throat. "I am so sorry about yer mem. I saw her around the Kraft and Grocery often. She was a *gut* woman."

"She is with the *gut* . . . good Lord now." Lydia lowered her head and kicked at a pinecone at her feet.

He wanted to ask where she lived — ask more about her — but now was not the time. Heat rose up Gideon's neck as he considered how he'd treated her. "You go past the Sommer place. It's the large house over there." He pointed to the log house with a passel of Sommer boys running around the front. "A ways down yet, the road will *T* at the Carash place. If you keep going you'll hit the lake — Lake Koocanusa — so you'll want to turn right."

"Turn right at the Sommer place? Is there a road there?"

"*Ne,* at the *T,* at the Carashes."

"You really don't need to tell me the names. I don't know these people, and that doesn't help."

"*Ja.*" His gaze narrowed. He knew many women like this. Impatient and quick tempered. Mem had told him that hard work and humility shaped a woman's character, and that's why soft, pretty girls were hard to live with. His sympathy lessened, and he wished his attraction would do the same. "I wouldn't expect it to matter to you."

The woman jutted out her chin, ignoring his comment.

He tried again. "Go past the first house. Turn right at the *T* at the second house. You should see yer parents' — yer dat's — house on down there in a small clearing."

"Great. That's all I needed to know." She lowered her head and slipped into her car without another word.

Gideon shook his head. Not so much as a thank you. He should have figured as much.

He stepped back from the road, and she started the car again and pulled away. He watched the yellow car speed up, its tires bouncing and splashing through the potholes. He hadn't met anyone like her — so independent, yet so in need. He could see that in her gaze. So beautiful, yet frustrating.

Remember Mem's advice, Gideon told himself. Stay away from a woman like that — far away.

No matter how she made his stomach ache.

CHAPTER 3

The place looked different than it had last year. The front porch needed a fresh coat of paint, and wild grasses and wildflowers had intruded, taking over where a manicured lawn had been before. Yearling pine trees crowded, and just north of the house sat the fenced-in pasture that that Amish man had been in — doing what, she had no idea. What did he say his name was? Gideon, yes. Living in Seattle she'd gotten used to incognizant people, but he didn't have to be rude.

She parked the car, but her hand paused on the door handle. Fatigue invaded her bones. She was almost too weary to walk up the steps to the porch. Partly because she'd driven all the way from Seattle — the most she'd ever driven in all her *Englisch* days at one time. But more than that, because of the realization that Mem's smile would not be waiting. No matter what choices Lydia had made, or how poorly she'd acted, the love in Mem's eyes had always been the same.

Tension and frustration of a moment before was replaced by a stab of longing. She thought of Mem rolling out a pie crust at the table and showing her how to transfer it to the pie pan. She considered Mem's laughter, ringing like the church bells down the road from their home when they lived back in Sugarcreek. Many people had said over the years they never knew a happier woman.

And yet at times Mem's happiness had brought only frustration. How could she be so full of joy when Lydia found so much of life a struggle?

"Lydia, dochtah, *you are home. Come here, baby girl,"* Mem had said the last time she'd been back. Mem had opened her arms and a smile had filled her face, as if it hadn't mattered that Lydia had walked in wearing *Englisch* clothes. And to Mem it hadn't mattered as much as it probably should. Mem had looked at her as if she was the most beautiful, special person on the planet.

Lydia released the handle of the door, covering her face with her hands as the tears fell. She'd chosen to walk away. She'd thought it out and had picked the better

path, hadn't she? She'd been so sure . . .
then. Her shoulders shook, and her throat
grew thick, hot as it clenched down to hold
back the sobs.

Then she heard it. A bumping against the
door. She wiped her eyes and looked out
the car window. Her dat stood ten feet away,
giving her space. The impatient one was old
Rex. He stood near the door his tail *thump,
thump, thumping* against her car.

She sucked in a breath and blew it out
again, holding back the tears. One of Dat's
Englisch friends had called her cell phone
yesterday. Hadn't she cried enough since
then?

She climbed from the car and was to him
in three long strides. Dat had never been
the affectionate one — not like Mem — but
he opened his arms and pulled her tight
against him.

"Oh, Lydie. She's gone, *kinder.* I don't
know what to do now. She's gone."

"Dat, I'm so sorry. I should have come to
visit. I should have made time. I didn't realize . . ."

"No one knew. The doctor thought she
was improving." His chin and beard quivered. "It was the good Lord's time."

Lydia pressed her cheek against Dat's
chest and nodded, wishing she had an

ounce of his faith. She'd never expected to leave her love for God behind when she'd picked up and moved to Washington state. Even though she wanted to live in the *Englisch* world, she'd hoped He'd go with her. He had, she supposed, but like most of her Amish traditions, God somehow became obsolete in a world where hard work, creativity, and knowing the right people got you far.

"Mem didn't have a lot of pain, did she?"

"One gasp, it was all I heard. Loud enough to wake me, but it sounded more like surprise than pain."

"That's good to know. I — I am glad in a way that her suffering is over."

"Suffering?" Dat pulled back slightly and looked down. "No one would call that suffering, not Mem. Once you came into our lives, daughter, then her heart problems weren't more than a bother. You were the best tincture anyone could ask for."

She nodded, gripping Dat's shirt. Then the sound of a horse whinnying caught her attention. She jerked back to look toward the pasture. Gideon strode toward her, the horse she'd seen running across the field following. She wanted to pick up a rock and hurl it in his direction. How dare he interrupt this moment!

"I'm sorry to bother." He held something up. It was small, round, and black, and she recognized it immediately.

"My lens cap!" She released her dat's shirt and strode toward Gideon. "I must have left it on the hood of my car." Lydia knew she looked a mess. Her face always became blotchy, as if covered with bright-red chicken pox, when she cried. It didn't matter. She didn't need to impress an Amish man.

When she got closer, he held up his hand, as if wanting her to halt just shy of the fence. "Hold up," he called.

She paused.

"I've just started working with Blue. He's a jumpy one. Can be mean too, from what I hear." The horse standing next to Gideon was beautiful. He looked gentle, tame — just like the Amish man.

Looks could be deceiving.

Gideon approached the wooden fence, placed one hand on it, and jumped over it as if it were a small mole hill rather than a tall fence. That was the second time he'd done that, and it impressed her still.

He approached and handed her the cap.

"I'm sorry, again, for interrupting. I jest knew you'd be missing it, and I didn't want you to wander back and look for it in the dark. There aren't any street lamps around these parts, and even the stars and moon are gonna be tucked away behind those clouds. It's dangerous on those roads. I mean, if you were trying to look around."

"Thank you. *Danki.*" She smiled in spite of herself and her mournful mood and tucked the cap in the pocket of her pants. "I'll take that advice from a local, and I'll make sure I don't wander the roadside after sundown."

Gideon ran a hand down the side of his face. "I'm not a local. Jest here for a season."

"One of the bachelors," Dat called.

She nodded and bit her lip. He'd been listening in. She didn't want to glance back at him. Didn't want to see hope in his gaze. Soon she'd be heading back to Seattle, and she didn't want to get anyone's hopes up.

"I appreciate you doing this, but . . ."

"*Ja,* I'll let you go." He climbed back over the fence and strode to the horse. Gideon didn't touch the animal, nor offer him a glance, but as Gideon continued, the horse followed behind at a safe distance.

In silence Lydia and Dat walked to the house. As soon as they entered the front door, Dat turned back to the window.

"I haven't seen anything like it."

She followed his gaze. "What?"

"An Amish man — any man — with that horse. He's a wild thing. Full of the *diebel.* I tried to pet him a few months ago. He'd come to the fence, and I was feeding him apples. Went from nice to mean in ten seconds, and bit my hand as I stroked his nose. Now, in two hours' time, the horse is following him around like a dog."

Lydia nodded, but she wasn't concerned about the bachelor. Instead she took her father's hands in hers.

"Are you okay?"

"My hand is fine. My heart . . ." He sighed, pulling his right hand from hers and placing it over his chest. "Part of it is missing. Forty years together. I'm not sure what to do with myself. I've been wandering in circles for a day and a night. I keep telling myself to stop looking for her —"

"Oh, Dat." Lydia sank down into the chair next to the window. "I feel so bad you had to be alone until I got here, but you won't be alone now — for a while. A few weeks at least. I'm going to stay until you get settled and find your own routine."

She'd expected him to disagree. To tell her he'd be fine. That had been common. He'd been the strong one. Even during all of Mem's illnesses he'd stood on his own two feet.

"*Ja, gut.* I will like having you here." His words were simple, but she read so much more in his gaze. He needed her. Dat needed her now like she'd never been needed. He turned and walked to his favorite chair and sat heavily.

This place would be her home — for a little while at least.

She stared at the window, and her gaze moved to the wild pink roses that bloomed near the well. Then she glanced to the east and north. The pine trees opened to reveal the pasture and the mountain peaks in the distance. Though it was June, snow still clung to those peaks. She'd come here only once a year and stayed a few days each time. She had forgotten how beautiful it was. Sitting on the front porch would have been the perfect spot to edit. Why hadn't she come more often?

Maybe because of the guilt of leaving.

She'd also assumed it was hard enough for her parents to try to fit into a new community without her presence. She didn't want to bring trouble for them by having an *Englisch* daughter hanging around.

There was a worn spot on the other side of the fence, and Lydia guessed the horses gathered there often for treats of apples. She pictured Dat feeding them, talking to them.

"This morning I wanted to tell Mem you were on your way . . . and then I remembered the reason why you were coming. She wasn't here to talk to —" He looked at Lydia, eyes focused. "She was happy with me, but you brought her pure joy. You made her a mother. God turned something hard into . . ." His words trailed off.

Lydia swallowed the ache and blinked back the moisture rimming her lower eyelids. Was the pain in Dat's eyes not only from Mem's passing, but from Lydia's knowing? Lydia wished she hadn't found out the truth behind her birth. Maybe then she'd still be Amish. Maybe then she'd call this beautiful mountain sanctuary home.

Then again, she doubted if she'd ever consider this place home. She'd been raised in Sugarcreek, Ohio, a place that couldn't be more different both in terrain and in lifestyle. While the people in West Kootenai considered themselves Old Order Amish, their lifestyle tended toward relaxed living among the *Englisch*. Since it was a young community compared to most, and everyone was from someplace back east, they welcomed outsiders.

Also, as she'd witnessed with her dat, since the men had to preach and lead in the community — while raising their families and working full time — they were thankful for help from new arrivals. A slight smile curled Lydia's lips as she remembered how her dat had found himself in the pulpit just two months after moving into the area, even though he wasn't a minister and had never preached an Amish sermon in his life.

For the last three years, instead of flying back to Sugarcreek, she'd driven from Seattle to West Kootenai. Dat claimed he'd always wanted to live in the mountains.

Not only was being around her parents awkward after leaving the Amish — Mem especially. Lydia didn't know this place — well, except for the stories her grandmother used to tell her.

"The people are too independent. My sister and her husband moved there in the seventies, wanting to be part of a new community, but all sorts of horrible, awful things happen there. Wild animals roam, and more than one Amish man has turned up dead from a bear."

Lydia hadn't stayed around West Kootenai long enough to find out more of the story, but this time she'd have to stay a few weeks to help Dat. She had no excuse not to.

Two sawhorses stood before the open door of the barn with fresh wood shavings at their base. The sight pinched her heart. She glanced back at him. "Did you make the coffin yourself?"

Dat nodded. "Some of our friends offered, but I wanted to do it for her. One last gift." Dat choked up this time. He lowered his head and stroked his beard. "Gideon came to help."

Lydia pointed back out the window. "That Gideon?"

"*Ja*. He was in the pasture when I was unloading the lumber."

"So he knew . . ."

"Knew what?"

"That you had a daughter who'd left the Amish?"

"*Ne*. I don't think I mentioned that you left. I talked about you, though."

"And you didn't think it was important to mention that?"

"Not really. There were so many more interesting things yet to share."

Lydia offered a sad smile. His words were true. He didn't hold back because he was ashamed of the truth. Dat saw the world in a different light. He focused on the good things, talked about what was right. Mem was . . . had been . . . that way too. And that's why Lydia never brought up any more questions about her birth mom. It was easier to run and to wonder than it was to ask her parents to share about the shame

51

and pain surrounding her birth.

And now half of that truth had died with Mem. She'd never know the secrets carried from one mother-heart to another.

Lydia rose and moved to the door. "I'll get my suitcase."

Dat stood, but she waved a hand in his direction. "No need to follow — it's just a small bag."

Dat nodded and walked into the kitchen, pouring himself a cup of coffee from the pot on the wood cookstove. "You know where to take it. The room is all readied up."

She paused with her hand on the front doorknob. "You got it ready for me?"

Dat took a sip of coffee and shook his head. "*Ne,* didn't you know? From the day you left, Mem always made sure your room was readied for your return. She'd dust, wash the linens every week, and in the summer she'd put in a vase of fresh flowers, jest in case."

Lydia's hand dropped to her side, and the sadness that had been there moments before grew to numbness. To feel any other emotion would be too overwhelming. Even now she questioned if she could sleep in that room, knowing.

"Yer mem never doubted you'd return to

the Amish for *gut.* She always felt you'd come back. That you'd make this place home."

Lydia nodded but didn't answer. How could she? She'd never have a chance at mending Mem's heart, and she didn't want to crush Dat's hopes too.

CHAPTER 4

Gideon couldn't get the woman off his mind. He hadn't met anyone like her. She'd acted so confident, so . . . *Englisch* as she'd parked her car, jumped out, and started taking photos. When he didn't know who she was, he didn't care for her at all, despite her beauty. But she was Jacob Wyse's daughter. That changed things. It confused him. Jacob had spoken of Lydie — his nickname for her — as if she was the most gentle, caring woman on the planet. She was not an old maid as he'd imagined, and she'd seemed anything but gentle.

Until he saw her with her dat, that was.

It was odd to see an *Englisch* woman clinging to her Amish father. Leaving the Amish usually brought distance to families, even in the closest of relationships — but not them.

Why had she left? Why would the only child of an Amish couple do that?

54

He'd made progress with Blue. For the rest of the day he'd worked to get the horse used to him. To see him as a friend and not a threat. Without a mother around, Blue had picked up a lot of bad habits. She hadn't been there to teach him who was friend and who was foe.

By the end of the day, Blue started seeing him as a friend. Over the next few weeks and months that bond would grow. Gideon needed to teach the horse that Gideon's way was the right way. Blue needed to unlearn a lot of bad habits. For the gelding, it made no sense why he shouldn't chase cows, nip at folks, change leads, or most of all, run and frolic without a care. The horse didn't realize there was a better way to interact. Blue needed to learn confidence in Gideon — and in humans. When difficult situations arose in the future — which they would — the horse needed to know who he should listen to and trust.

When he'd brushed down Blue and put him in his corral, Gideon couldn't help but watch the Wyse house in the distance. Lydia had only exited the house once — to get her suitcase from her car.

Should I head down there? Maybe offer help for tomorrow night's viewing?

He considered offering to hitch up their

55

buggy and drive them to the funeral the day after that. But his *farrichterlich* thoughts got the better of him. She'd seemed none too happy to see him the last time he'd shown up there.

Instead Gideon headed to the West Kootenai Kraft and Grocery for dinner. It was later than usual, and most of the other bachelors had come and gone, his cousin Caleb included. The only people sitting in the dining room of the attached restaurant were two older *Englisch* women deep in conversation and the older gentleman who tended to the front cash register. Edgar, *ja,* that was his name.

Gideon paused at the doorway to the restaurant, turning over his hat in his hand. Edgar motioned him forward, pointing to the dining room chair across from him, welcoming Gideon to sit.

Gideon's eyebrows arched in surprise — although on second thought he should have expected that. That's how things happened in this small community, he'd soon learned after arriving here. Amish and *Englisch* didn't just interact at a business level; many became friends. Some Amish even attended prayer meetings at the Carash house. He'd witnessed that with his own eyes when he'd stopped by to talk to Dave about training Blue.

Gideon removed his hat and sauntered over to the wooden table with the red-checkered tablecloth. Gas lanterns hung above each table from previous Amish owners, but electric Christmas lights had also been strung around the room by the non-Amish owner, Annie.

He sat, and an Amish waitress brought him a menu.

"We have everything tonight except the meatloaf," she explained. "That went quick like."

Gideon eyed the fried chicken, mashed potatoes, and green beans on Edgar's plate. "No need for a menu." He pointed. "I'll take what he's having, except I want the whole thing covered in country gravy."

The waitress chuckled. "The green beans too?"

Gideon nodded. "*Ja,* that's the best way. The only way, in fact, Mem could get me to eat my vegetables."

"You got it." The waitress shook her head and giggled as she hurried to the kitchen.

"She's a pretty one." Edgar pointed to the exiting waitress. "It's one of the Peachy girls — Eve. She's watched passels of Amish bachelors come and go fer years now with the same look of interest in her eyes."

"Really?" Gideon glanced back over his shoulder. "I didn't notice." Truth was there were very few women who caught his attention — except for that *Englisch* gal with the red hair and equally untamed disposition. Leave it to him to fancy the last girl in this area he should take a liking to.

Edgar's fork scraped on the plate as he scooped his mashed potatoes into a pile.

Gideon breathed in deeply, his stomach rumbling. Even though all the baking was done in the morning, the connecting kitchen and bakery still smelled of fresh bread, cinnamon, apples, and strawberry pies.

"What was yer name again, son?" Edgar asked. "There are too many bachelors to try to keep straight."

"Gideon."

Edgar nodded and then took a large bite of mashed potatoes. When he'd finished swallowing he dabbed his mouth with a napkin. "That's not a common name."

"Not too common. I knew one other Gideon back in Bird-in-Hand. An older gentleman." Did his parents regret naming him "mighty warrior"? Inside he felt anything but.

The waitress returned with a glass of water, then hurried off again.

Edgar rubbed his gray, bushy eyebrows. "I remember a lad called Gideon. His family vacationed here one summer."

Gideon chuckled. "Edgar, you have a wonderful memory. Do you remember the name of every visiting Amish child?"

"No, not close. But I'd never forget that name. Called it a thousand times at least during the search." Edgar took another sip from his coffee.

Gideon's heart cinched in pain, and a strange knowledge came over him. This man had been there — been part of the rescue team that had found him on that mountain. Surely there couldn't be two searches, two young boys with the same name.

He rubbed the back of his neck, and a thousand needles pierced the skin on his arms. He knew he should ask about that time. That's what he'd come for, wasn't it? To know the truth?

Instead he thought of the stone-cold glare in Dat's eyes. *Maybe I don't want to know.*

Gideon nodded but didn't speak. When his dinner came he ate half a piece of chicken and some of the potatoes. They talked about other things: the weather, the snow melt, and the results of the Amish auction a few weeks ago. Gideon knew if he asked a few questions, this man would be

able to tell him all he longed to know —
what really happened those few days — but
fear caught the words in his throat and
wouldn't release them. There was a reason
Dat hadn't wanted Mem to tell him the
truth.

Edgar watched him, a knowing look narrowing his gaze. "Yer not eating much."

"Actually, I'm not too hungry. My eyes
must be bigger than my stomach."

The waitress approached again. "Would
you like me to box that up, *ja*?"

Gideon nodded. If he didn't eat it later,
Caleb would. She returned a few minutes
later with a paper plate covered with foil.

"Best get back to the cabin." Gideon rose.
"Caleb will be wondering on me."

Edgar waved his good-bye, and Gideon
could feel the older man's eyes on him as
he left.

Did Edgar have any idea the young boy
was him?

CHAPTER 5

Lydia sat next to Dat as they drove the buggy the short mile to the neighbor's house where the funeral would be held. Mem and Dat's house was small, and when Amish friends offered up their place for the funeral, Dat had accepted. It made her feel good that even though Mem and Dat had only been living in West Kootenai for three years, most of the town would show up. She and Dat could have walked, but they needed their buggy to drive to the cemetery after the funeral.

Lydia pressed her sweaty palms flat on her thighs and smoothed the small wrinkles in her black dress. It was the plainest, simplest dress she could find, but it was not an Amish dress and cape. She'd pinned up her hair, but she had no *kapp* on her head. Guilt echoed shallowly in her chest. She should be thinking most about her mother, about her loss, but what weighed heaviest on her mind was walking into the Sommer house and noting everyone's eyes on her. She imagined their thoughts: *The* Englisch *daughter has come now, has she? Too bad her mother had to live her last years with such shame.*

Lydia took in a long, slow breath and told herself to suck it up. It didn't matter what they thought. She'd made the right choice. She had a great career and a good life in Seattle. She had friendships with her co-workers and knew a couple of neighbors in her apartment complex too. It didn't matter that she didn't have a fine and fancy *Englisch* house. She liked her place decorated simply. It was easier to clean. It gave her more time for reading and editing.

Still, as the metal buggy wheels rolled over the dirt road, it felt as if the gravel scraped her heart. They were right, in a way. She could have made a different choice. She could have been there during Mem's last days, last years.

The line of buggies came from both directions. Other folks walked, their heads low and their pace slow as if heavy hearts weighed them down. She supposed they were sadder for Dat than for Mem. Mem was a good woman — no doubt ushered through heaven's gates — but Dat would be living without the wife he'd shared his life with for forty years. Living alone, without a daughter to depend on.

One man glanced up as they passed on the narrow dirt road, and she could almost read his thoughts in his gaze: *what old man deserves this?*

She quickly looked away and glanced at the bunch of wild-flowers laid on newspaper on the seat between her and her dat. Bringing flowers to a funeral was an *Englisch* tradition, but she needed some excuse for getting out of the house this morning. Her dat's low sobs from the bedroom that he now slept in alone broke her heart.

If the rush-hour traffic had moved this slow in Seattle she'd have been tapping her fingers on the dash, but in this place it seemed normal — right even — that the idyllic scenery rolled by like a slow-motion film.

The mare moved at a steady pace, and the sun through the trees created a patterned mosaic on the road. Sitting next to Dat in the buggy brought a thousand memories. Growing up she'd never thought she'd leave, but after Lydia discovered the truth, she knew she couldn't stay, and she'd bought a ticket to a city as far west as she could go. Being a face in the crowd meant no one would ask questions. No one would ever know who she really was.

The thing was she knew. And in her running she'd spent too many quiet nights alone when she could have sat around Dat and Mem's table. When she could have curled next to the wood fire under a quilt and chatted with Mem about her day. Now it was too late.

A cool wind blew, caressing her face. Tears rimmed her eyes. The mare tossed her head slightly, seeing the line of parked buggies.

Visitation — and the first viewing — had been last night. She'd spent the whole day cleaning and then had made sandwiches for dinner. Feeling as if she was going to get sick — or maybe pass out — Lydia had pinned up her hair, washed up, and dressed in a simple garment before they'd welcomed folks into their home. Mem had lay in a plain pine coffin on the back, screened-in porch. Lydia had stood silent by Dat's side, the dust carried on the breeze through open doorway tickling her nose.

As the women from the community had passed the casket, she'd tried to remember which ones had helped wash Mem's body and dressed it in the long, white dress, *kapp*, and apron — the same *kapp* and apron Mem had worn on her wedding day. After

64

the viewing, the local bishop performed a short service. Even now Lydia couldn't remember the words. Had she been listening at all? Not really. Instead, her mind had replayed the many moments she'd spent in her mother's loving arms — memories she hadn't allowed herself to think about for years.

Last night, nearly one hundred people had strolled by her mem's open casket — almost everyone in the community, including Gideon, although Lydia did what she could to not make eye contact with the handsome bachelor. Everyone spoke to her and Dat about Mem's kind heart. Mem had that way with folks. You met her once and felt as loved as her best friend. It was a trait Lydia wished she had picked up . . . or did she? It was the *community* part of being Amish that Lydia had fled from.

And now the Amish funeral would finalize all Mem's years of living.

Dat parked the buggy next to the Somners' house. Two men waited to tend to the buggy for them. She took the wild-flowers from the passenger's seat, and after dismounting they walked to the front door. Neighbors already gathered inside. Lydia placed her free hand in Dat's, and they stepped inside together.

The casket had been carried to the Sommer house. A row of children sat with their mems. She remembered being their age and attending funerals just like this one. It had been a normal part of Amish life.

Lydia tried to ignore the stares. Dat released her hand and moved to the living area, where the men took their seats. There were two seats closest to the casket — one for him, one for her. At funerals family members of the deceased were allowed to sit together. But she couldn't make herself sit there yet — in everyone's full gaze.

Instead she crossed her arms over her chest as an older woman approached.

"Lydia, I'm Ruth Sommer. This is our place." She offered a welcoming smile and eyed Lydia's clothes. "That's a pretty dress."

Lydia studied the woman's eyes. Her comment appeared to be genuine. Lydia glanced down at her simple black frock. It wasn't typical Amish dress, but as close as she could find without pulling out her Amish clothes. She'd thought about wearing them — to honor Mem — but she didn't want to get anyone's hopes up.

Ruth motioned to the kitchen. "Lydia, this is my daughter, Marianna."

Lydia followed her gaze to a young woman by the kitchen sink — an *Englisch* woman.

She was pouring a cup of water for a toddler — a daughter, maybe, or a sister?

Marianna stepped forward and offered a sweet smile. "It's *gut* to meet you. I hope you'll stay around. And this is my husband, Ben." A handsome *Englisch* man with bright blue eyes stepped forward, and Marianna nodded knowingly. Even though Marianna didn't dress Amish, she wore a simple dress and a head scarf. Her mannerisms seemed Amish, too, and Lydia guessed it had been in the last few years that she'd left the Amish to marry this *Englischer*. What amazed Lydia most was that Marianna's mem seemed comfortable around her daughter despite her decision to not be Amish. Lydia thought her mem had been the only one who hadn't shunned a wayward child, as was expected. Maybe West Kootenai *was* a different place.

Lydia offered a slight smile despite the ache in her stomach. Under any other circumstances she would have enjoyed getting to know this family. But here, now, her legs grew weak under her long skirt, and her shoulders and arms ached as if she'd been trying to hold herself together within the grasp of her own embrace.

"Nice to meet you both. Thank you for opening your home. I best seat myself."

A silence fell over the place. The service was about to start.

"Here, let me get those." Mrs. Sommer reached for the wildflowers in Lydia's hands. "I'll put them in water."

"*Danki*. Thank you." Lydia offered them over. She guessed Mrs. Sommer would put them in a jar of water and keep them in the kitchen since the Amish never used flowers to decorate a casket or room where the funeral was held.

Lydia sat next to her father. So many *Englisch* in the room. How did they suffer through the two hours of songs and sermon in German?

They started by reading a hymn, and then the bishop stood for a sermon. Even though she hadn't attended an Amish service for many years, being amongst the simple people, with their deep faith, brought a peace she hadn't experienced in a while.

The bishop's voice rose as he scanned the room. His eyes paused on her for a moment and then continued on. "What a person sows in this life, he will harvest in *ewigheit*. So Jesus says further, *'Lasset uns gutes thun und nicht mude warden.'* "

"He will harvest in eternity," Lydia translated in her mind. *"Let us not be weary in doing good."*

"For the one who sowed good seed, he shall find grace at the time of judgment. He shall receive a home in heaven — something that can never be stripped away. But if one sows the worldly seed, his reward is destruction — eternity in hell."

Lydia's heart settled at the rise and fall of the bishop's words. The cadence was beautiful . . . not something one heard in everyday life, walking on city streets. Was it just four days ago she'd been dodging taxis to run across the street and grab a chai latte from her favorite tea shop?

Her shoulders straightened. Gideon sat with a few of the other bachelors. He glanced at her and offered a sad smile. Deep folds in his forehead displayed a pained expression and compassion for her — for her dat. Seeing that comforted her. Even though their first meeting had been filled with angst, at least there was a somewhat-familiar face.

Lydia held her emotions captive, binding them under lock and key, refusing to let them release. Heat surged through her from her effort, and she pretended someone else's mem lay in the coffin. Unlike the few *Englisch* funerals she'd attended in which most of the service memorialized the deceased, in this gathering there was no talk of Mem other than stating her name, the date of her birth, and the date of her death. Instead the bishop continued on, speaking of Genesis and God's creation of man for eternity. And then he shared the verses Lydia had heard at nearly every Amish funeral:

" 'Verily, verily, I say unto you, He that heareth my word, and believeth on him that sent me, hath everlasting life, and shall not come into condemnation; but is passed from death unto life.'

" 'Verily, verily, I say unto you, the hour is coming, and now is, when the dead shall hear the voice of the Son of God: and they that hear shall live.'

" 'For as the Father hath life in himself; so hath he given to the Son to have life in himself; and hath given him authority to execute judgment also, because he is the Son of man.' "

Tears filled the corners of her eyes. Lydia's heart warmed at those words as if someone had started a kindling fire deep in her chest. She let out a low sigh. This was a good message for Mem, but what about her?

When the sermons were done and another hymn was read, it was time to leave for the cemetery.

Four men, her dat's friends, carried the casket from the house to the black, horse-drawn hearse. They sat in silence as Dat drove the buggy. Lydia didn't know what to say to bring him comfort. She doubted any words could. And for the first time since leaving the Amish a deep missing came to her. As she drove in line with these faithful people she considered what returning — really returning — would be like. Not only to chronicle the "stepping into the old ways" as Bonnie encouraged her to do. But to consider the way of faith she'd left. To consider God.

They approached the small cemetery, and her eyes moved to the grave — an open chasm waiting for the simple pine coffin. Men from their church had spent the past two days digging it, coming as they could between chores, the sweat of their labor mingling with an occasional tear.

The black-dressed members of the community moved from their buggies and circled the grave. There were no tears now; those would be shared in private.

The bishop said a few more words at the graveside. The whole thing seemed part of a dream. Lydia had edited books about death, dying, funerals, and grief. Those concepts were easy to express on the printed page, but in reality the emotions jumbled together.

Anger, sadness, longing, mixed with a hint of joy that Mem no longer faced sickness or pain. Yet when they lowered Mem's coffin into the hole in the ground Lydia's knees trembled and her stomach turned. The blue sky and green of the trees faded to gray and the *kapp*s and faces of those around her blurred.

"I can't watch it. I can't . . ."

She turned and walked back down the road, the sound of shovelfuls of dirt hitting the wood behind her. She refused to look back, to see the reaction of the others as she walked away. Thankfully Dat didn't follow as she went to stand by the buggy. The sky was bright blue and high. Really high, as if God had attached strings to the heavens and hiked it up.

It was easier in Seattle to think that life was up to her, but here it was hard to think that. Being in her parents' home exhibited a faith lived out even more than spoken. Witnessing her mem's burial made her wish she could believe like them. How could they just accept it without question? Mem had told her faith was believing what she couldn't see. Yet what she saw — what she knew about herself — was what made the believing impossible.

"You all right?"

It was only as she heard the voice that she realized footsteps approached. Lydia turned. Gideon walked to her, his face a mask of pain.

She opened her mouth to answer, but no words came.

"Forget I asked. Of course you aren't all right. This day — I imagine this day is the worst one you can think of." His gaze told her he understood. What pain had he faced? She couldn't ask, not now. If she did the tears would come for certain.

"It's a bad day, all right."

"Can I walk you to the Sommer house fer the meal?"

"Walk?"

He sheepishly kicked at a rock on the ground. "I don't have my own buggy here in Montana."

"A walk, *ja* — yes. It's not far. It'll be . . . good to stretch my legs. To give my heart space to ache." She'd almost said *gut* instead of *good*. It surprised her how quickly her speech wanted to make the natural transition to the slower cadence and common Pennsylvania Dutch phrases she'd spoken for most of her life.

Gideon nodded, then turned back toward the cemetery. "I'll tell yer dat. I'll be right back."

She nodded and watched him go. She then lifted her head again toward the sky and smiled sadly. Lydia wasn't sure if folks got a chance to talk to God when they got to heaven. If so, she imagined Mem bending God's ear, telling Him with persistence her daughter, Lydia, needed a *gut* man in her life — an Amish man to bring her happiness.

Yet it wasn't Gideon's Amishness that made him so appealing. It was his nature, his temperament. Lydia had gone on numerous dates in Seattle with guys who had something to prove. Gideon wasn't like that. He was gentle enough to calm a stubborn horse, yet bold enough to stride across a pasture and tell an *Englisch* woman to stop taking photos. For the first time she understood why Bonnie asked folks about their life stories. Gideon was a protector, yet his gaze could be wary at times, and it made her want to ask what had happened to make him like that.

If she'd been looking for someone to draw her interest, Lydia would have come up with a different list of qualities in a man. Now she wasn't looking, yet in Gideon she saw qualities that wouldn't have made her list but would be there from now on.

And as Lydia watched Gideon return with

slow, deliberate steps, she imagined folks *did* get to talk to God. She also guessed He listened. Or at least He listened to Mem. How else could one explain a man like this walking into her life when she felt her weakest? How else could one explain that with Gideon she didn't mind being weak — didn't mind him seeing the tears that refused to be dammed any longer with missing Mem?

CHAPTER 6

They walked side by side, and Gideon pondered the look on Lydia's face and the knowledge that she'd wasted the last years of her mem's life living an *Englisch* lifestyle. The thought saddened him.

"It was a lovely service."

"The people here seem nice." She glanced over at him. "Have you made many friends?"

"A few. I wish more than I have. I tend to shy away from folks. I sometimes find horses easier to communicate with."

The path before them transformed from light to dark, light to dark as the shadows of the trees made a pattern on the dirt roadway.

"Why is that?" she asked.

He glanced over at her, not expecting the question. "Huh?"

"What you said. Why is it that you can communicate with horses better than people at times?"

Gideon tucked his hands into his pockets. He was quiet for a moment, trying to figure it out, but he couldn't think back to a defining moment.

"I jest suppose it's the way the Lord made me. He made some who are *gut* with woodworking, and my dat could make a crop grow in the desert. I was always drawn to horses. Maybe because they're misunderstood at times. People think horses are naughty on purpose when really they just have a small need that no one's paying attention to."

Most of the troubled horses he'd worked with were eager to please under the right circumstances. With people that wasn't always the case. They could turn around and hurt or disappoint you even if you did everything right.

Lydia shifted on her feet. Gideon eyed her, and she looked away. Did he see a wounded, misunderstood creature who ached from her mother's loss? Did it matter if he did?

"Well, *ja*, that makes sense," she finally answered. "I feel honored . . . that you are willing to risk my friendship."

"You make it sound as if yer a horrible risk."

She glanced down at her garment and touched her *kapp*less hair. "Aren't I?"

"I have to say that my mem wouldn't be smiling if she saw this — me with an *Englisch* woman — but if I've learned anything about living in West Kootenai for the last few months, it's to consider what's inside more than what's out."

She nodded. " 'Don't judge a book by its cover.' "

"What?"

"It's an *Englisch* phrase."

"I know the phrase, but yer not a book."

Humor crinkled his eyes, and the tension in her neck lessened. Yet even Gideon couldn't ease the tautness of returning to the Sommer house for the funeral meal. While Dat knew these people, she didn't. What had they heard about her? What did they expect? Did they know she was leaving in a few weeks? Did Gideon know?

She'd gotten used to spending most of her time outside of work alone. But she realized in this moment she craved companionship. And Gideon gave her comfort. He was a safe, solid presence, taller than she remembered. There was something about his dark features that reminded her of Mark Ruffalo. Not that Gideon or any of the Amish folks would know who that was. A film star was opposite of all they believed in.

As they walked, buggies filled with families passed. Lydia pictured Mem's grave a mound of dark soil now, but she pushed that thought away.

She glanced up at a few buggies and saw eyes set on her. As she made eye contact the passengers immediately looked away.

"I wonder what they'd think if I decided to stay?" The words escaped from her mouth, and when they were met with silence, she questioned if she'd really said them.

"Do you care what they think?" Gideon's voice was raised as if he wanted the closest buggies to hear.

"Excuse me?"

"Do you care? I mean, I'm sure you weren't concerned with what others thought when you left the Amish."

"*Ne.* I wasn't."

"So, I would guess that if you considered staying — returning — it would be because it came from deep within, and not because you were trying to make others happy."

Lydia nodded and then paused and cocked her hip with a knowing glance.

Gideon took a few more steps before he stopped and looked back. "What?"

"And you said you can't communicate."

"Oh, I can state my opinion, *ja*. I never denied my ability to do that." One corner of his lips lifted in a smile. "But the back-and-forth talks are what get me in trouble." He tilted his head. "After all, I didn't ask what you thought about returning to the Amish . . . and that would be the only right thing to do."

She stayed there, watching him walk away, unsure of what to do. When she'd said *stay,* she meant staying to care for Dat. Why had Gideon assumed she meant returning to the Amish? She remembered Marianna. Surely in a community like this, one could be *Englisch* without the same shunning one received in a community back east. But the way he reminded her that her choice to be Amish or not was her decision made it almost sound appealing.

The way Gideon *interacted* with her was appealing. Mostly because even though he'd offered to walk her, he wasn't coddling her. He'd offered her friendship and not pity on the day of her mem's funeral. He wasn't ashamed to be seen with her even though she didn't wear a dress or *kapp.*

But how could she tell him her talk of staying in West Kootenai longer than two weeks didn't mean she was returning to the Amish? She'd made a point of never saying that. Never acting like it was such. The last thing she wanted to do was break her dat's heart again.

Unless . . .

She thought of the book Bonnie talked about. Maybe it would be good enough to write about returning to the community as an *Englischer.*

Lydia sighed and started after Gideon, picking up her pace as she hurried to catch up. She enjoyed her job in Seattle, but she loved the idea of writing a book even more. She enjoyed her friends, but there was no one there like Gideon. And then there was her father. He needed her, and she held the ability to bring him joy within her grasp.

Maybe Gideon saw something within her gaze she'd yet to acknowledge. Maybe this trip wasn't just about burying Mem. Maybe it was about breathing life into parts of her she'd allowed to die.

She could almost imagine Bonnie's words. *"Did you run to something or away from something, Lydia?"*

She hadn't wanted to think about that. It was easier rewriting someone else's story than penning her own.

The shared meal was eaten on the church tables — made when extra legs were added to the church benches — set up around the Sommer house. As with all church meals, the men sat with men, and the women and younger children sat together.

Lydia sat mostly to herself near some of the other women, taking in the sight. Even as she sat there she imagined what words she'd use to capture this scene. With black type on white paper, she'd be able to describe enough of the setting for readers to be a part of this gathering. Harder to describe would be the jostling of hope and loss within. The darkness of never again feeling a mother's embrace contrasting with the eagerness to find a home with her father again — at least for a while.

Take a step of faith. Be brave. Pick up the pen to your own life. Her lower lip trembled at the thought.

With one phone call Bonnie could pack up that box of Lydia's things, load her houseplants, and rent the place she'd considered home. With one conversation with Dat, she could call the people in this room her neighbors.

Lydia watched the women in the kitchen and the men finishing up their plates of food. These folks were all here to honor her mother, yet she only knew a few names. She thought of their old home in Sugarcreek.

82

Mem was a friend to many there — did they also grieve or was Mem's passing just unfortunate news to be shared at a quilting circle?

An *Englisch* woman with a slight build and a long blonde ponytail approached. She had the swagger of a cowgirl but a smile that made all at ease in her presence — Amish and *Englisch* alike. Lydia had met Annie, the owner of the West Kootenai Kraft and Grocery, only a few times, but it was obvious that a few times was all Annie needed to make someone a friend.

Annie approached and extended her hand. Lydia placed her own in the woman's. It was warm. Yesterday, as she'd been enfolded in her dat's arms, Lydia realized how little those in her new life had offered a warm touch. Her heart hungered for more.

Annie smiled. "Your mother was a very special woman."

"Thank you, Annie. I appreciate that."

"No, dear, I'm not just saying that. She was a special friend, and we grew in our love of the Lord together. In fact, every Monday after the breakfast rush I'd grab some pastries made that morning, run over to her place, and we'd have a little Bible study."

"My mother . . . She had Bible study with

an . . . ?" Lydia paused, studying Annie's face, realizing what words almost emerged.

"With an *Englisch* woman? Yes, or as she would say, *Oh, ja.*" Laughter bubbled from Annie's lips. "Ada Mae kept to herself mostly when your parents first moved here, but she warmed up — they usually do."

"They?"

"Our Amish friends. It's hard to open up to outsiders. Well, with what they've been taught all their lives. But she came around."

"So when you studied together . . . did you study anything special?" Lydia was still trying to let the idea of her mem studying the Bible with an *Englisch* woman sink in.

"Oh, just what we'd been reading that week in the Bible and studying on our own." Annie's smile faded, and her lip quivered slightly. "I'm going to miss that — miss hearing your mem's promises."

"Her promises?"

"Yes, it was one of her favorite things to share. Seemed not a week went by that she didn't point out another promise from God to us. Your mem's faith was a beautiful thing. She trusted God even with her health. Even with —" Now it was Annie's turn to get a sheepish look on her face.

"Even with me, her only daughter, forsaking the Amish and living in Seattle?"

"Yes. That was heaviest on her heart. Part of it was that you left the Amish community, but mostly she hoped you would someday love God like you did when you were a child. She said —"

"Lydia?" A woman approached and placed a hand on her arm. "I'm sorry to interrupt, but yer dat is looking weary. Gideon said he'd drive you both home. I'll send some food with him. You don't mind, do ya?"

"Mind? *Ne*. I mean no." Lydia shook her head, and a red curl slipped from its pin. She quickly tucked it behind her ear.

She glanced over at her dat, and the pain of the day crashed down upon her to see his thin frame and pale face. When had he gotten so old? Lydia offered a hurried good-bye to Annie and the other women and then rushed to his side, thankful that Gideon was already there, leading Dat to his buggy.

Could something happen to Dat too? Her heart dropped into her stomach. She'd never forgive herself if it did.

Still, as the buggy wheeled out of the yard, Lydia glanced back. What truth had Annie been about to share? What had been so special to Mem?

CHAPTER 7

Lydia sat up straight and listened. The dark night outside the window had only one sound, the occasional hoot of an owl. Her mind was far from quiet. Thoughts pressed in. Thoughts of life and death. Of being birthed into darkness and fighting it off her whole life.

Footsteps creaked on the floorboards outside her bedroom door. Was that what had woken her? West Kootenai was far quieter than her apartment in Seattle. Because of that, every single noise seemed amplified, drawing her attention.

Dat was up, stoking the fire. He most likely hadn't been able to sleep. After coming home and resting he'd gotten some of his color back, but he'd hardly eaten a thing. She'd have to watch that — watch him. But tonight, at this moment, he was the one still caring for her and she liked it.

Lydia snuggled into her blankets. She

wasn't alone tonight. Dat was doing his part to keep her warm. He always did his part.

When she was small, he'd come in to sit and watch her sleep. She must have been ten years old the first time she realized he was doing it, but even when she felt his presence there she kept her eyes closed and pretended she was sleeping. Sometimes he'd hum his favorite hymn, barely audible as it leaked through his lips. It took nearly six months for her to get up the nerve to ask Mem about it.

"Why does Dat watch me? Do I talk in my sleep or somethin'?"

"Ne." Mem had chuckled. "Sometimes he still finds it hard to believe the *gut* Lord gave you to us. He says his prayers seem to be closest to God's ear near you . . . because your adoption was our first answered prayer."

Lydia had known from early childhood that she'd been adopted. Mem always called her "their gift." It wasn't until her teen years she understood she'd been a curse first.

"The first answered prayer?" Lydia had asked. "Surely there were more before that."

Mem had smiled at that comment. *"Ja,* there were other answered prayers, but you were the first that mattered. Really mattered."

Another tear slipped out and tumbled onto her pillow. Why hadn't that memory replayed when she was sixteen? During her *rumspringa,* she'd thought more of what *Englisch* things she could get away with. She could listen to music. She could drive a car. She could leave.

As if leaving Mem and Dat would change anything about her birth.

She hadn't gone far at first. She stayed with a family in town. The husband traveled for work, and his wife had an online business. Lydia had watched the kids, cleaned, and soon started editing the woman's presentations. It got her foot in the door with the right people, and she never looked back. At eighteen years old when she was offered a job in Seattle, she left without question. But being here now made her ask herself: why had she turned her back on the two people she loved most?

Why did I waste all those years with Mem? Years that'll never come again.

Lydia cooked Dat breakfast the next morning — eggs, bacon, and toast. He dug in with gusto, giving her a sense of satisfaction that he found such joy in a simple meal.

She yawned. In Seattle she got into the office by eight o'clock, which meant getting p at six o'clock. To Dat, that would be eeping in. As he grew older he started tak-g more naps, but he hadn't yet gotten out f the habit of waking up before the roost-s. Mem used to tease Dat that he needed wake up early so he wouldn't miss his rst nap.

Mem. The house was filled with her things. Iem's mending in a basket by the rocking air. Her favorite mug hanging on a hook the cupboard. Her shawl folded on the ble by the back door. Lydia pictured Mem rapping it around her shoulders to go out feed the chickens or check on the squash the garden, or just to step onto the porch watch the mountain finches flutter ound the yard. But this was Lydia's tchen now, at least for a while. She jotted own notes in her green spiral notebook — emories mostly, and thoughts about what was like to be here again. Then she pushed e notebook to the side.

She'd started a grocery list and considered riving down to Eureka. If she was going to ay here, she needed a few things from the ore. Things she doubted they carried at e West Kootenai Kraft and Grocery.

Her stomach growled as she thought out the Shoo-Fly Pie Mem had taught r to make. Mem always called hers the

Wet Bottom Shoo-Fly, which wasn't the same as the Dry Shoo-Fly that *Oma* Wyse made, which was better for dunking. Lydia made a mental note to check the cupboards for the ingredients for Shoo-Fly Pie — and then changed her mind. Maybe she should wait to make Mem's favorite. Give their hearts time to heal.

She took a sip of her coffee and glanced at her father. His eyes were fixed on Mem's rocking chair. Could he see her there still?

Shoo-Fly Pie. It was the last recipe Mem had sent Lydia in the mail. Lydia had pulled out the recipe card from the envelope, read the latest West Kootenai news, and had thrown the letter away. She tucked her fist under her chin and rested on it, thinking of that now. What had the letter said? She wished she had kept it — kept all Mem's letters.

"Penny for your thoughts."

Lydia glanced up at Dat. His eyes were on her. Warm, gentle, mournful.

"That's an *Englisch* phrase if I've heard one."

He chuckled. "We've lived around here three years yet. Things as these git picked up."

"I was trying to remember the last things Mem wrote to me about. A wedding, I think. And did someone stop by to help you take down a dead tree in the back?"

"*Ja.* It was the tree yer mem used to have her clothesline on. It had to come down, otherwise a bad wind would have sent it into our back porch. A number of the bachelors came by to help . . . including Gideon."

Lydia pretended hearing his name didn't bring a fluttering of butterflies to her stomach.

"Seems like something that would happen. Folks are nice around here. Gideon was kind to walk with me yesterday, although I hope he didn't get too much of a teasing from his bachelor friends."

They'd had a nice walk, a nice talk, and that was all. But curiosity brightened Dat's eyes. What would Dat think if he knew that she and Gideon had briefly discussed her staying?

Coming Home. It would be a good title for a book. She'd already started writing down the jumble of thoughts, feelings, and emotions balled up within her like the yarn in the basket. Maybe she'd find some answers if she had a chance to get words on paper. Maybe writing about Mem would ease the loss.

"I was wondering about something, Dat. About Mem's last words — or your last conversation. Since she didn't know what was to come . . ."

He paused and lifted his head, scanning the timbered ceiling. It took him a few minutes to answer. It wasn't because he'd forgotten, she guessed, but because speaking of Mem was hard.

"She was snuggled into bed already when I came in." Dat's emotions sat heavy in his throat. "I heard something outside and hoped it wasn't deer because I hadn't fixed the fence 'round the garden yet."

"Was it deer?"

"*Ne,* jest the neighbor's dog."

Lydia nodded.

"And she asked about the beans."

"The beans?"

"*Ja,* the beans in the garden. There was a frost coming, and she was worried about them. I told her not to fret, that I'd already covered them in plastic."

She had to check on Mem's garden tomorrow. Mem had been a wonderful gardener during Lydia's growing-up years, but her plot had shrunk over time as it became harder for her to tend to it.

"Oh." Dat sat up straighter and ran his free hand down his beard. "And she had a note for me. Something to put in the Promise Box."

Promise Box. The words sent a tingling sensation down her spine, and she straightened in her chair. "The Promise Box?"

Dat's eyes brightened. *"Ja."* He slowly placed his fork on the table. "I thought about telling you about it last night, but, well, we both needed quiet, time to grieve."

"Okay, but what is it?"

He stood and offered the softest hint of a smile. "It's something I've been wanting to tell you about for a while."

"Tell me about?"

"It was yer mem's most special treasure."

"How come I didn't know, then?" None of the things her mother had owned were worth anything. They were just ordinary household items. None were special. Unless her mem had been hiding something. But why would an Amish woman do that? To live a Plain and simple life was all her mem knew.

"What could she have that would be considered valuable?"

Dat took slow steps toward their bedroom. "It was a gift fer you," he called. "She had a plan yet to give it to you fer your birthday this year."

Warmth filled Lydia's chest. She wanted to see it but was almost afraid to. What did that mean — *Promise Box?*

In less than a minute he returned. In his hands was a simple wooden box. Lydia thought she'd seen it a few times — sitting on the table next to Mem's Bible or on top of her nightstand.

That is the treasure?

He handed it to her and she took it. The wood was smooth but aged as if it had been held in her mother's hands a thousand times.

"Did you make the box?"

Dat nodded. "*Ja,* years ago. For our first anniversary, I think. Ada Mae used to use it to keep stamps and change until she found a better use."

"Then what did she use it for?"

He shrugged. "You'll have to find out. Open it . . . but not here. Later. Give yourself time. You'll want quiet. You'll want to . . ." He smiled. "I don't need to tell ya everything. Jest make it special."

Lydia spread the old quilt under the tall larch tree and settled under a swath of sunshine that had managed to slip through the branches. She curled her legs to the side and tucked her long skirt under her. The breeze was warm. In the distance, Blue whinnied in the pasture. Lydia was only slightly disappointed that she didn't see

Gideon in the field with the horse. Although she would have liked to see him, she mostly wanted to be alone. To discover what was inside the box.

Lydia opened the lid, and her brow furrowed. She'd expected it to have keepsakes, but instead folded pieces of paper were tucked inside. She opened one. A Scripture verse.

"Lo, I am with you alway, Matthew 28:20," was written in Mem's neat script. There was nothing else.

Is this what Mem thought was so special?

Lydia sifted through the papers. Most of them had dates. One of them was thicker, as if it were a few pieces of paper folded together. A tremble moved up her arms, through her chest, and settled in the pit of her stomach. The date on the outside: almost exactly two months after she was born. What secret was tucked inside?

Baby girl, I've been praying for the day I would hold a *kinder* in my arms. A *boppli* of my own. I can't believe yer mine. I've been waiting all my life to have a child, but you are more than I ever dreamed. Even the *Englisch* stop and tell me what a beautiful child. I agree. I hope they do not think me too prideful.

I thought it would be something special to have a daughter, but to be chosen by a mother . . . I cannot describe the feeling of knowing another would choose me to care for a child she carried and birthed. I feel unworthy. I feel special. I know there will be hard days, but I cannot imagine a moment I do not wonder of this gift. Of you.

I considered myself prepared to be a mother. With younger brothers and sisters I knew about the feeding, and bathing, and holding. But I wasn't prepared for the swell of love deep inside. Sometimes I expect my dress not to be able to pin because I'm certain my heart has doubled inside my chest. I hold you more than I ought because I don't want to lose a moment. I know how quickly the time passes.

You'll be soon crawling around on yer own. Yet with each moment I have your head tucked under my chin — breathing in your scent — I think of another woman. A woman with empty arms. Does she wonder about you? Does she hold you in her dreams? I have no doubt of both.

Yer dat feels the same love as I. I've caught him more than once in the night just sitting by your cradle and watching you. He told me the other day that he didn't feel worthy of such a gift. I told him that's why it's called a gift; it's something given, not earned.

You are so lovely, daughter, so innocent. I only wish you could stay as such. I hate to think ahead to the day when I'll explain to you about the circumstances of you coming to us — of you knowing the truth. Hopefully when the time comes the truth of the love your dat and I have will overshadow the pain. It is my greatest wish.

Love, Mem

Lydia stared at the words. She read the letter three times, trying to take it all in. Her mother's words of love weren't surprising. She'd known that love. She'd felt it. She'd seen it in Mem's gaze. What surprised her was that from those first months, Mem was already concerned about her discovery of the truth. It wasn't an easy truth to understand.

Lydia placed the letter on the quilt and looked past the pasture to the trees and hills, to the tall, jagged mountain peaks that jutted into the sky beyond. One could see the beauty of the mountains, yet the hardship of the climb up into them wasn't known until the hike started. One could know the pain of revealing the coming truth; feeling it was something different. Mem had hoped her love was enough to keep Lydia in their home, to keep her Amish. The hardship of watching her daughter walk away must have been overwhelming to bear.

Lydia lifted the letter and pressed it against her chest.

Why didn't I appreciate you more?

A small sob broke through with her words. "Why didn't I accept your love, stay rooted in it and protected by it, when I had the chance?"

Her mem's greatest fears had come to light the day she turned sixteen. Lydia wished she could go back. But there was no going back. There never would be.

Her fingers flipped through the other folded up pieces of paper. Would all of these make her equally sad?

Lydia prepared to close the box when the note on the very top caught her attention. The handwriting was shakier than the other ones, and it was dated . . . just four days ago. The day of Mem's death. It was the last note Dat had tucked inside the Promise Box for Mem.

She picked it up, turned it over in her

hand, and then put it down again. They were her mem's last words, and she doubted that she'd written about beans. Lydia put the note in the box, closed the lid . . . then pulled it out again and opened it up before she lost her nerve.

Dearest Lydia,

If you found this box, it means that my time on earth is through. I have been a selfish woman. For most of the day I've felt my life slip away. I've battled sickness all my life, but nothing like this. It's as if the pull to heaven is stronger than the pull to earth.

I thought about having Dat use a neighbor's phone to call you and tell you to come, but I convinced myself to wait until tomorrow. I want to see you, dear daughter, but not the sadness in your gaze. And I want one more day with your father just to appreciate the ordinary, simple moments of our life.

Although it has not always been an easy life, I don't regret one day of it. I am thankful to the Lord for many things: To live the Amish lifestyle. To be surrounded by a gut community. To have been taught to know the Lord and love Him. And last — and most — for your father and you.

Some women have ten children, but I wouldn't trade ten for you. Though you are far from me in miles, you are not far in heart. With each promise I write, I not only thank the Lord for His goodness, I also pray you can find hope in these words.

Out of all the promises one is my favorite:

"Be strong and of a good courage, fear not, nor be afraid of them: for the Lord thy God, he it is that doth go with thee; he will not fail thee, nor forsake thee," Deuteronomy 31:6.

No matter where you go our good Lord will be with you. He will never leave you. My prayer is that you don't feel as if you left Him when you left the Amish.

Dear Lydia, I don't know what words a mother is supposed to share with her daughter, but the ones I share here, within this wood casing, are those that have meant the most to me. They are not thoughts or quotes, they are promises. This is my Promise Box.

I didn't understand God's promises for many years. I assumed our Lord giving us salvation and the hope of heaven was enough. But through the years God has promised so much more. And I learned this promise because of you, the first promise offered.

Within these notes is your story, daughter. The promises from God are for you.

Love, Mem

The letter ended. Lydia wished there was more. She wished Mem had called. *I'd give anything for one more day with her.*

Her heart sunk with heaviness, but the joy of finding this box of treasures was like helium balloons, holding it up from sinking completely.

Annie had mentioned something about Mem's promises too. *Promises? What promises?* What did Mem mean?

Lydia put the letter back into the box and closed it. She couldn't read more now. Not yet. Mem's words were alive to her, as if she was sitting right next to her. She'd have to take them slowly, treasure them. Or at least that was her excuse.

She rose and folded up the quilt . . . and noticed Gideon striding across the pasture, approaching Blue. Lydia had books to edit. The wise thing would be to go shopping in Eureka and then spend some time working

101

on a manuscript. Yet the sight of the man and the horse tugged at her like a magnet. She approached the fence and watched as Gideon tied a loose rope around Blue's neck. The horse acted like Gideon had done so every day of his life.

Lydia knew the truth: Blue was untamed and unreliable. Gideon knew that about the horse and understood.

She pulled the quilt tighter to her chest, running her fingers over the straight hem. Did Gideon read people as well as animals? What did he see when he looked at her? Her mem saw someone worthy of God's promises, but Lydia hadn't seen that in herself. Not for a very long time.

CHAPTER 8

Gideon straightened and adjusted his hat, willing his heart to calm its double beat. Lydia watched from a distance. Beside him Blue's ears twitched, and the horse tossed his head. Gideon chuckled. "You felt that, did you?"

If he wanted to succeed with Blue, he'd better pay the pretty redhead no mind. The horse picked up Gideon's piqued emotions. Confidence and calmness were the two most important qualities of a horse trainer.

Blowing out a long, deep breath, he wrapped an arm around the back of Blue's neck and rubbed him briskly on both sides of the neck. To get ready for the halter, the horse needed to understand Gideon could touch all around his neck without startling him. Gideon had seen more than one person trying to reach around a horse's neck only to have the horse get spooked, plowing him over. Being calm didn't mean that the horse wouldn't jump and be scared . . . but it helped.

After a few minutes, Blue warmed up to him, and Gideon took the halter and rubbed it on the side of Blue's face, getting him used to the feel. When Blue was comfortable, he attempted to wrap the halter around Blue's neck and buckle it. The jingling of the harness caused Blue's ears to prick. He jerked. Gideon swooped the halter off, grabbing the rope just in case Blue bolted. Sure enough, the horse started out on a trot. Gideon held onto the rope, letting Blue know he wasn't going to get away. The horse tugged slightly, and then submitted, running in full circles around Gideon. He released a breath and held on, knowing the horse would calm. Thirty seconds later Blue paused and glanced over at Gideon again. Gideon reeled in the rope as if he were pulling in a large fish. Blue came with no problem.

Gideon tried to ignore Lydia, but he couldn't help but glance at her out of the corner of his eye. She watched with interest, and Gideon liked having her there. He liked that she appreciated his work. Lydia would make a great friend. He had many *Englisch* friends in the area. One more wouldn't hurt, right?

Gideon again forced himself to stay calm and focused on the horse. He didn't make a big deal of the fact that the jingle of the harness had spooked Blue a few minutes ago. Everyone deserved a second chance.

This time he placed the noseband on Blue first, then reached to the other side of Blue's head and grasped the crownpiece and buckled it. He looked to Lydia again, expecting a wave or thumbs-up. Instead she stood chatting on her cell phone. His heart ached as if Blue had bruised it with a wild kick. Who was he fooling? They were too different. He was just someone who'd occupy her time until she headed back to her city life.

The truth hurt.

That's why he hadn't approached Edgar to get more details about that event twenty years ago. The truth would hurt. Wasn't that why Mem and Dat had kept quiet all these years?

Yesterday, after the funeral, he'd gone back to the bachelors' cabin and sat on the front porch, boots kicked up on the porch railing, looking into the hills.

He'd sensed Edgar's eyes on him during the funeral, but he refused to make eye contact. Why did he have to be the stupid kid who had gotten lost in the woods?

Who'd disobeyed his parents and caused trouble in the whole community? His mother had reminded him many times where disobedience had led him. How could he forget?

Couldn't he have been remembered for something good? Something noble? Guilt harnessed itself to his heart, and he wished he could shake it off.

"C'mon, Blue." He led the horse through the pasture away from Lydia. Leading with a rope was an important part of the training. It put a connection between him and the horse; through it Blue learned trust.

They walked through the pasture and then toward a hill, passing under the trees. It was dimmer there. His mentor's words trailed through his thoughts:

"The horse needs to learn that no matter what you bring into his life, you will not purposefully hurt him. In fact, the trust built might even save a horse's life one day."

"You're trusting me, aren't you?" Gideon spoke the words to Blue, but he also couldn't help but feel as if God was speaking the same words to his heart.

"Trust isn't really trust when you're allowed to roam free in the sunshine, is it?" he said in a whisper. "You're gonna learn trust by walking in the shadows. By feeling constrained. By letting me lead."

After guiding Blue for fifteen minutes, Gideon took off the halter and untied the rope around the horse's neck. With a pat on Blue's hindquarters, Gideon let the horse know the lesson was over for the day. He carried the tack across the pasture and thought about heading back to his cabin to write a letter to Mem and Dat. Maybe he'd give them a chance to tell him the truth before he asked Edgar.

Gideon had made it halfway across the pasture when he glanced over at the Wyse place again, fully expecting to see Lydia still talking on the phone. Instead, she stood near the front porch with two other bachelors — Amos and Micah. Micah's buggy was parked out front, and his horse nibbled on the grass by the fence line.

Lydia's head tossed back, and her laughter spilled onto the breeze. His gut tensed. He pulled off his hat and wiped his brow with the back of his sleeve. What were those two doing there? They hadn't cared enough about Mrs. Wyse to show up at the funeral, and now they were going to stop by?

Gideon lowered his head. Of course — like his mem always told him — another's actions weren't his to judge.

He kept walking, tried to ignore them, but

Gideon knew the beautiful redhead stood behind the purpose for their visit. *I should just let them be.* But something inside propelled him that direction. He approached the fence, and Mr. Wyse's dog, Rex, bounded toward him. Gideon reached down to pet the dog, and then climbed over the fence and approached the others.

He fixed his eyes on Lydia, and she glanced his direction. "Is there an ice cream social I hadn't heard about?"

"Oh, no." Lydia placed a hand over her chest and then looked back at the two young men. "They've come bringing Dat home. He walked down to the Kraft and Grocery, and he stumbled off the porch and banged up his leg. Annie had called my cell and was going to drive him home herself when Micah offered. Which was so kind." Lydia smiled at him. "I can't believe —"

"Is he all right? Yer dat?" Gideon looked to the doorway.

Lydia frowned. "I hope so. He limped inside and wouldn't let me take a peek at his leg, but I'll check on it. Said he tripped over a loose board on the front step. I hope that's all it is."

"It's been a hard few days for him." Gideon glanced to Amos, Micah, and then back to Lydia. "But it was good to see you smile.

I heard your laughter all the way out in the pasture."

"*Ja,* well it's Micah's fault." She narrowed her gaze at the blond bachelor. "He's the one who told me what Dat said."

Gideon pushed his hat farther back on his head. "What's that?"

Micah smiled. "When I asked Mr. Wyse if he wanted a ride, he said, 'Suppose so. Seems to me my git ain't goin' very far.'"

Lydia laughed again. "It's funny because Dat always used to ask me, 'Lydia, are you ready yet? We best git going.' I'd always tease him and ask what his 'git' was."

Then as quickly as the smile brightened her face, it faded. A shadow of memory moved across her eyes. "And then Mem would always respond the same." Lydia sighed. "She'd always say, 'My husband is getting so *crittlich* of late. Give yer daughter a moment.' " Lydia lowered her head. "It's amazing how those little things that didn't seem to matter mean the most now."

Lydia reached up, as if to fiddle with her *kapp* strings, and then dropped her hand. Gideon tried to picture her in Amish dress. He liked that thought.

Lydia forced a smile and looked back at Micah. "I'll get in now and check on Dat.

Thank you so much for giving him a ride home."

Amos nodded. "*Ja,* of course. I hope he feels better soon."

Micah took a step closer. "Won't you let us know?"

Lydia nodded. "Of course." Then she glanced to Gideon. "See you tomorrow . . . in the pasture, that is."

"*Ja,* me and old Blue . . ." He waved as he strode away, wishing he'd come up with something wittier to say.

The other bachelors followed Gideon out from the front lawn. When the front door of the cabin shut behind them, with Lydia inside, Micah turned to Amos. "Oh, boy, what I would give to have a *buss* from her!"

Amos winked. "Just one kiss? I'd like to make her my girl."

"*Ja,* but she's *Englisch.*" Micah glanced back over his shoulder. "Too bad." He climbed into the buggy.

Amos smirked. "Maybe so, but I've not been baptized yet. There's no one who says I couldn't make her my girlfriend."

"I say you can't." The words shot from Gideon's mouth.

"You?" Amos looked back at him. "Don't tell me yer fancy on her. You've been baptized. I heard you preach that day when the bishop was out of town."

"*Ja,* that's true." Gideon's mind scurried to find an excuse. "But have you thought of this . . ." He paused, considering. "Her mem passed jest days ago. You should wait two weeks at least before making a social call."

Amos lifted a brow and eyed him. "Is that a church rule?"

"*Ne,* jest common courtesy."

Micah climbed into the buggy, and Amos did the same. "All right, then, I'll be watching you too, Gideon. Making sure yer *courteous.*" He motioned to the backseat. "Coming?"

Gideon shook his head. "*Ne,* I'll walk. I have to stop by the Carash place and tell Dave how the horse training's coming."

Micah nodded, but Gideon could tell Micah knew he was just blowing hot air about the common courtesy. Gideon couldn't believe how he was acting either.

Why had he been so bold and forceful about Lydia? He knew why. He couldn't bear the thought of these other bachelors playing with her emotions. He didn't know her too well, not yet, but something told him that Lydia was special. More special than to be treated with disrespect.

It wasn't that he had any intentions. As a

man baptized into the church, he couldn't.
Shouldn't.

CHAPTER 9

Pat sat in the rocking chair, and Lydia opened the white curtains in the front windows wider, then sat down on the green padded footstool before him, determined to look at his leg.

He waved a hand her direction. "It's fine, really."

Lydia placed her elbow on her knee and her fist under her chin to wait. "I'm not going to move until I look."

"Didn't ya have laundry to take down from the line?"

"I did — I do, but it can wait." She grinned up at him. "You should be *donkbawr* I don't jest call the doctor."

"Thankful? *Ne.* There's no need for a doctor! It's only a bruise."

"If that's the case, then let me see. You know how *fartzooned* Mem would be if I didn't insist. She'd be sitting here doing the same."

Dat nodded and his gray beard brushed against his homemade shirt. "All right, then, but just because yer doing so well with your Amish words. I thought you'd forgot yet and got all fancy like."

"How could I forget?" She reached forward and grabbed his pant leg, slowly rolling it up. "I'm actually enjoying letting my words relax. There was much about my upbringing I missed."

He cleared his throat. "Enough to make you want to come back?"

Lydia paused her movement.

His lips pressed into a thin line, and the wrinkles around his mouth splayed out. His top lip had a small nick from his razor, and she remembered Mem had always shaved him. She hadn't thought about that. Who would help him now, and as he aged? How could she turn her back?

She took his hand. It trembled in her grasp. "You finally asked. I was waiting for you to. Mem was the one who always held you back from asking me before — held your reins from prodding me so." She bit her lip, then lowered her voice. "I'm not sure, Dat. There's a lot to think about. I'm still trying to figure out what I want from life."

Gideon's face filled her mind, but she

quickly pushed his warm smile and chiseled features out of her thoughts. If she returned to West Kootenai for good, the handsome bachelor wouldn't be the reason. Besides, at the end of hunting season, he'd find his way back to his own home.

No, family — and maybe even faith — would guide her decision. Gideon's dark brown eyes and gentle demeanor might be able to tame a horse, but she couldn't let him wrangle her heart so easily.

"You mean you will consider it, *ferleicht*?"

"Perhaps. But it's something I need to think about."

Dat leaned back in his rocking chair, no longer hesitant about letting her check his leg. She returned to her examination.

"Will you pray about it too?"

Lydia finished rolling up his pant leg and winced. "*Ja, ja.* Of course." Dat's shin was bruised from the top of his foot up to his knee.

"You got yourself good." She prodded gently and then clucked her tongue. "But nothing looks broken. Just a nasty bruise."

"That's what I get for trying to go grocery shopping. I couldn't even make it to the front door." He had a soft smile even as he said the words, and she knew it was from

her admittance that she'd consider returning.

Still, consideration was not a decision.
Lydia tucked a strand of red hair behind
her ear. She nibbled on her bottom lip, and
her heart turned to a stone in her chest.
How disappointed he'd be when she decided to return to Seattle after all.

*I didn't promise. I told him I'd think about it.
And . . . pray.*

Did she even think prayer worked anymore?

Lydia placed her hand on his and forced a
smile. "Don't worry about doing the shopping. I'll get some groceries tomorrow. I'm
so sorry. I should have taken care of that
today. I just . . ."

"I saw we were out of coffee. Your mem
did so much — managed our home so well
— even on days she couldn't get out of bed.
I was trying to help." Color drained from
his cheeks. His face took on the gray shade
of grief.

Moistening tears caught her by surprise.
"I didn't get to the store because I looked
in the Promise Box. I read a few of Mem's
letters."

"Beautiful, don't you think?"

"The letters?"

"*Ja,* and the woman who wrote them.

More beautiful through the years."

Lydia nodded, thinking of her mem. Dull brown hair, a plain-looking round face, heavy around her middle. She'd been beautiful to Lydia, to Dat.

"She was simple and ordinary by the world's standards," Dat said, as if reading Lydia's thoughts, "but she had such spunk. I remember when I first laid eyes on her. It was at a volleyball game. She ran and dove for the ball as if there wasna anything more important in the world. I liked that about her, but I mourned when she became the ball, being hit around by life."

He fisted his hands in his lap and pounded them softly once, twice. "The weakening of her heart over the years pained me to see. Each year she put aside doing more things she loved, but the worst was when year after year passed and no children came."

Lydia released his pant leg and swallowed down her emotion. "Nothing could be worse for an Amish woman . . ."

"For any woman with a loving heart like Mem's." He unclenched his hands, sighed, and leaned back farther into his chair. "For years she was jest going through the motions. And then the promise came."

"The promise?"

"*Ja* . . . that's what started the box. One

117

promise Mem clung to as if it held her very breath of life. More promises came after that, but the one promise softened her heart to hear the rest."

"It sounds like you're building up the plot in a mystery novel." Lydia chuckled. It was the only thing that kept her from crying over missing Mem.

"It's a mystery, all right. God's promises are always a mystery. A *gut* God like that. He didn't have to offer anything, but He gave us Himself, and so much more."

She scooted the stool closer and placed her cheek on his knee like she used to as a young girl. When she was younger, he'd just pat her *kapp,* but now her dat ran his finger through the red curls that framed her face. She imagined his smile. Maybe he even remembered her red curls from when she was a baby?

"Was that first promise in the box?"

"*Ja.* I remember the moment we arrived home from church service — yer mem was writing it down. She didn't want to forget one word."

Lydia wanted to ask more questions, but she doubted her dat would tell any more than he already had. More than that, she wanted to read more of Mem's words. The promise — whatever it was — would mean more coming from Mem's heart.

Rex approached and curled by Lydia's side, and she ran her fingers through his fur. She lifted her head and looked into Dat's eyes. "That first promise must have been pretty important."

"I'd say so." Dat winked, then cleared his throat. "And I have another promise I must keep." His brow furrowed.

She scooted back and stood. "What's that?"

"I promised Annie from the store that I'd get help with the chores for the next few days."

"That's a good promise. I'm glad she's watching out fer you. If you just remind me of everything, I can do it. It's been a couple of years."

Dat shook his head. "Annie made me promise something else too: that you wouldn't do them. She says you need time for your own healing."

"Yes, okay, but then who?"

"*Vell,* Ruth Sommer asked to come by with dinner. Her daughter, Marianna, has already offered to help with the chickens and garden." Dat rose and hobbled to the window. "I was thinking Gideon for some of the work in the barn. I do need help with the harnesses." He flexed his fingers. "I don't have as much strength as I used to."

"Gideon?" She walked up to Dat and stood by him, shoulder to shoulder. Her stomach churned at his growing expectations. "What about Micah and Amos? They seem nice enou—"

"Ne." His refusal shot between them. "They are nice, but Gideon will be working right at the Carashes' house. It's so close. No need for another to make an extra trip."

"Gideon, eh?"

She opened her mouth to remind him that a good Amish bachelor would never be interested in an *Englisch* girl, but a passel of dresses and *kapp*s coming down the driveway kept the words balled up in her mouth. Dat had told her Ruth Sommer and Marianna would be coming by. They led the procession, and six more Amish women with them, each one carrying a basket filled with items.

Dat nodded toward the approaching women. "I think that's my cue to find something to fiddle with in the barn." He limped toward the back door and slipped outside.

The women's voices carried up the long driveway, even though they spoke in low tones. They came because they'd cared for Mem. They came because Amish cared for one another.

Lydia opened the front door, tucked her hands in her apron pocket, and stepped out onto the porch. White clouds had met up against the mountains, casting a shadow on the valley, but seeing the women's faces brightened the day.

"I hope we're not intruding." Ruth Sommer held up a basket filled with canning jars — plum jam, cherries, beets. "We brought you some things. It's not much, but . . ."

"It's wonderful. You've already done so much." Lydia stepped inside and welcomed them in. Without hesitation, the women hurried to the kitchen. All but one.

"I thought I saw Marianna . . ." Lydia scanned the room.

"She's already gone back to check the garden," Ruth explained. "She sometimes came down and weeded while your mem watched." Ruth placed a hand on Lydia's arm. "Marianna was afraid she'd tear up if she came inside — although I told her there was no shame in shedding a tear for a friend."

Lydia nodded, taking a deep breath. The women's smiles lightened a load she didn't realize she'd been carrying.

A tear fell from the corner of her eye. She

wiped it with her knuckle. "That's *gut* — good — advice." She shut the door, and then followed the women into the kitchen. "And I want to thank you for your friendship. The way you cared for Mem. She wrote often about how you visited, helped. She hasn't been well for a very long time."

"That's what the good Lord expects." A small woman with grayish blonde hair placed an apple pie on the kitchen counter. "I've received help myself more than once." The woman peered up at Lydia, concern narrowing her gaze. "And what about you — is there anything we can do to help you? I'm not *gut* with words, but if you need someone to visit with yer dat so you could get time to work on those books, I can send my husband down."

"I'll be fine." She waved a hand. "Dat goes to bed early, and I'm eager to work by lamplight. Maybe it'll add more creativity to my edits."

"Not that you need that." Ruth Sommer crossed her arms over her chest. "Your mem told us of your work. She tried not to talk pridefully, but you should have seen the way her eyes glowed."

Lydia tried to think of something to say but didn't know what. Weariness descended upon her and the fresh reality of her loss hit her again. No one would ever care as much about her work as Mem had.

A younger woman, also with red hair, approached. She introduced herself as Eve and then pointed to the kitchen. "I placed some bread on the counter. I'll make sure a fresh loaf is delivered every morning for the next week."

Lydia shook her head. "No, that's too much."

"It's not too much. It's just bread. Besides, I asked Gideon, and he offered to deliver it."

Lydia's brows furrowed. "But why Gideon?"

Eve pursed her lips. "He's at the restaurant for breakfast, and he works right next door." Eve's expression told Lydia it would be foolishness to consider Gideon's visit as anything more than just a helpful gesture. Eve also had a look of superiority in her gaze. Maybe Eve — and the other women — didn't think Lydia could make bread, being *Englisch* and all. Maybe they felt it was their duty to make sure her dat didn't starve.

"Yes. Of course." Lydia took a step back. Her father might have high hopes for her return to Amish society, but he was the only one.

Eve cast a sideways glance at her, and Lydia felt as if an army of ants crawled up her spine.

The women didn't stay long. They hurried out as quickly as they hurried in. As their cluster of white *kapp*s moved past the Carash place and disappeared down the road, Dat returned to the house and cut himself a large slice of apple pie. He sat at the kitchen table, and his shoulders slumped as if eating the pie seemed like too much work. He only picked at the golden brown crust.

Lydia chatted about the kindness of the women, but Dat didn't answer. Instead he pointed out the window toward the pasture.

Through the tall grass, Blue trotted toward the Carash house. The horse's gaze was on Gideon. Blue was most likely ready for dinner, to be brushed down, and be put into the corral for the night. But instead of paying attention to the horse, Gideon's eyes were on the women as they walked past.

Eve waved at him, and Lydia quickly looked away, surprised by the prick of jealousy that jabbed her heart. She crossed her arms over her chest and strode to the kitchen, eyeing the perfect loaf of bread. There was no reason why someone like Eve and someone like Gideon shouldn't be attracted to each other. No reason at all.

"Do you think you can talk to him about choring?" Dat asked. "I'd be happy to pay."

"Ask Gideon?" She lifted her chin, determined not to let jealousy stand in the way of friendship. He'd been good to her — to her dat. "*Ja*, of course. I'll head down soon."

Lydia waited until Gideon moved to the barn with Blue. Then she made Dat a cup of tea and went to her room to freshen up. She ran a brush through her hair, telling herself that her emotions were a tangled mess after losing her mem and she shouldn't get wrapped up in Gideon. Or who caught his fancy. Her heart raced as she thought about staying here and helping Dat. Would she have to face emotions like this every day? Being around people meant dealing with them . . . and figuring out her temporary place in the midst of them.

In three days she'd remembered things she hadn't in six years. She remembered the joy of being a daughter, a like-minded friend. She remembered the care of a community. She remembered the soft touch of her dat's hand on her cheek. She remembered the joy she'd brought her mem — joy she shared openly in her Promise Box letters and notes. She'd never experienced such emptiness as she did over the loss of her mem.

She also remembered what it was like to be interested in someone. She'd been so focused on her career she hadn't given herself time to date, no matter how often Bonnie told her she "needed to get out and meet a nice guy."

Lydia twisted up her bun, pinning it, and then put on a long skirt and T-shirt. She remembered, too, how it felt to be an outsider. In Ohio she'd looked the same on the outside but internally was vastly different than those good people in her community. Here people knew she was different. They had no expectations she couldn't fulfill.

Lydia sauntered to the hooks hanging on the wall and grabbed a sweater, knowing the air would grow chilly in the afternoon.

She headed down the dirt road, thinking of the editing work waiting for her back at the house. What would life be like without constant deadlines? While it was work she was good at, since being in Montana she hadn't missed it. Instead it seemed like an unnecessary chore. How many beautiful summer days had she spent inside poring over ink on paper? Too many.

She lifted her face to the fading sunlight,

as if discovering its warmth for the first time, and quickened her steps.

In the three days since she'd arrived, she'd buried her mother and discovered a secret gift. A box of promises.

In these three days she'd been part of this community — their burying and their caring. She'd forgotten how the Amish supported each other.

Gideon stood by the corral. Seeing her, he lifted his hand and waved.

She'd also forgotten how attraction could reach up and grab one's throat, seizing excited breaths. And while many men had warmed her with their smiles, Gideon lit a match, tossed it inside her heart, and heated a blaze. And the thing was . . . she couldn't imagine Gideon not being Amish. It was who he was. His mannerisms, his speech, his care for horses, his care for others. Lydia wouldn't be as attracted to him if he were just another guy she'd met at a coffee shop.

What did this say about her?

Lydia approached and leaned against the top rail of the corral. "You're really making progress here, aren't you?"

"*Ja,* I'd say so. I didn't even have to call, and I saw bright eyes and a happy gait coming toward me."

She chuckled. "Are you talking about me

or the horse?"

"*Vell,* I hadn't thought about it before, but now that I am, maybe both."

"Oh, *gut.* We're on an equal playing field, vying for your attention — me and Blue."

A chuckle burst from his lips. "I wouldn't say it's equal. I'm getting paid to care for Blue."

"Hey, not so fast." She held up her finger. "How come you just assume I'd come for a social visit? Turns out I've actually come to offer you a job — tending to *me.*"

"You? Do you have a horse you're hiding somewhere? With yer vehicle, I'm not sure I'm the man for your task."

"Not that. My dat asked if you'd be interested in helping with the chores. After he fell, he promised Annie he'd get help."

Gideon took a large brush and set to work at brushing Blue down. "*Ja,* of course, but I should have offered."

"Just as long as you say yes." She reached out and pet Blue's nose. "I'm not one to muck stalls, especially after being away from it for so long."

"Can I tonight, after I finish here?"

"*Ja. Gut,* then, I'll make dinner. I insist you stay."

He paused. "That'll be nice, but just as long as it's *only* work."

His words shot like an arrow to her heart. She took a step back, and her shoulder bumped against the wooden post of the corral. "Of course. I understand. Me being *Englisch* and all."

"Oh, it's not that." He reached a hand toward her as if wishing he could take back his words. Then he shook his head and turned back to Blue. "It's jest that Micah and Amos, well, they were both talking about callin' on you. I told them that it seemed only proper to give you time and space to heal after just losing your mother."

Gideon looked like a nervous boy whose mother had just found a frog in his pocket. "Oh, really? How much time did you tell them I needed?"

"Two weeks."

She ran her fingers over the rough wood on the corral railing. Why did he want the other bachelors to stay away?

Does it matter?

It did. It mattered a lot. And that's what worried her. She was intrigued by this kind, handsome Amish man.

"Two weeks. I see." She crossed her arms, guarding herself from reading too much into this. "So you'll be by later?"

He ran a hand down Blue's velvety coat. "*Ja,* I just need to finish up here."

"Dat'll be happy." She wanted to say more — that she'd be happy too — but she couldn't.

She'd walked away from being Amish. That was her decision. And she couldn't live with herself if she thought she had any part in drawing someone away. To open her heart up to Gideon would cost her nothing. For him to open his heart up to her, everything — all he was — would be at stake.

Lydia offered a quick wave, turned, and headed back to her parents' house.

Then again . . . maybe she was actually the one being drawn.

CHAPTER 10

Lydia opened the door to the pantry for the third time. Although she saw the items, they blurred before her. Her mind was not on dinner. Not at all. She'd never be able to get the cooking done if she didn't talk to someone about all that was happening — so much in her mind and heart.

"Dinner can wait ten minutes." She hurried toward her bedroom, where she opened the bottom drawer of her dresser and pulled out her cell phone. She had less than half a bar of battery. She should save it since there was no place in Dat's house to plug in the phone and charge it, but she couldn't wait. If she didn't talk to someone, she'd burst. She pressed the speed dial for Bonnie, then crawled onto her bed and pulled the quilt over her head to muffle her voice.

"Hello?"

"Bonnie, it's me."

"Lydia, are you all right?"

"*Ja* . . . yes," she mumbled.

"Are you sure? You said you were going all the way during the few weeks that you were with your dat — no cell phones, no driving."

"I know, but I had to talk to you. Otherwise I'm going to go crazy."

"Is it that bad?" She could hear an echoing sound as if Bonnie was driving down the highway.

"It's worse. I've got a crush."

"What are you talking about?"

"Okay, maybe not a crush-crush, but there is this guy. I've never known anyone like him. He's so handsome and kind. He seems to have a good heart, but maybe it's just attraction. Dumb, confusing attraction."

"Uh-oh, that's going to cause a problem."

"What do you mean?"

"I was serious about what I told you as you left. I think you should stay there, start being Amish again, and write about it. I don't want a guy — a handsome cowboy — distracting you."

"You don't understand. He's Amish."

Bonnie chuckled. "Amish. You have a crush on an Amish man?"

Lydia balled her fist and pushed the quilt back from her face. "Why did you say it like that? Do you think you — *your* people —

132

are the only ones who got the beauty gene? He has dark hair and eyes that are almost black. You'd think he was cute if you saw him — homemade shirt and suspenders included."

"Yes, maybe I would. But is that all you like about him? His curls and sexy swagger?"

The quilt pressed heavy on her body, and Lydia pushed it to the side. "I said nothing about his swagger."

"No, you didn't need to. I can hear it in your voice."

"You can?"

"Yes, and I'll stop bothering you now about returning to the Amish. I have a feeling circumstances will make that inevitable."

"It's not that easy. Not at all."

"But you've been thinking about the book — your story — right?" Lydia could hear a smile in her voice.

"I've been jotting down notes."

"Notes? Are you kidding? We've had long talks about this. Remember? Your 'someday' book? You have something to say —"

"They're just musings, observations about the Amish lifestyle from someone who's been away far too long."

"Do you hear yourself? That's amazing stuff. I'm not saying you make this a sensational, tell-all book about the Amish. But carry us — the reader — into the world with you. Share inside facts only someone like you could know. Let us feel your struggle, your conflict."

"Observing brings no conflict," Lydia stated flatly. "It's only a story if I return — go all the way. And I won't do that unless I feel this can be my home."

The other end of the line was silent, but she knew Bonnie was still there, giving her time to think. Allowing time for truth to seep in like rain on freshly tilled soil.

She liked the idea that at any moment someone "out there" could be reading her words. It had given her some satisfaction when she'd edited, but it wasn't the same. There was a difference between making spaghetti sauce from the tomatoes, onions, and peppers she'd grown in her garden, and opening a can of prepared sauce and adding a few seasonings. Even if she made the sauce better with her seasonings, it still wasn't her creation.

Lydia had known that about cooking for years, but she appreciated it with her words now too. In the last few days she'd jotted down little notes about the community, the people, and questions about where she really belonged.

"Maybe I'll write my story, but it'll be just for me — and maybe for my husband and children someday, if God ever blesses me with such."

"That sounds like a good idea." A horn blared through the phone, but Bonnie paid it no mind. She chuckled.

"What? What's so funny?"

"If you start writing, a book will come out of it. Circumstances will make that inevitable too."

Lydia bit her lip and knew Bonnie was right. Even as she wrote down her thoughts, she could already see how easy it would be to structure them into scenes, chapters.

"You process through your pen, Lydia," Bonnie continued. "Don't run from that. Put your words on the paper and see what they tell you. I have a feeling you're on the right path. You just have to give yourself permission to follow your heart."

"Circumstances will make that inevitable." The words replayed in Lydia's mind as she peeled potatoes and started scrambling eggs. With their chickens out back, eggs were something she could always count on.

She whipped up some biscuits and took out a jar of Mem's apple butter. *Inevitable?* A book? A romance? A new life? If it was only that easy.

If Bonnie had used the word *inevitable* last week, she would have argued. But now . . . Lydia couldn't describe how comfortable she felt in Mem's kitchen. Joy seeped through her veins at the thought of waking up tomorrow morning and sipping coffee on the front porch with Dat. Of walking to the grocery store for supplies and offering a wave to Ruth Sommer as she passed her house. Of looking out into the pasture and seeing Gideon there, working with Blue.

But if she did that, something else was inevitable too: in a small place like this, she couldn't hide from her past. Maybe Mem had already told Annie the truth behind Lydia's adoption. Annie knew about the Promise Box, didn't she?

Her breaths came short, quick, but she told herself not to think of that now. Tonight she didn't have to dwell on the pain. Today — if she allowed it — could be the first step into a new beginning.

Lydia peeked out the window. Gideon stood out back with Dat, and for some reason it seemed right that he was here now. There weren't many chores. Dat had only his mare for the buggy, one cow, and some chickens. There was a small garden to tend. Dat limped around, pointing out the rows of squash, beans, and carrots as if the garden were a blue-ribbon affair. Gideon nodded and smiled at Dat, warming Lydia's heart. She leaned over the sink and swung open the kitchen window.

"Dat, if you see any tomatoes, I can use them in my scramble!"

Dat eyed the tomato bushes and nodded, but it was Gideon who kneeled down and inspected the plants, choosing the reddest tomatoes.

Ten minutes later they were seated around the table. Dat lowered his head in silent prayer. Lydia and Gideon did the same.

Thank you. The words were heavy in her heart. She was thankful to be here. To have time with her dat, and to be able to hold Mem's promises in her hands. She was also thankful for Gideon's friendship. Even if their relationship never got beyond that, she was thankful.

They lifted their heads, almost in unison, and Lydia filled their plates.

"Looks *wunderbar*!" Gideon took a deep breath and then forked a large portion into his mouth. When he finished chewing, his eyes locked with hers. "*Danki* for insisting I stay."

Heat rose up her cheeks, and Lydia waved a hand. "Nothing special. I really need to go shopping, but Mem's tomatoes do make a delightful touch."

The mood sobered, and Lydia glanced to her left. It was hard to ignore Mem's empty chair.

"I could see your mem loved to garden and tend her chickens, but who's the reader?" Gideon pointed to the glass-encased bookshelf by the fireplace.

The shelf had been there for as long as she could remember. It held her favorite childhood books and stacks of *Family Life* magazines.

"I've always been a reader. Without siblings, books became —" Lydia's words paused as she eyed the shelf behind the glass doors. Many of the old books were gone, and inside was another stack. How had she not noticed that before?

One book was on decorating. Another a memoir about a service dog who worked in hospitals. The third a mystery novel for kids — not the type of books one would typically find in an Amish home.

Lydia gasped. "Dat . . . you . . . those . . . Who bought copies of my books?" She placed her fork to the side of her plate.

Gideon's eyes widened. "Your books?"

"Not mine. I mean, I didn't write them. But I worked — work — for a small publishing company in Seattle, and those are books I edited. I just had no idea . . ." She blinked back the tears.

"It was your mother." Dat placed his fork on the table and smiled, as if she'd just caught on to an inside joke. "Any time you mentioned a book in one of your letters she had me take her to the Kraft and Grocery, and she'd ask Annie to order it on her computer. She couldn't even wait until Mondays when Annie came to the house. She was so proud."

Lydia lowered her head, fiddling with her napkin on her lap. "I — I didn't know. I didn't think you understood my work." She focused on her lap, forcing herself to breathe.

The feet of a chair scraped against the wooden floor, and footsteps sounded. Lydia lifted her head and watched as Gideon walked to the bookshelf. He gingerly opened the glass and pulled out a book, holding it up. *Montana Hunting Stories.*

"You edited this?"

"*Ja,* it was one of my first projects. I wrote a few of the stories too. But don't tell the author I confessed that."

"I have this book. I read it. I bought it in the train station in Whitefish. It's a great book."

Butterflies danced in her stomach, and the sadness of a moment before was replaced with awe. "I can't believe you've read a book I edited." She sat up straighter in her chair. "Do you read much?"

"Not as much as I'd like. Dat never understood boys who would rather sit under an apple tree with a book, so I usually only allow myself the pleasure before bed or sometimes on a lazy Sunday afternoon."

He returned the book to the shelf and then hurried back to the table. "Sorry. I didn't mean to ruin dinner. Where were we?"

Lydia picked up her fork, but the food no longer held her interest. She felt so unlike herself — or rather the self she'd been the last six years — but in the same way strangely at home. "You didn't ruin dinner. You made my day. I've never met anyone — outside of the publishing house — who has read one of my books. It's just amazing that it was you."

They continued dinner, talking about many things, but throughout the meal Lydia caught Gideon glancing in her direction. Did he feel the attraction too? Was he concerned she was *Englisch*? He should be. Now what? Did she really want to return to Seattle? What about Gideon and the book?

What about Dat?

Gideon hadn't stayed long. He ate dinner, and they chatted for a while before he took a shortcut across the pasture to the cluster of bachelor cabins located just up the road from the Amish school and the West Kootenai Kraft and Grocery.

She'd watched until she could no longer make out his form in the darkness, then bid Dat good night and retreated to her room.

Even though she'd packed a flashlight, Lydia lit the kerosene lantern on her nightstand. It seemed like the right thing to do when reading more notes from Mem's Promise Box.

Her story started with Mem's story. She knew it was within this box that her book would start.

She opened the box with expectancy and looked through the dates until she found the oldest one. It was a note written almost six months before her birth. Lydia gently unfolded it and smiled again to see Mem's familiar script.

I'm not sure how to write this note. It seems to me I never liked to consider myself cursed, but when the smallest glimmer of hope has appeared I see that fact more clearly.

When folks look upon the Amish, they think us to be all the same. We see the differences. The size of a hat brim, the hooks or buttons on a garment, and the style of the buggy classify better than words. Yet no matter if one is Old Order, Swartzentruber, or even Mennonite, there are things the same: trying to live Plain and growing large families. And there is no curse greater on an Amish woman than to be barren. It's a thunderstorm in one's mind and heart even on sunny summer days.

That's why the promise means so much. It was given to me by a visiting bishop just today, and I want to get every word down before I forget a syllable. He was an old man, older than our bishop by many years. If he were any younger than that I wouldn't believe him, but I figured at his age he knows not to take promises lightly.

I was minding my own business, helping in the kitchen. Since he was new to our church, I don't understand how he knew my fate, except for the fact I'd been slicing pies in neat, even pieces for twenty minutes and hadn't one kinder tugging on my apron. The other ladies were placing thick loaves of bread on the tables. The bishop walked straight into the kitchen as if he owned it. That's when I knew his words were important. No man — bishop or not — enters a woman's kitchen when her mind is intent on getting food on the table.

"What is yer name, ma'am?" His voice had a rumbling to it as if it were filled with marbles. I realized once I looked up that it was emotion making that sound, for his eyes watered too.

"Ada Mae Wyse."

He nodded once. "Our good Lord has a promise for you, Ada Mae." Then he said by this time next year I was going to have a baby. I felt like Sarah from the Bible at that moment. I didn't know whether to laugh or cry. Laugh for joy. Or cry because I couldn't take my heart aching when it didn't come true.

Instead I just nodded and turned back to that pie. I know pies. I don't know what to do with promises. With this promise.

The words ended there, and Lydia turned the paper over in her hand. The last few penned words were squiggly, filled with emotion. The handwriting was always the same as it had been. Even in the time of Mem's great illness, she never lost her penmanship.

Lydia refolded the letter in its perfect ninety-degree creases, trying to decide what she thought of that. Had the bishop heard of her birth mother's pregnancy and also Ada Mae's childless state? Had he used his influence to bring a baby into Ada Mae's arms? Or . . . was it possible that God was behind it?

A chill moved down Lydia's arms. She knew about Sarah in the Bible, or at least she remembered some of the story. Sarah was barren, and God sent an angel to tell her she'd have a son. It seemed easy to think of such things happening long ago. Biblical characters seemed almost more than human. But could such a promise be sent by God to someone today? Sent to tell of her coming? Her birth?

Impossible.

Lydia placed the paper back in the box. What did the other dozens of folded notes say? Today just one occupied her thoughts. Mem's words weighed on her mind. Her heart quivered in her chest like an aspen leaf on the wind.

Lydia swallowed hard and turned off the kerosene lamp. Then she snuggled down under the covers as the last rays of light peeked around the curtains. That's one thing she remembered about Montana: the sun set late here in the summer months. Yet she couldn't keep her eyes open. Her day had been full of hopes and promises. When was the last time she could say such? Too long ago to remember.

And it was one promise that filled her mind most as she drifted off to sleep.

She'd been the promise — the promise from a man of God to Mem.

CHAPTER 11

Lydia woke before dawn and finished the edits on a novel about a group of women who crossed on the Oregon Trail. She liked that the novel was inspired by true stories. She was also excited to add depth to one section that involved a ranch hand, Chuck Trent. As she edited the part where Chuck tried to calm a wild horse, she couldn't help but think of Gideon. The gentle way he'd handled Blue yesterday was a perfect illustration for the fictional character in the book. As she thought of Gideon, "Chuck" came to life on the page.

As much as she enjoyed others' words, her own pulsated through her mind. She was eager to get her contracted work done and sent. Her own sentences, paragraphs, trailed behind her like a lost puppy, begging for attention.

Lydia bundled the manuscript to send back to Bonnie. After breakfast with Dat, she walked with eager steps to the West Kootenai Kraft and Grocery. The log cabin-style building was set at the end of the muddy parking lot. A wooden-planked walkway, just like the ones she'd read about in Wild West books, led her to a glass-front door. Her favorite part, though, was the tall log post near the store. On it were arrows pointing toward various locations and the distance to them: *North Pole 2,750 miles. South Pole 9,500 miles. Honolulu, Hawaii 3,912 miles. Canada 2 miles.* It was good to know your place in the world.

Lydia entered and approached the older man at the counter.

"Hey, there." She held up the package. "I'd like to overnight this to Seattle, please."

"Nope. Not going to be able to do that." He didn't glance up from the copy of the *Daily Interlake* newspaper that he was reading.

"Do you have a priority option?"

The older man with gray hair shook his head. "I have a scale and stamps. If you'd like to do any of those fancy options, you'll have to go down the hill and cross the bridge over to Rexford."

"Just to mail something?"

He looked up at her then and tilted his head, eyeing her curiously. "You Jacob

Wyse's girl?"

"*Ja . . .* yes."

"Then why don't you jest drive your car there?"

He wasn't harsh with his words. The way he said it made her want to chuckle.

Lydia twisted a strand of hair around her finger. "I'm, uh, not in a driving mood."

"I have stamps, then." He turned the page of the newspaper.

Lydia looked down at the package. In addition to the manuscript, she'd also sent a note that she might be a little late on the other two manuscripts too. Just as she wasn't in a driving mood, she wasn't in an editing mood either.

"Wonderful, that'll work. Stamps, then."

The older man weighed the package, and she paid him for the stamps. He tossed it into the outgoing mail pile and a weight lifted from her shoulders.

What she was in the mood for was to get back home so she could watch Gideon in the pasture with Blue and to read more letters in the Promise Box.

She glanced at her watch. It was early. She had time to have a cup of coffee — to watch the people in the community as they shopped and ate. To take the first steps of getting to know the folks who called this place home.

Lydia hadn't thought twice about leaving the Amish, but returning filled her mind to the top — just like the way Mem filled jelly jars, so that the extra fillings squished out when she put on the lid.

The breeze ruffled Lydia's peasant skirt as another customer stepped through the front door of the West Kootenai Kraft and Grocery. The logger who moved past her smelled of Old Spice, like her neighbor back in Seattle. Back home, Mr. Montgomery's scent always hung around the glass and metal elevator. But here the scent was a brief introduction. The scents of bacon, coffee, and last night's fried chicken punctuated her further steps.

After him, an *Englisch* woman and her daughter walked by.

"Good morning!" Lydia chirped. She pushed her lips up into a smile.

The woman's steps were lighter as she picked up a grocery basket. "Good morning to you too."

Bonnie had told her to take a step of faith. Dat said God had a plan for her. Her father's sable brown eyes twinkled when he'd said that. His plan meant here, with him. What would that look like?

She stepped lightly to the restaurant area,

and even though she'd just eaten, the scent of cinnamon rolls and peanut butter wooed her. More wonderful scents. The kitchen was open, and an *Englisch* woman rolled cookie dough into balls, setting them onto the pan in nice, even spaces.

The Amish waitress sat at the table closest to the kitchen, filling salt shakers. Lydia recognized her.

She didn't look up. "Sit anywhere you'd like."

"Thanks, Eve."

Head jerked, gaze narrowed, and Eve's eyebrows turned down.

Lydia took the table closest to Eve, her skirt catching slightly on the rough-hewn wooden bench. Light glinted off the window, causing her to blink. She shielded her eyes and peered out at the rays of light stretching into the lavender-gray sky.

Hope stretched out of her heart, and joy mixed with regret. Joy over imagining Dat's face when she told him she most likely would be returning. Regret that she hadn't come home sooner. That her stubborn will had enveloped her like a force field. Yet instead of offering protection, it had kept love and family and community from penetrating its solid defenses.

"Coffee?" Eve lined up twelve shakers in a

neat row but didn't move.

Lydia shifted in her seat and pressed her open hands on her legs. "Tea, please. Do you have Earl Grey?"

"Most people drink coffee around here." Eve rose and set the salt shakers on the other tables, ignoring Lydia's table completely, walking around her with a wide berth.

Lydia stomach knotted, and she clenched and unclenched her fists. Had she done something or said something wrong?

"Whatever tea you have is fine." Her singsong tone fell flat. "And thank you . . . for bringing that bread by the house yesterday. I know it's out of your way."

"It was a nice day out. I wanted to see the lake, so I thought I'd come with the other ladies."

"Tomorrow Gideon —"

"No need to waste his time. I can come again." Eve turned over Lydia's coffee cup with a clatter.

Lydia cleared her throat and jutted out her chin. "I know you said Gideon would bring it by tomorrow, but I told him not to worry. I'm going to bake two loaves later today. My mother did teach me how to bake."

"If you say so."

"I did appreciate your help, and that from the others. All your help. The plum jam was delicious —"

"We did it because of your father, *ja*. For yer mem's memory too."

"I'm thankful my father shared."

"Dat says we're to be separate from the world. Folks haven't paid that enough mind. I'm not going to fool you to think we could be friends, Lydia."

And next week? And the week after? What about when — if — I decide to begin wearing my dress, kapp, *and apron?*

Lydia straightened her shoulders, focusing on the woman's face. She lifted the white porcelain coffee cup. "About the tea?"

"I have chamomile. I'll be right back."

Lydia pushed back, her shoulders pressing into the hard wood of the bench. *Shouldn't they think about putting cushions on these benches?*

Eve returned with a cup of hot water and a tea bag that looked as if it had been sitting on the shelf for ten years. She placed a menu on the table, still without a word. Obviously not everyone would be thrilled by her choice to return.

Lydia pulled out her notepad and pen from her purse, and with one more glance to Eve she began to write.

■ ■ ■ ■

Two cups of tea later, Lydia looked at the words in front of her. With pen across the paper, she couldn't come up with one reason why she'd want to go back to Seattle. Yet returning to the Amish, there was something holding her back: faith. Her dat had asked her to pray about returning, but for some reason, praying was the hardest thing to do.

Eve was busy in the kitchen, and she'd left Lydia's tab on the table, informing her to pay at the front cash register when she left. Lydia wasn't going to hold a grudge. She understood the fear of outsiders — especially those who chose to leave the Amish way.

She grabbed a small handheld shopping basket and considered what she wanted to make for dinner the next few days. One of her favorite things was potato *gnepp,* which Mem called "old shoes." She got the ingredients for the dough and more potatoes for the filling. She also got items for chicken loaf and beef and bean soup — a few of Dat's favorites.

By the time she'd finished shopping, the older gentleman was gone, and a young

Amish woman rang her up.

Lydia paid and scooped up the two paper sacks. *"Danki."*

The young woman eyed her. "Did you used to be Amish?"

She had opened her mouth to respond when she felt a hand on her arm. She turned to see a short, older woman in Amish dress with strawberry blonde hair peeking out from under her *kapp.* She seemed pleasant enough, and Lydia offered a smile.

"Lydia Wyse?"

"Ja?"

"I'm Sallie Peachy. I know your parents." The woman scanned Lydia's loose sweater and long skirt, but instead of judgment in her eyes, a soft smile touched her lips. "You're sort of like Marianna. She left the Amish too."

Sallie turned slightly and pointed to a woman in the kitchen. Instead of a *kapp,* the woman wore a handkerchief over her light brown hair, and she hummed along to the radio as she kneaded a ball of dough. Her long dress and apron wasn't Amish, but it was close. When she turned, Lydia realized it *was* Marianna.

"Uh-huh," she answered, not knowing how to respond. "So she left the Amish?"

"*Ja,* to marry Ben. Their wedding took place just a few months ago — the most beautiful wedding. For an *Englisch* one, of course."

Lydia smiled. "*Ja,* I imagine so." Was there a purpose for this information? She was certain Gideon was already out in the pasture with Blue. Had he scanned her parents' place looking for her? "Marianna, uh, seems to enjoy her job," she said, attempting to be nice, then readjusted her bags in her hand.

"Oh, it's not her job. She's just filling in for Sarah, who's in Ohio right now working at a bakery. She's engaged now, too, from what I hear. The two women are best friends, and when Marianna was in Indiana, Sarah ran the bakery and now with Sarah gone . . ."

"Marianna is in charge. How wonderful that worked out." Lydia took a step closer to the door.

Sallie Peachy frowned. "Are you heading home already?"

"Yes, to put these groceries away and check on Dat."

"Oh, *ja,* how is Jacob? I heard he had a horrible spill yesterday."

"He's *gut* . . . staying off his feet. A kind

155

bachelor named Gideon is filling in for him."

"Gideon, eh?" Disappointment on the woman's face was clear. "I have two daughters, and my daughter, Eve, considers him a fine man . . . one of her favorites among the bachelors."

"He is nice." She forced a grin. "I'll let him know you send your regards."

The woman nodded and then reached out and grabbed Lydia's arm. "I do have two questions before you go."

"Sure." Lydia paused.

"First, every Saturday all us ladies from the community come for breakfast here at the restaurant. The Amish ones tend to show up first; I suppose we're early risers. But the *Englisch* ladies like to join us too. It's a nice time of shaaaaring . . ." The woman stretched the last word out, and Lydia guessed their sharing time was more effective at spreading local news than that newspaper Edgar had been reading. Maybe more accurate too.

"I'd like that."

"And that last thing . . ." Sallie narrowed her gaze. "Yer not sweet on Gideon, are you, because in my opinion there have been enough young people leaving the Amish lately. No offense."

Lydia shrugged. "None taken." She bit her lip, trying to figure out how best to phrase her response. Finally the words came to her.

She cleared her throat. "Mrs. Peachy, I do consider Gideon a nice friend and you can be rest assured that I have no intention of persuading anyone to leave the Amish."

"That's *gut* to know, dear." Mrs. Peachy patted her arm. "You just never know about young folks these days. Things aren't like what they used to be when the thought of not being Amish didn't cross our minds. Faith, friendship, community . . . what's not to appreciate?"

"Ja." Lydia nodded. "I'm starting to see."

"We aren't perfect. God doesn't expect us to be," Sallie continued. "Faith isn't about having all the answers. It's about taking one step. The *first* step."

Lydia moved to her chest and pulled out her Amish clothes.

It had taken her just a few minutes to put the grocery items away. Each moment, urgency pushed her forward, confirming what she needed to do. Had God sent Sallie Peachy to the store at that moment to talk to her — just as He had sent that bishop to talk to Mem all those years ago?

The fabric of the dark-blue Amish dress

was light, but the weight of it tugged at her arms. She slipped out of her skirt and sweater, then slipped the dress over her head, pinning it up the front. Putting on the Amish clothes was more than just a way to dress. With it came expectations. A way to live, a way to think, a way to believe.

Belief. That was still growing in her. Faith would come, she hoped.

Lydia moved to the window. From where she stood she could see only a fraction of the pasture where Gideon now worked with Blue. Yet just because she couldn't see him didn't mean he wasn't there. And just because she'd run away from the Amish community — and from God in a sense — didn't mean He had left her.

Lydia's hands trembled, and she turned back to the bed, noting the quilt Mem had made. Her heart ached knowing that Mem always had the room ready for her. Had Mem known what she hadn't — that Lydia could run but God would follow? That she could turn her back on her Amish ways but the love of her parents and community was a rope, tethering her to them?

Lydia moved to her bed and sank to her knees, resting her forehead on the mattress, breathing in the scent of sun and pine from the clothesline. How long ago had Mem washed the bedding, hoping for her daughter to return? Did Mem have any idea what would bring her back? Had she understood the bravery it would take to stay?

The Scripture verse she'd read from Mem's Promise Box replayed in her mind: *"Be strong and of a good courage . . . for the Lord thy God, he it is that doth go with thee."*

It's too hard.

She waited for a sign from heaven. A knowing inside. A clear revelation in her mind. It didn't come.

Can I ever know for certain? What if it's the wrong choice? Staying meant a different life, but did it mean an easier one? She knew that wasn't the case.

She thought of both Eve's distain and Sallie's welcome. Both would be a part of life here. *The choice is not an easy life. The choice is . . . God.*

She pressed her palms onto cool, wooden floorboards. That was it. The heart of what she'd been running from. She'd felt betrayed. Growing up she followed in Dat and Mem's footsteps and loved God with her whole heart. She listened to the preacher's words and worked so hard to obey. She'd tried to be good. She *had* been good. But did it mean anything? No matter what she did, nothing could make up for where she came from. Or the pain she'd caused her birth mother.

Did she deserve what she got? No.

Lydia covered her face with her hands and lowered her head. Pain moved from her temples to her jaw as her teeth clenched. She remembered this conflict, these questions. It had been easier to run than to stand up to God. To tell Him she didn't understand. To feel the disappointment that in all His creating and managing and overseeing He'd let her — and her birth mom — slip through the cracks.

A silent sob shook her body, but instead of the tears that usually came, a new thought shed light into the dark places. She moved to the Promise Box again and pulled out the first note, rereading it. Her life had brought pain to one . . . but joy to another. She tried to imagine herself from Mem's eyes. A gift. A glimmer of light. A promise.

God knew me. He had a plan.

Why pain had to be part of that plan she didn't know, but could it be enough to embrace the truth of what Dat had said: that her life had been the gift to Mem that allowed her to trust in God's promises again?

Gentle, soft — like an angel's kiss — peace settled in Lydia's heart.

160

She pictured God. Waiting, just like Mem had, with open arms. Instead of preparing a room with flowers and fresh sheets, He'd prepared a life for her.

She wanted to return to her faith, and deep inside she had a feeling that returning to the Amish was the way God was asking her to do that. Not because God could only be found in the Amish community, but rather because He wanted her to be a part of a people who dealt with their angst and hopes together.

Lydia blew out a breath, considering what this meant. She'd rent out her condo. She'd park her car. She could work, *ja,* some . . . But again she had a feeling that the work she'd been doing — crafting others' words — was going to take a backseat to writing her story, living the story first penned by God.

This meant opening her heart, knowing others and letting herself be known, at least in part. She couldn't imagine confessing her whole truth, but she could look to God. She could believe He'd given her to Dat and Mem for a purpose.

And for the first time in her life, that seemed enough.

Gideon sat down with a piece of paper and

pen, wishing he could be more like Lydia — a natural with words. He wanted to write to Dat and Mem — to urge them to share the truth of that day he got lost in the woods, but he couldn't figure out how to say the words without them feeling as if he was judging them, blaming them. If Lydia was here, he could ask her to write the words for him. Although . . . could she? How could she help when he'd rather listen than talk, than confess?

Tonight at dinner she'd entertained him with stories of ferry crossings, tomato ice cream, and dozens of other interesting facts about Seattle. What he found interesting, of course, wasn't that Lydia enjoyed talking about the place, but that she talked about it in past tense. As if it was her former life. Did she plan to settle in West Kootenai? Stay here?

Caleb slept soundly in the top bunk of their cabin, but Gideon couldn't sleep. As much as he enjoyed training Blue and helping Mr. Wyse with the chores, the truths he and Lydia both battled never strayed far from his mind.

He knew Lydia was adopted. Her dat had shared that information, speaking of the gift they'd been given. But he'd also overheard it in whispered words: "That's why she's different. No wonder she doesn't fit in." No one knew for certain if her birth mother had been *Englisch,* but that was the assumption. Amish mothers didn't give up their babies.

He could read her story in her eyes, just as he'd read her edited words in that book. She didn't feel as if she fit in. Even the immense love of her parents couldn't make her believe otherwise. He wanted to tell her the truth — that she had value — but how could he when he ran from his own past? Maybe that's why they got along so well. They'd become experts at pushing everyone else to the edges in order to protect the thin veil of self-dignity that hid their pain.

I can't help her until I discover my own truth. I have to face the pain Mem and Dat don't want to share. I have to know.

He looked at the piece of paper on the table before him. And although he'd planned on writing a letter to his parents, he thought instead of the words to a hymn from the Ausbund that his mem used to sing.

When he was younger, Gideon hadn't understood why she didn't sing about happier things. But now it made sense. It was easy to sing to God in the joyous times, but true faith came when one sought God, praised Him, in hardship. The words from the Amish hymn moved from his mind to his pen.

Everlasting Father in heaven,
I call on you so ardently,
Do not let me turn from you.
Keep me in your truth
Until my final end.
O God, guard my heart and mouth,
Lord watch over me at all times,
Let nothing separate me from you,
Be it affliction, anxiety, or need,
Keep me pure in joy.
My everlasting Lord and Father,
Show and teach me,
Poor unworthy child that I am,
That I heed your path and way.
In this lies my desire.
To walk through your power into death,
Through sorrow, torture, fear and want.
Sustain me in this,
O God, so that I nevermore
Be separated from your love.

Gideon finished the last line and exhaled. He read the words over, letting them sink in.

There was a stirring from the top bunk, and Gideon glanced up. Caleb turned to his side and glanced down at him. His dark brown hair stuck up in all directions.

"Are you writing a love letter?"

Gideon shrugged. "Of sorts."

"Are you fancy on her?"

"You talking about Lydia?"

"Who else would I be talkin' about?"

Gideon set his pen on the table. He'd have to put off writing Mem and Dat until another day. "Of course not. She's *Englisch.*"

"Yer mind says that, but what about yer heart?"

"I've only known her a week. Less than that. Besides, she's going to be back in Seattle soon and in six months — at the end of hunting season — I'm heading back to Pennsylvania."

"No one says you have to return. You can work here as well as there." Caleb sat straighter and leaned his back against the wall. "*Ja,* my dat said he knew from the first time he saw Mem that she was to be his wife." Caleb chuckled. "Of course it took three years for her to figure out the same thing."

"*Ja.*" The crisp evening breeze shimmied through the open window, and Gideon latched the window closed and perched on the end of his wooden chair. He didn't know how to respond. Didn't know what he thought. His greatest joy of meeting Lydia mixed with discovering a man who knew about his past. And finding out he was too coward to face it.

"I do think she's special." He put the cap on the pen and tossed it onto the cluttered counter. "I just wish we were more alike than different."

And more different than alike.

"And if things change?"

An image of her in Amish dress and *kapp* filled his mind. He swallowed and told his heart to calm its quickened beat. He wiped his sweaty palms on his pants and shrugged. It was the only answer he could give.

"Gideon . . ." Caleb frowned. "You can talk to me. I'm not going to run off and tell her how you feel."

Gideon's steepled fingers rested against his lips while he studied the tack hanging on the wall of the cabin. His brows lowered as he tried to put his thoughts into words.

"Change can come, but not all change is good." He rose and slid suspenders from his shoulders. "The trick is in where you put your trust. Whose voice yer listening to. If anything, a woman like that could do me in.

"The worst horse isn't one who tugs on

the ropes, Caleb. It's one that refuses to submit to teaching. That tries to race off his own direction, not understanding that true safety comes from one who guides with a gentle hand. There's nothing I can do but wait . . . and pray that God will take these feelings away."

"You can pray she'll return Amish," Caleb mumbled as his head returned to the pillow.

"*Ja.* There's always that." Gideon wasn't going to get his hopes up. And even if she did return, that didn't mean she'd care for him as he was beginning to suspect he cared for her. It would hurt even more knowing he'd be rejected without Lydia not being Amish as an excuse.

And his feeling for the beautiful redhead would be yet another part of his heart he'd have to hide and ignore.

CHAPTER 12

Lydia arrived at the Kraft and Grocery just past nine o'clock wearing a skirt and simple shirt. Even though she'd tried on her Amish clothes to see if they still fit, she decided not to wear them out of the house yet. Instead she thought of the perfect way to tell Dat. Tomorrow, as he hitched up the horse to the buggy to head for Sunday church, she would come out dressed in her Amish clothes. Other than Mem's funeral, she hadn't been part of an Amish service for years. He didn't expect her to go. It would be a joyful surprise.

But today . . . today she'd still be considered *Englisch* in their eyes. And in a way she liked that. It would be interesting to see who accepted her as Lydia and who would only accept her once she again wore Amish clothes.

She liked that the women got together every Saturday. She pushed open the glass door to the Kraft and Grocery and listened as women's voices and laughter filled her ears. Even though it was summer the woodstove in the dining area had been lit against the bite of the chilly morning air.

Many sets of eyes turned her direction as she entered, and conversations paused for just a moment. There were mostly Amish women there, and Lydia figured that in the next thirty minutes or so, *Englisch* women would filter in.

Mrs. Sommer had an empty chair next to her and motioned to Lydia. Her heart leapt slightly and she hurried forward. To her mind, it seemed a small thing to be accepted into this group, but her heart felt otherwise. While she had friends in Seattle, there was something special, different, about the Amish community. Had she missed being known? Belonging?

"I jest don't know what we're going to do." Sallie Peachy patted her *kapp* as her voice raised above the group. "School starts in less than two months. Do we have time yet to advertise in *The Budget*?"

"Maybe so," an older Amish woman was saying. "But what young woman would be interested in coming all this way jest for an interview? And I don't feel comfortable hiring someone without meeting her first."

What had gotten the women as frazzled as spotting a fox near the chicken coop? Lydia scooted nearer to Ruth, leaning close to her ear. "What are they talking about?"

"Oh, we jest discovered Emma Litwiller, our teacher, is moving back to Wisconsin to care for an elderly aunt. We need a new teacher for our school, and no one around these parts is a *gut* fit."

"Are you sure there isn't anyone in the community who'd consider the job?" another Amish woman asked. Lydia had yet to remember everyone's name but she knew that would come with time.

"*Vell,* there is Marianna," Ruth Sommer chimed in. "Just to fill in until we can get someone. A few months, maybe. She'll be traveling to California with Ben for part of the winter. He's written some songs and . . ." Ruth's voice trailed off, and Lydia put the pieces together. Marianna's husband Ben must be the same musician Mem had written about. Lydia was familiar with his song "Every Warm Cabin," and she was surprised that he'd come from the small community of West Kootenai. After Lydia knew a bit more about him, and his connection to her parents, she had smiled whenever she'd heard the song around Seattle.

Sallie Peachy lifted an eyebrow and cleared her throat. Her face reflected pity. "But, Ruth, this is an Amish school. Marianna is no longer Amish."

Ruth's mouth opened slightly, then heat filled her cheeks. "Oh, *ja.*" Her words were simple but they carried bucket loads of pain. Lydia's shoulders tensed and her heart grew in its ache. She'd brought the same embarrassment on her mem. The same shame.

Ruth lowered her head and fumbled with a handkerchief on her lap.

Sallie Peachy picked up the conversation, trying to get the attention off her friend. She spoke of a niece in Ohio who was good with children, but she didn't know if she'd be able to come since her mem had just had another baby.

"Besides," Sallie added, "she lived in the world for a time and has jest recently been baptized."

"Jest as long as she *is* baptized. *Is* Amish," an older woman piped up. "I don't see the problem. Isn't it true we are a new creation when we turn to God . . . and He remembers our sins no more."

Lydia placed her palms down on the cool wood of the table, and excitement tightened her chest. Is that what mattered? Not where you'd been, but who you became before

God. Before the church?

Dear Lord, is this part of Your plan? Did You bring me back for such a time as this? Will they really accept me?

"I'll write a letter, then." Sallie gave a firm nod. "I'll let you know what she says."

Lydia hoped the young woman wouldn't be able to come. In her younger years, before the pain of her past was known, she'd dreamt of being a teacher — for a few years at least. She'd thought that having a job like Miss Yoder, her favorite teacher, would be both fun and worthwhile. To spend time with the students in and outside of the classroom. To get to know their families. To travel with *Englisch* drivers on field trips and open up the outside world to the young students in a fun and safe way, just as Miss Yoder had done for her.

Hearing about the need of the community was as if someone had taken ammonia to the window to her dreams and cleaned off the layer of film that had built throughout the years. Walking in the world, driving through rush-hour traffic, losing herself in the latest sitcom had built up layer after layer of grimy self-interest, blocking her view into what really mattered.

As the women discussed the role of the teacher, Lydia thought back to a book she'd edited. The author had urged women to follow their dreams. Through the pages, the author asked readers to think of their first dreams, as a child, and test them to see if they were still valid. Whether it was to be an artist, a musician, a baker, or even the mem of young children, the dreams from one's young self often aligned with one's God-given gifts and pointed to God-penned desires that were cast aside or forgotten in the reality of life.

She also thought of Bonnie and could almost picture her boss's wide-eyed excitement. Not only would Lydia return, she'd also become a teacher? It sounded like the making of a great book.

As they talked, more women joined them, and excitement built as Lydia listened. Her mind was racing with lesson ideas when Mrs. Sommer reached over and patted her hand. Lydia glanced over at the older woman and noticed the woman's gaze was directed behind them.

Lydia looked over her shoulder. Gideon had just entered. He looked surprised to see her sitting among the other women, yet a pleasant smile lifted his lips. He moved to the back restaurant area, separated from the main dining room by a curtain. Was it only her imagination, or was there an extra lightness to his step?

She motioned to the waitress and asked for a cup of hot water and a tea bag, trying to distract herself from the tension building inside. Did the tautness inside come from a hope that God was leading her? It seemed almost too good to be true that she could stay and serve in a way that would not only bring joy to her father but help the community too.

Yet would they accept her? she wondered again. Lydia looked down at her brown skirt. Not now. Not yet.

Inside, she felt like Blue on that rope, wanting to run back to Seattle but feeling a powerful source holding her back. Her mind raced in circles, yet was it possible that Someone held the lead? Someone who loved her very much?

Even though Gideon was on the other side of the restaurant, partitioned off by a half wall and curtain, knowing he was there took the chill off her heart, just as the woodstove did in this room. If he was that happy to see her interacting, trying to fit in, then what would he think when she arrived at church tomorrow in Amish dress? What would he do when he discovered she wanted to apply for the teaching job too? Would she tell him right away? Or should she prove herself to be a trusted part of the community before she brought it up?

Lydia readjusted in her seat, chiding herself for worrying about Gideon. She hadn't asked much about his family back home, his dreams, his goals. She was foolish to think he'd be willing to take a step closer to her if she chose to be Amish. What if his possible attraction was only that — something he kept from afar? And after hunting season would he stay? Or would he return to his friends and family back in Pennsylvania?

She touched her fingers to her lips, knowing she'd still make the same decision. The decision to return to the Amish wasn't about him, after all.

More women showed up, and the conversation moved away from the topic of an Amish teacher, but the women's tight-lipped smiles proved the worry remained heavy on their minds. And why wouldn't it be? A schoolteacher was one of the greatest influences on the lives of their children. And as she considered that, Lydia's stomach knotted. It didn't matter if she changed on the inside; what mattered was if the others in this community believed she had.

Would I trust myself if I was in their shoes? Trust enough to let me guide young children?

She lowered her head and folded her hands on her lap. *Ne.* Not yet, but hopefully that would change. Maybe if she sought God more, like she had as a child, and read about His promises in Mem's box, the change would come — not by force but through the gentle, quiet direction of a loving Savior.

Lydia made her dat a sandwich of homemade bread and hamburger soup made with leftovers for lunch. She set the table with the special red plate Mem had bought years ago. They used it every birthday and during other important events. As she'd walked home from the store, Lydia knew she could no longer wait until before church service tomorrow to talk to Dat. She needed to talk to him about their community's need, and the only way to do that would be to tell him her decision.

It was a special day — one Dat had waited years for. Her future would forever change after this moment.

Lydia ignored the nagging thoughts that reminded her a book was at stake too. She had that to look forward to also, but she wouldn't tell Dat about that now. Not yet. A soft smile played on her lips as she imagined the back-cover copy: *"Lydia Wyse returns to bury her mother, and in rediscover-*

ing her Amish roots she finds her faith again. More than that, she finds her influence matters in the lives of the children in the community."

Lydia nodded. It sounded good to her, and it would sound even better if she also found the love of her life. But love could not be scripted. It was far too fickle for that.

She shook her head, as if knocking away her fanciful thoughts, and turned to Dat. "Dinner's ready!"

Dad rose from his favorite chair, sauntered over, and sat at the kitchen table. After their silent prayer, he picked up half of the sandwich . . . and saw the red plate in front of Lydia. He paused, sandwich mid air, and fixed his eyes on her. "Have we something to celebrate?"

"*Ja.* I went to the store today, and I hung out with the other ladies. I can understand why Mem enjoyed living here. There is quite a feeling of diversity — unlike where we lived in Sugarcreek, where everyone was the same." She picked up a strawberry and placed it in her mouth, chewing slowly.

Dat stroked his long beard and eyed her curiously. "And . . . are you going to have me sit all day before you tell me what the celebration is about yet?"

Her heart fluttered, and her finger followed the edge of the red plate. "I heard some news. The schoolteacher is leaving, heading back east."

"That's a shame. I heard she's done a fine job."

Nervous energy bubbled up in Lydia's stomach. "*Ja,* well, I was thinking, Dat, that I'd like that teaching position." She nearly bounced in her chair like when she was ten and asked her dat for one of the neighbor's puppies. Rex had grown and aged, but the exhilaration that surged through Lydia made her feel young again.

"*Ne,* that's not possible." He shook his head and took a bite of his sandwich. "An *Englisch* woman cannot teach Amish children."

She tilted her head and sighed. Mem would have put two and two together. One look at Lydia's face aglow and she would have figured it out.

"I understand, Dat. Do you not think I know that?" She brushed scattered sandwich crumbs from the plate onto her hand. "And that's what this is all about. Being back here — reading Mem's notes and thinking about life — well, things have changed."

Dat glanced up at her. His eyes widened slightly. He stopped chewing for a moment, then placed the sandwich down again.

Thick, gray eyebrows lifted. "What are you saying?" His words escaped as a breath.

"I've been thinking about it. Being back here has brought so many good memories. Even though I jest started reading Mem's letters, I'm seeing myself — the Amish world — differently than I have for many years."

"Just say it." Dat pushed back from the table. "Yer fluttering around the answer like a butterfly on Mem's rose bush out back."

Lydia smiled, feeling her cheeks plump. "I'd like to rejoin the church," she said in a rush of words and air.

Her dat nodded, lowered his head, and then dabbed the corners of his mouth with a napkin. If it wasn't for the slight trembling of the napkin in his fingers and the softest gasp of air, she never would have realized her father was crying.

"Dat, are you okay?"

He lifted his head slowly and met her gaze. His eyes glimmered with emotion. Seeing tears brought moisture to hers.

"If only your mem . . ."

"I know. If only Mem could have seen this day, she would have been so happy. It was all she wanted." Pain jabbed Lydia's gut like a pair of knitting needles. Heat traveled up her arms — guilt — but she pushed it away.

She had to trust in God's timing.

"But I wasn't ready then. I didn't know I was ready until I came back. Something changed when I first spotted this house from the road. I felt a sense of returning . . . even when I hadn't realized I'd been gone."

Dat pushed the plate away from him, and Lydia looked down at hers, no longer hungry either.

"Mem . . ." The word swelled and filled her throat. She swallowed hard and forced herself to continue. "Mem wanted it more than anything, I know."

He folded his hands on his lap, then unfolded them as if trying to decide what to do. A longing came over her: Lydia wanted to run to him and climb into his lap like she had when she was five.

"Daughter, are you sure you want this? It will change . . . everything."

She nodded. "I want . . . yes. I'm ready to do this." As she said the words, a peace she wasn't expecting fell on her. The truth was she wasn't choosing to be Amish as much as she was choosing God. God's plan. It was the right choice, she knew.

"I know the days and weeks to come won't be easy. There are things to take care of back in Seattle. It'll be like trying to fit my foot into shoes I wore six years ago. But I trust

I'll get used to the old ways again."

Dat nodded, and tore off a piece of crust from his bread.

"A teacher, then?"

"Well, I would like to apply. There is a need, and I've —" She was about to mention the years of college she had, but she knew that would most likely be a detriment rather than a benefit. Growing up in the middle of an Amish community, teachers served as role models in Amish society. They taught not only with their knowledge, but with their lives.

"It might take awhile, but I'd like to earn their trust. I really do think I could be a person who could reinforce what the people in this community teach at home."

Dat eyed her. His thick gray eyebrows twitched slightly, and she guessed what he was thinking. *You're still in* Englisch *dress, and you think you can be an example?*

He cleared his throat. "*Ja,* I'd focus on that. Before you talk to anyone about your desire to teach this fall, I'd focus on the returning."

She understood that his trust would be the one she'd have to gain first. Even though he loved her, she'd hurt him and Mem in so many ways — moving out, not writing often, visiting even less. It would take work to rebuild the relationship with him. To reclaim the close relationship they used to have. But at least she was being given a second chance to try.

Lydia wasn't going to turn her back on that.

"*Ja.* I understand." Lydia rested her chin on her balled fist as if truly letting it sink in that this was happening. "I was thinking the same. I'm going to have to trust that God can help me with that."

During her teen years, God was the last thing she'd wanted to think about. She was more focused on getting her driver's license, working, saving money for a car, and trying to fit in with her *Englisch* friends.

Being back this time, she was reminded of some of the things she had enjoyed about being Amish and about what she'd liked about God — before her heart was hardened and she became mad at Him. Mad that God would allow evil men to rape innocent women. Mad that God would put her birth mom in a position to force her to give up her only daughter. Mad that she had to be raised by strangers. Yes, they were good people, but life wasn't supposed to work that way. Life was supposed to be fair. God was supposed to be good.

Lydia reached over and patted Dat's hand.

"I won't say anything to them yet. I'll work to live the life — the life you and Mem had always dreamed for me. It's a promise I'm going to keep."

Promise. The word filled her mind, and she knew it was the promise Mem had clung to. Lydia imagined her smiling in heaven even now, and she supposed some promises were worth writing down, praying about, keeping.

CHAPTER 13

She'd been awake even before the crow of the rooster, excited for the day. The day of her return.

Yesterday she'd made dinner for Dat and Gideon — and left it simmering on the stove — and then she'd traveled down to Eureka to get her car serviced. She needed to have it ready to sell, but more than that, she didn't want to be around when Gideon came over to help with the chores. One look at him and she wouldn't be able to keep the secret. She had asked Dat not to tell, and he agreed. Lydia had plans to do it herself at church.

Lydia combed out her hair and pulled it back away from her face and behind her ears, fastening it on both sides of her head with barrettes. Then she pulled it all back with a simple hair band. The ponytail was thick and close to her head, and the rest of her curls trailed down her back like a waterfall. She then folded the ponytail twice and rolled it up into a bun to pin it up. She used three large pins and a gray hairnet. She'd found both the pins and the hairnet in her mother's things. With determination, Lydia pushed the pins toward the center of the bun, while also grabbing some of the hairnet and some of the hair to make it stay. She used nine pins total. She could have done with eight, but she added an extra for good measure. She didn't want to make any mistakes today.

When her hair was all pinned up and tucked under the hairnet, she placed a *kapp* over it all. It was the same *kapp* she'd worn in Sugarcreek. She hadn't been surprised to find it. Mem had kept all her things. Mem was the one who'd taught her how to put up her hair proper like. And as she glanced at her final appearance with her outfit and *kapp* she smiled as she also remembered Mem's words to Dat every Sunday morning.

"Comb your hair, Jacob. You're all strou*bly!"*

Dat would always nod and groan as if he was put out, and then he'd head back to their indoor bathroom for a brush. Lydia hadn't understood why he didn't do it without prodding, but now she did. Mem's

185

reaction was part of the fun of it. It had been a special tradition — if you wanted to call it that — within their family, no matter how silly. It was part of what made their home *home*.

After a quick breakfast of biscuits and jam, Dat headed out to hitch up the buggy. The church service was to be at the Peachy place today — too far for Dat to walk with his bruised leg.

She took another quick glance at her dress, her neat hair, her face without makeup, and then covered the mirror with a scarf. That was one tradition she'd kept even when she'd moved to Seattle. Growing up Amish, she'd been unfamiliar with looking at her reflection any time night or day. Or was it more than that? Perhaps what she didn't like was the underlying feeling of guilt every time she saw herself in *Englisch* clothes.

She moved to the front porch but stopped short when she heard two men's voices. Lydia hurried down the porch steps and around the side of the house toward the barn. Gideon was there, helping Dat hitch up the mare. Lydia paused and stared. Her throat knotted. Her face flushed.

Gideon glanced at her, looked back to the mare, and then, as if not believing what he'd just seen, turned back and eyed her again. Rex trotted to her side, tail wagging as if equally surprised.

"Miss Wyse . . . How . . . how nice you look today . . . in Amish dress." He tried to hide his smile, but it was pointless.

"*Ja.*" She placed a hand over her heart. "And that's kind of you. To come all this way . . ."

"I'm here to help with the chores, remember. I wouldn't want to slack on my work."

Lydia paused before him, lifting her face and looking into his eyes. The emotion there pierced her. "That's one thing I'd never call you: a slacker."

His Adam's apple bobbed, and he took a step back. "I have the buggy ready, if yer set to go. I didn't expect you to be going, but it appears that I was wrong."

"It wasn't that you were wrong." She smiled. "I wanted it to be a surprise." She could tell from the look in his eyes that he understood.

"It is a wonderful surprise. Welcome home. Can I help you up?"

Lydia hadn't needed help climbing into a buggy since she was a toddler, but she accepted his offered hand all the same. He gripped it and guided her up, his eyes lingering on her face, her *kapp*.

She sat in the middle of the seat, and a moment later the two men sat on either side of her. Dat seemed to enjoy the nervous energy in the air. He enjoyed turning over the reins to Gideon. Enjoyed, too, the bits of small talk that mattered little.

Dat grinned like she hadn't seen in a while, seeming more like the man who'd come in every night from the fields when she was a child. If hope could be captured in a gaze, it was in her dat's as they parked at the Peachy place, where he insisted on helping Lydia down from the buggy and walking by her side.

His daughter was there, with him. And even as her dat wore black from her mother's passing, on his face he wore a smile.

They arrived at service just moments before it started and the surprise of the members of the congregation was evident as she patted Dat's arm before hurrying to the kitchen side of the room to find a place on the bench beside the other women.

The bishop was the same one who'd spoken at Mem's funeral, and his messages were good. The songs were the same as the ones she'd sung as a child, and as she looked around the folks here weren't much different from the families she'd grown up with.

The biggest difference was within her. The difference of choosing her path toward God, instead of doing what she did because that's what her parents had taught her. The difference was she listened to the bishop's message, and when she felt a stirring within her heart, she understood the message was for her.

Unlike when she was a child, and a young teen attending services, this time she paid attention to the words she sang — penned from their martyred ancestors — instead of just moving her mouth out of habit. They rose, and Lydia lifted her voice with the others. She'd sung the words many times, but this time she translated them from German to English in her mind.

In the beginning, God created me to be his child.
He created me clean.
He gave me his image when I was still in my mother's womb . . .

The hymn continued but she couldn't move past the words still caught in her throat. Had she translated that right? *God created me clean. God created me clean.*

They knelt for silent prayer, and Lydia was sure her heart would stop from the emotion surging through her. Why had she not paid attention to the words of that hymn before? Why had she been so hard on herself?

She remembered the heartache in Mem's gaze when she'd told Lydia about her birth. Mem had ached with her. There had been no accusation. Did God's heart ache the same?

Lydia covered her mouth with her trembling hand.

Trust the truth, Lydia. Truth will set you free.

What was the truth?

For so many years what she thought impure — her birth — God had seen as clean and pure. She lowered her head even farther, letting that realization sink in.

She'd been an innocent child in her mother's womb. The sin hadn't been hers.

She'd used her pain to set off without God. To prove she could depend on herself, provide for herself.

Forgive me . . .

It was a simple request but one that flowed down into the deepest parts of her, washing out her murky soul.

After joining the congregation on their knees for a silent prayer, they sang again.

Lydia lifted her voice, her soul soaring high with her words:

When the law wounded my conscience I
    began to cry for God's grace and mercy.
I began to cry to him to help me out of my
    sin and to accept me once more as his
    child for his mercy's sake.
God in his grace, heard through Christ my
    cry.
He brought me out of death, forgave my
    sins, took me again as his son, and
    through him I overcame sin when he
    made me new.
Because I had fallen from God through sin
    and come under his wrath, he bore me
    again as his child.
He bore me in his Son, the Lord Jesus
    Christ, who is the man in between, so
    that I would not be lost.
No one comes to God unless God draws
    him.
Therefore he shows us Christ so that none
    of us will run away from him when we
    see through the law the punishment we
    deserve.

The words of the song overwhelmed her. She'd known about the sacrifice of Jesus, but now the head knowledge moved to her heart.

Put Me first.

The words filtered into her mind as a gentle message. She opened her eyes and looked across the room to where Dat sat.

I am your heavenly Father.

She looked to Gideon who sat a few rows in front of Dat.

I am your first Love.

Her soul swelled as if all the sunshine from outside the window were trapped inside her chest. The feeling — as if God were really there with her — both scared and thrilled her. What would He ask of her? What would He expect? That was the scariest part.

And although no voice shouted from heaven, Lydia had an inner knowing of what she needed to do. She could care for Dat. She could be a friend to Gideon. But Jesus wanted her whole heart first.

Chapter 14

Gideon watched Lydia walk from table to table, wiping down the wooden planks of the table tops, and he was amazed by how comfortable she seemed in her Amish dress and *kapp.* He reminded himself that she'd been raised Amish, but the woman driving into town just one week ago had seemed far from Plain.

He'd had a hard time getting her off his mind the last few days, and he'd been sorely disappointed when he showed up at her house last night and she wasn't there. And that's what bothered him. His mem had pestered him for years, asking him what young woman had caught his eye. One finally had — an *Englisch* woman. Or least she'd been *Englisch* when their gazes first met. Now . . . did it help or hurt matters that she'd returned to her Amish heritage? That there were rumors circulating over lunch that Lydia was going to be baptized into the church? It was worse, he decided. Gideon knew he could convince himself to stay far away from an *Englisch* woman, but now . . .

Something inside told Gideon to wait and watch. Lydia had only been here a week. If she were putting on a show or trying to gain favor, the truth would be found out. Then again . . . He glanced over at Amos and Micah, who also watched Lydia with interest. If he waited, he had no doubt another bachelor or two would step forward and try to win her heart.

"Gideon, I've seen you out in the pasture with Blue a time or two. How's it going?" Mr. Peachy's question interrupted Gideon's thoughts. The older man had a round face and ruddy complexion, and his long beard was more gray than brown. He looked like a younger version of the Santa Claus that Gideon often saw decorating *Englisch* businesses at Christmas.

"*Gut, ja.* I knew Blue was an intelligent horse. He warmed to the halter well."

"Do you have any secrets?" Mr. Peachy asked. "I'm amazed in the change already — Blue's always been a wild horse."

Gideon shared some of the tricks he used with horse training, especially with horses as strong-headed as Blue. Mr. Peachy

194

listened intently. Every few minutes Gideon's eyes left Mr. Peachy's face to scan the room in search of Lydia. She talked with Hope Peachy for a time, and then she chatted with Mrs. Sommer. After a few minutes he watched as she approached her dat, whispering something into his ear.

"I've been thinking of buying myself another horse." Mr. Peachy ran a hand down his beard. "I was wondering —"

Lydia walked out the front door without a glance over her shoulder. Her steps seemed determined. Gideon scowled.

"Let me know if you'd like me to check the horse over," Gideon interrupted.

Mr. Peachy's brow furrowed. "Well, not anytime soon —"

"*Ja,* not soon, but if I'm still here . . ." Gideon patted the man's shoulder. "But I'm going to head outside for a time. Talk to a few folks and then see if they, uh, need help loading the bench wagon."

"*Ja,* I'll contact you . . ." Mr. Peachy's words trailed behind Gideon as he hurried outside. He paused on the porch steps. In the distance, Lydia walked down the dirt road toward the store and school.

"She said she was going to peek in the window of the school," a soft, warm voice said.

Gideon turned to see Eve Peachy sitting in a rocking chair, holding one of the neighborhood children. Eve and the toddler boy watched some of the other kids pushing each other on a tire swing. Children's laughter filled the air.

"Oh, I was jest . . . worried about her. I mean after losing her mem."

"She didn't seem too sad. Happy like." Eve stood, placing the toddler on her hip. "I heard some of the women talking to her in the kitchen. Lydia said she'd been running for so long, and she's happy to feel as if she's come home."

He nodded and turned his gaze back in Lydia's direction. She continued down the road, the summer sunlight highlighting her *kapp.* Her black dress was down to mid-calf and unlike the thick black shoes most Amish woman wore, she wore brown slip-on shoes with a swirl design on the side. He supposed one couldn't give up all things *Englisch* overnight.

With a slight shrug of his shoulders he turned back toward the front door of the house. The men were beginning to carry the benches and table tops to the bench wagon, where they'd be taken to the next house for service in two weeks.

"I'm sure if you hurry you can catch up

with her." Disappointment was evident in Eve's voice.

"Nah." Gideon waved a hand. "I was just concerned about her, that's all. If she's doing well, she doesn't need me."

"You know you want to."

He rubbed his jaw. "I want to be a friend."

"I figured as much. From the way you look at her, you appear very friendly."

He looked closer at Eve. She blinked quickly, as if struggling to hold back tears.

Caleb had teased him weeks ago that he held Eve's fancy. Gideon hadn't believed it until now. But what could he do? One's heart wandered where it desired. He shuffled from side to side. As eager as he was to see Lydia — to talk to her — he was also eager to get out of view of Eve's disappointed grimace.

"Well, maybe I should go down. She might want company. I mean, being new to town . . ."

Without saying another word, he hurried down the road with a quickened stride, and in less than one minute he caught up with her.

Hearing his footsteps on the gravel, Lydia turned. He grinned, but his smile faded when she looked into his eyes. Lydia's gaze reflected disappointment. Was she disappointed he'd interrupted her walk?

"I saw you heading off. If you need me to drive you anywhere . . ."

"In the buggy?" She cocked an eyebrow. "Oh, no, I don't need a ride. Just heading out for a walk. Enjoying the beauty. Talking to God." Her words trailed off and heat rose to her cheeks. "That sounds strange, doesn't it?"

"Not to me." He waved a hand down the roadway. "Do you mind if I join you?"

"Actually . . ." Lydia bit her lip and glanced down the road to the school. "I was just thinking of Mem and my own first day at school. She came to see me —" Lydia's voice cracked and she took a deep breath and found her composure. She crossed her arms over her black apron, the color she'd be wearing for a year as a sign of mourning. "Mem missed me. She sat in the back. The teacher didn't seem to mind, but I did. I wanted to be grown up. Like the other kids." She looked up at the sky and closed her eyes, allowing the rays from the sun to pour over her.

"I'll let you be, then. Give you time." He took a step back and expected her to argue. To say that she wanted him with her after all.

Instead she opened her eyes and looked at

him. "Thank you. And thanks for the ride today too. I appreciate all your care. Getting to know you has meant so much."

Gideon studied her gaze. The nervous attraction that had reflected from her eyes the past few days had been replaced with a mix of peace and wonder, making her even more beautiful.

He waved a good-bye and hurried back toward the Peachy house. When he got there a few minutes later, he grabbed up one of the last benches and carried it out to the bench wagon, joining the other men. He supposed he should be happy. Lydia had made a good choice. She'd chosen to follow the way of faith. He knew it was what really mattered. Yet part of him also felt sad. Lydia was growing closer to God and to her dat. Would there be a time when she'd no longer need his friendship?

After he finished helping loading up the benches, he hung around longer than the other bachelors, waiting for Lydia to return, just in case he needed to drive her and her dat back. At least that was his excuse. As he was talking to Mrs. Peachy about her garden, Gideon felt a hand on his arm. He turned expectantly, believing it to be Lydia. Instead, Mr. Wyse stood there.

"I do appreciate your help this week." Mr.

Wyse extended some folded-up bills.

Gideon pulled his hands back, showing the man he would not take it. "*Ne,* I wanted to help. It was just a small way . . . a small offering in your time of loss."

"Thank you." Mr. Wyse tucked the bills back in his pocket. "I appreciate that. And I was going to tell you there's really no need for you to drive me home. No need to help with chores. My leg's doing better."

"Are you sure?" The words spurted from Gideon's mouth.

"*Ja.* I feel better — both my body and my heart. It'll be good to roll up my sleeves again. To feel useful."

"All right . . . if you have no need."

Then, with a final wave, the older man moved toward the hitching post for his horse. It wouldn't take him more than ten minutes to hitch the horse to his buggy.

How things had changed.

Just hours ago Gideon had worried about how to keep his heart protected from falling for Lydia when he was destined to be around her so often. Now he didn't need to worry about that. He could spend his days like he had before she arrived — talking with the other bachelors, planning for the hunting season, shooting practice over by Alkali Lake, and thinking again about the truth he'd wanted to discover while he was here.

The *lost* feeling surfaced. So familiar. Gideon hadn't realized it had lessened for a week. Even though they were just new friends, being with Lydia had helped that.

But now, as he walked down the wooded trail toward the bachelors' cabins, he felt disoriented. He was still in the same community, but the disconnection grew with each step. It was the same as when he was with his family. With all his brothers and sisters he was always surrounded by people, but he was just a seat warmer, a place filler. That time alone on the mountain haunted him in ways Gideon didn't understand.

Should tomorrow be the day he talked to Edgar and discovered the truth? Gideon had a feeling it was.

Lydia walked up the steps of the small log cabin school and looked into the window. Peering inside, she saw that three rows of small desks, a teacher's desk, a woodstove, and a chalkboard on one wall made up the room. Her mind wanted to run ahead and imagine what it would be like to teach there, but she stopped herself. As she had felt during the church service, her returning had to be about what God desired for her. If she considered anything else, then her return could be as futile as her leaving. And that was the last thing she wanted.

Lydia turned and gazed out at the metal swings, the slide, and the merry-go-round that looked old enough for her dat to have played on as a youngster. Then she pulled a slip of paper out of the pocket of her dress. She'd been looking through the Promise Box this morning when she spotted it. This letter had more than a date on the front. It also had a note written under the date: *Lydia's first day of school.*

She'd felt bad not letting Gideon join her, but since she'd woken this morning, she'd planned on coming down this way after the church service. Her chest still felt full of God's light, and she was eager to connect with Mem.

Dear Lydia,

You insisted on walking to school with the Slabaugh children next door. The oldest, Hester, is nearing twelve and fully capable to watch after you. She's cared for you on numerous occasions when my weak heart put me in bed for a spell, but I still didn't want to see you go. Maybe it's best, though, that I didn't walk with you. I might have followed you inside and sat right beside you.

The chores are done. They were done quickly without my "helper." It took twice as long to hang the wash and tidy up with your help . . . but who was in a hurry? Not me. I miss your voice telling me about the stories you think up and the songs. The lines from the church hymns sound best from yer lips.

I begged yer dat last night for him to allow you to stay home another year. He told me you needed to grow up into the woman God designed you to be. I could see the words hurt him to say them, but he spoke truth.

I complained to the Lord about it, and I pulled out my Bible hoping to find some peace. I cling to God's promises to be with me, to keep me, to have a good future for me. I needed to find a promise to help me on this day too. I read in the German Bible first, and then I pulled out the *Englisch* Bible our driver let me borrow. He was right — the English words do make it easier to read.

I started reading the Proverbs, and the fifth verse caught my attention: "A wise man will hear, and will increase learning; and a man of understanding shall attain unto wise counsels."

I found peace then. It was as if God was telling me that your hearing and learning would move into the hands of another now. I do like Miss Yoder. She is a godly young woman. I'm praying for her now, and praying for you. Praying that your greatest knowledge will settle on the love of God.

God says, *"Vie Gottlofen haben jein jri-erlen, wider mit Gott, oder ihr gewissen,"* which means the ungodly have no peace with God or their conscience. No matter how we raise our *kinder,* each child must respond to the love of the Father. I am praying for that day. I pray for your choice, Lydia. I pray you claim God's promises for yer own.

I know not whether that day is later or soon, but may all you are taught about our *gut Gott* take root deep in yer heart.

And I must close now because I realize you forgot yer lunch pail on the front step! I can't say I'm saddened by the discovery as it will give me an opportunity to check in on you.

Love, yer mem

Lydia's hands quivered as she read those words. She folded up the paper and slipped it back in her pocket, realizing that the day

Mem prayed for her to claim God's promises for her own was today. *This day.*

Had God known that? Of course He did. And Mem's desire for her was Lydia's desire now. To hear and increase in learning. To attain wise counsel from this new community of the faithful who God had brought her amongst. And maybe to get the chance to pass on what she'd learned.

She looked around at the playground and smiled. In time, perhaps, she'd be found worthy.

Gideon tried to ignore the rejection he felt. He'd thought for certain that he and Lydia were growing in their friendship, but maybe he'd just been mistaken. She was returning home, but that didn't mean she wanted him to be a part of it. The way she'd pushed him away on their walk today proved that.

He was alone in his cabin. Caleb and some of the other bachelors were out at a Youth Sing. Maybe he should have gone. Maybe spending time with some of the other young women in the community would have helped him get his mind off of Lydia. Eve would have been happy to see him.

Instead he pulled out a piece of paper and a pen, again determined to write the letter.

It would be easier to tell Mem and Dat now that he knew rather than wait until he returned to Pennsylvania and saw them face-to-face.

Dear Mem and Dat,

I am sure you figured out by now that I didn't come to Montana to hunt. While I will enjoy hunting, that is not the point. I came to know the truth of the past. I've known for many years that more happened in the hills of West Kootenai . . . things that you didn't tell me. Maybe soon I'll I understand why.

I didn't go asking around — don't worry about that. I know how Mem always says to keep my nose in my own business. Instead, I sat down with a man who recognized my name. As one of those who'd been on the rescue party he called my name a hundred times. Tomorrow I will ask him the truth of what happened.

I was jest a young boy who got lost. I suppose you felt as if you were protecting me by not explaining everything that happened, but sometimes one needs to know the truth to be able to face it with courage. I might regret knowing, but at least I'll stop making up my own scenarios in my head.

I hope everyone is doing well. Montana is beautiful, even though memories come back every time I look at the hills. I bet the little girls are growing up. Tell Rachel I might not be able to throw her up as high in the sky when I return. I imagine Glen's Esther has had her baby by now. Was it a boy or a girl? It seems that all the new babies in our family have been boys of late — not that I mind.

I have made new friends, and the church here is nice. The gatherings are smaller than in our community. I worked at Log Works for a time, but lately I've been training a horse, and I have other jobs lined up. I like those types of jobs better.

I hope you are all doing well.

Your son, Gideon

He read the letter over three times. What else could he say?

He was thankful he hadn't written a few days ago. If he had, he might have been tempted to mention Lydia. One mention of a young woman and he would have gotten his mem's hopes up. No, it was better just to face the truth all around.

Like his grandpa used to say, "You can

tell when you're on the right track. It's usually uphill." Would there ever be a bright spot of hope — an easy, sunny path? Would he return to Pennsylvania as empty, as lost, as he felt now?

Would he regret finding out about the hidden truth?

CHAPTER 15

Gideon was the first person in the store the next morning. He was waiting on the front porch when Edgar turned the sign from *Closed* to *Open.* After writing the letter he'd been worried about approaching the older gentleman, but after praying about it Gideon slept well. There was some benefit that came from not knowing the truth, he supposed. What you didn't know couldn't keep you up at night.

Edgar sat on a stool behind the counter. Behind him was a small desk with a computer and a chair where Gideon often saw Annie answering emails and placing orders. Edgar motioned to the chair, and Gideon walked around the counter and sat. Two bakers chatted in the kitchen and the scent of peanut butter cookies wafted through the air.

Edgar ran a hand down his freshly shaven face. His cheeks were pink. The end of his nose was too, as if he'd been standing in the open oven sniffing the baking cookies.

"I was wondering when you'd come by and want to talk about it."

Gideon's eyes widened. It was almost as if Edgar had been expecting him. "How did you know I was the Gideon who got lost in the woods?"

"Other than the fact that your face turned as white as a sheet of printer paper?"

Gideon shrugged. "I guess there's always that." He kicked his boot on the wooden floorboard, too embarrassed to look in the man's eyes. "Sir, I should have said something . . . should have confirmed that boy was me. That's one of the reasons I came here to West Kootenai. I know I got lost all those years ago, when I was jest a *kinder,* but . . . I know there's more that happened."

"What do you mean there's more that happened?" Edgar interrupted. One of the bakers approached and set two cups of coffee before them. Without saying a word, she hurried back to the kitchen. Gideon paid the coffee no mind.

"There's more than me jest getting lost. More my parents never told me. That's why I came back. I figured that if they didn't tell me the truth there'd be someone around who would."

"They never told you the story?" Edgar shook his head and took a sip from his steaming cup. "I wonder why your folks never told you."

"That's what I've been wondering too."

Edgar ran a finger across his chin as if considering the right words. "What do you remember?" he finally asked.

"I was only four, so the images are fuzzy. I remember the train ride from Pennsylvania to Montana. Me and my brothers and sisters filling the seats, and our dat telling us to behave. That meant no shouting — no matter how excited we were — which was hard. I'd never been on any trip like that before.

"I remember people staring at us. And for the first time realizing how different we were being Amish. I hadn't thought much of it before that because everyone at home that I knew was like us."

He blew out a breath, getting to the part Edgar was most interested in. Gideon forced a nervous laugh. "I remember the first night we stayed at the place of folks who'd lived in Bird-in-Hand but had moved to Montana. Their place was small, and all us kids slept on blankets lined up in front of the fireplace. We were supposed to be sleeping, but I was listening instead. In the adjoining kitchen the men were talking about bear hunting. I decided then I wanted to get me a bear. I wanted to be big like those guys."

Gideon paused. He also remembered wanting to stand out — be special. With twelve brothers and sisters he often went unnoticed. He'd been just one of the boys, a name and a face among many. He blinked once slowly, and then turned to Edgar. He couldn't tell the older man that. It seemed so foolish now.

He cleared his throat. "The next morning I headed out not long after breakfast. With twenty kids running around it took them awhile to realize I was gone — or so Mem told me later."

"Do you remember anything else?"

Gideon nodded, his forehead furrowing as he tried to reconstruct things. "I remember trying to find my way back. Being cold. I fell in a small creek . . ." He shook his head. "Most of it is blurry." He crossed his arms over his chest as a shiver ran up his spine. "I remember being alone. I wasn't used to that. I remember crying and calling for Mem."

"They organized a search party." Edgar looked up at the ceiling as if the memory played out there on a screen. "They looked around the lake first because the property you were staying at was close. Some of the men didn't think you headed that direction because one of the boy's BB guns was missing."

"Ah, *ja.*" Gideon ran a hand down his face. "I'd forgotten about the BB gun." He chuckled. "See, I told ya I was going bear hunting."

The front door opened, causing the bell to jingle against the glass, and a few of the other bachelors entered and headed into the dining room. They waved at Gideon, and then continued on. Many of them ate at least two meals a day at the restaurant. It was easier than trying to cook in their small cabins.

"I don't remember being rescued. I think I was sleeping when they found me. I remember being carried. I remember waking up sleeping next to my mem."

"It's a good thing you don't remember more."

Fear tightened the muscles in Gideon's neck. "What do you mean?"

"You were looking for a bear, but one found you. A few of the guys some him approaching. They distracted him. They called to him, got the bear to chase them instead." Edgar cleared his throat.

A hollowness filled Gideon's chest as his mind tried to comprehend what Edgar was saying — that the older man was talking about him.

"They split off in two directions and the bear followed one of the guys — a father of twelve himself," Edgar continued. "It was dark, you see, and the mountain — even the hills — are dangerous. The visiting Amish men weren't used to the area. The man who was being chased stumbled in the dimness of the afternoon. He fell down a steep incline."

Gideon wanted to tell Edgar to stop. On one hand he didn't want to know more. On the other hand he needed to know.

"It wasn't that far of a drop. Woulda been fine except that he landed wrong."

A groan escaped Gideon and he covered his face with his hands as a pang of guilt struck hard. The event had happened twenty years ago, but the telling of it made it feel as fresh and painful as if it had happened yesterday. No wonder Mem, Dat had hidden the truth. How could you tell your *kinder* something like that?

"They found him twenty minutes later. They found you too, still sleeping. The bear was gone." Edgar shook his head. "A tragedy to be certain."

"You say he landed wrong." He didn't know how to ask the rest of the question.

"When they found him he was alive." Edgar shook his head. "But his injuries were too severe. His neck was broken. He died as the rescue workers were trying to get him to the hospital."

"And the family — the woman and children of the man who died?"

Edgar clucked his tongue. "A sad story indeed. She married another Amish man, so I heard. I don't know the details, but it wasn't a good situation. I suppose you can't be choosy when you have twelve mouths to feed. Her name was Myrna. I remember that because it's my sister's name."

"Myrna." Gideon's voice trembled. "It's my mother's closest friend. They were children together and Mem has gone many times to visit her in Lancaster." Gideon thought about the sad stories he'd heard about Myrna's life. All those times he'd never known that he had a part in her heartache.

"Her husband is cruel," he confessed, "and most of her children have left the Amish. I never realized I was the reason why."

Edgar placed a hand on Gideon's shoulder, squeezing. "You can't take that guilt.

You were only just a boy. It was an accident." Edgar released his grip. "Don't your people believe that everyone's life is in the hands of God? If anyone is to blame you can talk to God about that."

Gideon rubbed the back of his neck. It was tight. His chest felt tight, too, as if it was trying to deflect the truth he'd just heard. He rose and moved to the counter, spreading his hands across the cool surface and leaning against it.

"You all right?"

"*Ja.*" Gideon nodded. He wasn't all right, but how could he tell Edgar that?

"So, it seems things are going well with Blue." Edgar was trying to make small talk, and Gideon felt sorry for the man. It should have been Gideon's parents who told him the truth.

He imagined returning home to Bird-in-Hand. Imagined striding up to the porch and opening the front door. In his mind's eye he could see Mem in the kitchen stirring the pot of soup on the stovetop. He imagined Dat reading *The Budget* in his favorite chair. He pictured them looking at him. Would they look at him differently now that he knew the truth?

Gideon also knew why his parents hadn't told him before. Who wanted to see guilt, like a wild pony, crushing their son's heart?

"Thank you, Edgar." Gideon straightened and then headed to the front door. Today he'd work with Blue. Today he'd gaze at the Wyse place, wondering what he'd done to push Lydia away.

Today he'd pray for Myrna — his mother's friend — and also ask himself why he thought knowing would be any better than the silence.

Gideon turned toward the door, but the rumbling of his stomach caused him to pause. He turned instead to the restaurant. Eve waited tables this morning, and even though she stood before another table of bachelors, with order pad in hand, her eyes fixed on him as he entered.

"Sit anywhere you'd like," she called to him. Then she turned to gaze to the table where the salt shakers were lined up, waiting to be filled. Gideon knew it was an invitation for him to join her rather than the other bachelors, and as he looked into her dark brown eyes his heart warmed. Eve's acceptance of him was like a healing balm. A smile slid onto his lips, and he pushed down the pain of the truth. Then, with quickened steps Gideon moved to Eve's table. With Eve he always felt valued — and this morning he needed that more than ever.

Lydia's face filled his mind, but as he pulled out the chair he pushed the thought away. His heart couldn't risk rejection . . . not now. In life the easiest things were the certain ones. And right now the only thing he could be certain of was that during breakfast he'd have a fine conversation with a woman who wouldn't draw him in one day and push him away the next. A woman who'd chosen to be Amish all her life and whose smiling eyes rested on him even now.

CHAPTER 16

Dirt rose from the dusty road, and Lydia told herself not to think about the fact that getting to the West Kootenai store and back would have only taken five minutes if she could have jumped in her car. But the car had been gone three weeks already, sold to a high school student in Eureka with a generous grandmother.

The road was lined with trees. Pine, larch. The wooded path opened to a field where two horses nibbled on bright green grass. At the edge of the road, between the dirt and the fence, was an apple tree. Its leaves were covered with dust from the road, but its branches were filled with small reddish-beige apples. Lydia stepped over a few of the rotten fruits lining the ground and then paused. She glanced up at the branches. A small gray sparrow fluttered from branch to branch as if overwhelmed with all the fruit too.

It seemed a waste that so much fruit fell to the ground.

A basket swung on her arm — the one she used to carry her shopping to and from her home. She set it down, plucked a dozen apples, and set them in the basket with the rest of her groceries. She'd make an apple pie later and bring a smile to Dat's face.

Picking this fruit was similar to Mem's letters in the Promise Box. While most people drove by this tree in a car or buggy, she'd stopped to pick the fruit. Mem had done the same, pausing to capture the memories, writing them down and tucking them inside her box. Lydia was grateful that she had. Though Mem was gone, Lydia knew her more than ever. Appreciated her more than ever too.

Dust in the air tickled her nose. Lydia blew out a breath and pulled out the small notebook and gel pen that she kept inside the basket. She wrote down her observations about Mem. She also wrote of the smell of the dusty ground and the lightness of the wind that brushed her cheek like a kiss. She looked at the clouds around her. They looked like the cotton-candy puffs she'd eaten at the carnival she'd gone to with Bonnie, and she wrote that down too.

She'd been working on her book diligently.

When she wasn't doing the wash, feeding the chickens, cooking, Lydia wrote down her memories and contrasted them with her return. She translated her conversations with Dat, and recorded her reflections on the letters and Scriptures from Mem's Promise Box.

The story of her life filled notebook pages, as if she wrote about another. Words for the next sentence, next paragraph, trailed through her mind throughout the day. It was almost as if God was walking beside her, pointing out the beauty of everyday life, and breathing inspiration into her heart. It was new and different. She was new and different. If someone else would have declared such sudden changes she would have scoffed. Yet maybe all the time God had been waiting, ready for her to open her heart.

Lydia knew that not all writing came in such idyllic moments, and she didn't want to take it for granted. She didn't want to waste her time following her fleshly desires when God had so much He wanted to share. She told herself that if God had a plan for her and Gideon to be more than friends He would make that clear in His own time. His promise to His people was that He would be with them always — not that He'd grant them desires from their preestablished list. She had learned that from the promises jotted down in Mem's box.

As she turned at the *T* in the road at the Carashes' house, Lydia looked to the pasture where Gideon worked with Blue. Gideon had a saddle on the horse. She stopped in her tracks and smiled. The horse training seemed to be going well. She grinned at the thought of seeing Gideon up in that saddle.

When she neared home, Blue trotted her direction. Gideon followed at a distance. Lydia hadn't talked to him much lately. He hadn't been coming around the house, and when she saw him in the pasture, he rarely paused to visit with her. While her heart pinched a bit that his interest in her had waned, she knew it was best. Moments with God and Dat were her first priority, and her time slipped away with the motion of the pen over paper. The right man would be there at the moment her soul was ready for him. Shouldn't she trust God with that?

Blue approached the fence and tossed his head as if in a greeting. She reached up to pet him and he scooted, enjoying it. Then, with a toss of his head, Blue stepped back and eyed the basket at her feet.

Lydia chuckled. "Oh, *ja,* I understand.

You see my apples." She reached down and grabbed one and then placed it on her open palm, offering it to Blue. He eagerly took it from her hand and chewed it with gusto, eyeing the basket again. She laughed and reached for another one.

"Stop!" Gideon's voice split the air. Lydia jumped. Blue didn't seem bothered by it. He pawed the ground with his front hoof.

"What?" She placed her hand on her hip and watched as Gideon came her way. The way he stomped over reminded her of the first moment she'd seen him. For the second time, she couldn't believe how utterly handsome he was with an angry frown on his face.

Lydia shrugged. "I was just giving him an apple."

"Just?" Gideon shook his head. "You rewarded Blue for disobeying me. I was teaching him to listen to my voice commands and when he saw you he bolted."

"I can't help it if he likes me." She offered a coy smile. "It must be my *kapp*. He's liked me much better since wearing one."

"I don't mind that he likes you, but he must learn to listen to me first."

"*Ja.*" Lydia lowered her head, considering his words. "But —" She looked up again. "— I'll make up for it by inviting you to dinner. I'm making fried chicken with apple pie for dessert."

"I, uh, wish I could." Heat rose to Gideon's face, and he ran a finger under the collar of his shirt. "But I already accepted an invitation to the Peachys'. In fact . . ." He eyed the sun lowering in the horizon. "I best get going and wash up."

Lydia's jaw dropped, along with her heart, falling to the ground like one of those apples. "*Ja*. Have a nice evening." She didn't know what else to say. She wasn't a fool. Eve's eyes had been fixed on Gideon. Eve had been watching him playing with the kids after the last church service at the Sommer house.

Lydia took a step back and picked up her basket. With a wave, she turned and hurried back to her house. She'd only done what she felt God was asking her to do. So why did she feel a jab of pain with every step? Why the sudden tears? One escaped and tumbled down her cheek and she wiped it away.

As she'd sought God and leaned on Him, she'd secretly hoped He had a plan that involved Gideon in her life . . . and that the time for them to build on their friendship would be soon. She was fine allowing space between them, but if she was honest with

224

herself, she didn't want to think of him turning his attentions to another young woman.

She thought about the Scripture verse she'd read this morning, written by Mem's hand: *"For I know the thoughts that I think toward you, saith the Lord," Jeremiah 29:11.*

This morning the Scripture's promise had given her comfort, but now she didn't know. What if the plans God had for her didn't involve Gideon? What if she'd been clinging to the promises too tightly? *What if they . . .* She didn't want to consider that they might not come true.

Lydia blew out a breath. Could the promises be trusted? In all the weeks since she'd decided to return home, return to God, this was the first time the doubt had grown loud, echoing in her head.

She hurried up to the front door and pulled open the screen. In ten steps she'd crossed into the kitchen and placed the basket on the floor. For some reason she was suddenly too weary to think about placing the basket on the counter. Too weary to think about making an apple pie, much less dinner. She needed comfort. She needed Mem's words.

The bishop's words were given to me a

week ago and daily it's a battle between fear and faith. I have no doubt that if it's a promise from God it will come to pass. But can I trust a man's words? How could one hear from God more than another? How could the bishop have been so sure of something that's been an impossibility in my life? It sounds prideful to me to say God has spoken a message to me alone. I try to remember the bishop's face. Did he appear to be a prideful man? I can't be sure and that worries me.

More than that, I wonder if it was a promise for me, then why didn't God jest tell me? Don't I have two ears on the sides of my head? Was it an audible voice the man heard? The questions keep me awake at night. If only I had answers.

But the more I think about it all, the more I realize I have to have faith. Doubt and tears haven't got me nowhere. Both have been my companions for years.

Maybe faith and trust will do their good work. That's what I keep coming back to. That's why I'm praying that God will take me to the next step of this faith business. I'm a woman who does right by church and the Plain ways of the community. Is there more to be done? Is there a way to have more faith?

I was wondering all these things when Augusta Primbridge stopped by. She owns a book shop on Oak Street and is always passing along books for me to borrow. Suppose she thinks since I have no children to tend to I have extra time fer reading, which isn't far from the truth. In the box were two fiction books, a cookbook of chicken recipes, and a Bible. An *Englisch* Bible. I was about to put it in a brown sack to return to Augusta when I glanced in the front and back to see if there was a name in it. There was no name, but a heading read "The Promises of God." That caused me to pause because in church I hear much about requirements, but talk of promises doesn't come often. And why does God need to promise anything in the first place? He does what's right by us; isn't that enough? It's not like He owes us more than our breath, this world, and the heavenly place which we all strive to know some day.

I read a few of the promises, but I'm not sure if I can keep this *Englisch* Bible around. What would the bishop say? I wrote down a few of the promises, the ones that spoke to my heart the most, and I returned the books to Augusta.

I have to say that reading these verses

has helped me to believe more than doubt. Maybe that's what faith is all about. Believing a pea-size more today than yesterday.

"For unto us a child is born, unto us a son is given: and the government shall be upon his shoulder: and his name shall be called Wonderful, Counsellor, The mighty God, The everlasting Father, The Prince of Peace," Isaiah 9:6.

"And all thy children shall be taught of the Lord; and great shall be the peace of thy children," Isaiah 54:13.

"A word fitly spoken is like apples of gold in pictures of silver," Proverbs 25:11.

Eve waited for Gideon on the front porch of the Peachy house. The front door was closed, but the windows were open, and Gideon could hear the sounds of Mr. and Mrs. Peachy chatting inside.

"Dinner is ready," Eve said as he approached. "I made a cherry pie. I heard it was yer favorite." She perched forward on the rocking chair but didn't stand.

Gideon mounted the steps, but his boots felt as if they'd been filled with lead. He rubbed his brow, head aching. He hadn't

228

slept much from worrying about Lydia, but most from fretting over how he'd ruined so many lives. Myrna, the children, the community. One Amish life lost had a ripple effect, but the loss of a father, a husband, was like a tsunami.

"You do like cherry, don't you?" Eve's words interrupted Gideon's thoughts.

"Oh, *ja.* I'm sorry." He widened his eyes and pushed his hat back on his head.

"Is it that horse? Is he what troubles you?" Eve rose. "Everyone — my father especially — is amazed by how quickly he's falling into line yet. We haven't seen such a thing. Sadly, I've seen too many untamable horses have to be put down."

"Wasn't thinking about the horse. Blue is the least of my worries."

The scent of fried pork chops and corn on the cob caused his stomach to rumble. Gideon took a step toward the door. He knew it would be polite to greet Mr. and Mrs. Peachy since they'd been the ones to invite him to the meal, but Eve hurried toward the door and placed her hand on the door handle, halting his entrance.

"Is it a *her,* then?"

Gideon cocked an eyebrow, guessing who Eve was talking about, but not wanting to admit it. "Her who?"

"Lydia Wyse, of course. I see the way you watch her — so enamored by her in Amish dress."

Gideon took a step back. He knew he was going nowhere until Eve gave him permission. His thoughts had been more on the truth of what had happened on the mountain all those years ago. Nightmares had plagued his few moments of sleep. Worries had filled his waking hours. Yet he didn't want to tell Eve that. Let her think that Lydia weighed most on his thoughts.

He rubbed the back of his neck with his hand. "There's a big difference between dressing Amish and committing herself to the lifestyle. We've both known youth during *rumspringa* who'd wear *Englisch* clothes all week and then show up to Sunday service dressed all prim and such in their Amish dress."

Eve cocked her head. "Do you really think Lydia Wyse is doing that?"

Gideon didn't answer. He didn't need to. He'd been watching. The town had been watching — as he'd expected they would. Lydia's changes over the last few weeks seemed sincere. *"Ja,"* he finally said. "She has changed, but just living as an Amish woman and being baptized into the church are worlds apart. One is a lifestyle, the other a commitment. I think she's far from entrusting herself completely to the community, to our ways."

Eve opened the door just a crack, and the scent of cherry pie wafted out with the other wonderful smells. He brushed his muddy shoes on the boot brush, nailed to the wooden planks of the front porch, and waited.

Eve studied him. "I wish I could agree with you." She sighed. "But I have a feeling that we'll be arriving at a church service in coming weeks to discover that Lydia has decided to become baptized."

Gideon's heartbeat quickened. "Have you heard something?"

"Ne." She bit her lip and turned her wide blue eyes toward him. "But if I was in her shoes that's what I would do." Eve tucked a strand of reddish-brown hair behind her ear. "Some things are worth committing your soul to God for. Things that really matter more than we thought. People who draw you in without meaning to . . ."

Is she talking about me? Does she see something I can't?

He stepped forward again, forcing Eve to open the door and step inside. Her father's greeting welcomed him, followed by a wave from Mrs. Peachy.

"I think yer seeing things," he mumbled under his breath. "Maybe you should try to pen one of those fiction books Lydia has done worked on."

Eve chuckled. "I'm not a novelist but an observer of life. I saw the coming chapters when Marianna Sommer first laid eyes on Ben Stone. It's almost as if some things were set in motion by God or something . . . and folks just can't help but get all caught up." Eve shrugged. "I'm jest wondering when it's my turn to take a ride on that merry-go-round."

CHAPTER 17

Church service was being held at Lydia's house. It was the first time Jacob Wyse had hosted it, but all agreed it would only be fitting, considering the occasion — even if they all had to squeeze in. All their furniture had been put in the barn and they'd packed as many benches into the house as possible. When the congregation stood for the first hymn, Lydia rose and followed Bishop Alton Plank out the front door. They walked around the side of the house, and Lydia smiled at seeing the buggies lined up and the horses nibbling on grass in the Carashes' pasture, with Blue right in the middle of them.

"Lydia, when I saw you at yer mem's funeral with your set chin and *Englisch* clothes, I have to say I never expected this day."

"I know, Alton. I mean Bishop Plank." She saw him so often in town in his logging clothes, not to mention having had his wife over for tea more than once, she forgot at times that he was the spiritual leader of their community.

"Are you sure of this? Sure of getting baptized into the church?"

"*Ja,* I am." Lydia nodded. "I didn't know what I'd lost until I found it again." She bit her lip, forcing herself to remember their words. Life had been an exercise in memory of late, as she worked to preserve her conversations, thoughts, emotions within the pages of her book.

"I wish yer mem could have seen this day."

Lydia lowered her head. She wished that too. She had to believe, though, that Mem had trusted in God's promises and had known deep in her heart that this day would come.

"Well, if you're certain, then I'll tell you what I've told all the others. Joining the church through baptism has great importance. Over four hundred years ago our ancestors were tortured and killed because they believed in adult baptism. They didn't think being baptized as an infant was enough. They felt one had to make a choice — one's choice in Christian belief."

"Yes, I remember that. I'd learned it —

Mem made sure I knew the history of our faith."

"Gut," Alton continued. "By being baptized into the church you'll have to live up to the rules of faith. It's our duty to keep you accountable, and if not . . ."

"There will be church discipline, I know."

"Since you already studied the Dordrecht Confession of Faith growing up, well, I find no need to do that again."

She cleared her throat. "That's kind of you. Mem and Dat taught me right. I just wanted my own way."

"But you can make this commitment now?"

"Ja."

"This is a promise for life." Alton looked deep into her eyes.

She balled her fists at her side. "I know."

"And if you're uncertain, it's time to reconsider and turn back."

Lydia breathed deeply. "I'm not uncertain . . . not this time." Joy bubbled up within.

"Gut. Then we better get back in there."

Lydia followed him back into the church service, head lowered, praying she wasn't making a mistake. And even though she knew that she only had to accept the life, sacrifice, and forgiveness of Jesus for salvation, she wanted to be part of this community. She believed in it — believed in the people.

They sang familiar hymns and Alton preached the same sermon she'd heard at every baptismal service growing up: the story about Philip's encounter with the Ethiopian.

" 'What doth hinder me to be baptized?' " Alton said with emphasis. "To which Philip answered, 'If thou believest with all thine heart, thou mayest.' And the Ethiopian replied, 'I believe that Jesus Christ is the Son of God.' "

Lydia had heard the same words dozens and dozens of times, but this was the first time she understood. She did believe. Because of the promises Mem shared, she understood God's Word more than ever before.

After the hymns and sermons had finished up, Lydia knew it was time. At Alton's direction she approached the front, kneeling on the rag carpet — the carpet Mem had made, in the home Mem had cared for. Breaths came hard.

"You are making a promise to God, as witnessed by the church. Do you have anything to say? What is your desire?"

Lydia cleared her throat. "My desire is to

renounce the devil and all the world, accept Jesus Christ and this church, and for this church to pray for me."

She knew then it was time for the four questions.

Instead of looking to Alton, she fixed her gaze on the wall behind his shoulder. Tingles moved up her arms.

"Do you believe and confess that Jesus Christ is God's Son?"

"*Ja.*"

"Do you believe and trust that you are uniting with a Christian church of the Lord, and do you promise obedience to God and the church?"

"*Ja.*"

"Do you renounce the devil, the world, and the lustfulness of your flesh and commit yourself to Christ and His church?"

"*Ja,* I do."

"Do you promise to live by the standards, the Ordnung, of the church and to help administer them according to Christ's Word and teaching, and to abide by the truth you have accepted, thereby to live and thereby to die with the help of the Lord?"

She paused only slightly. "*Ja.*"

With a gentle motion Edwin removed the prayer covering from her head. His soft fingers curled under her chin and lifted.

Footsteps approached and without glancing over she knew it was Gideon. Lydia's dat had asked him to participate, and Gideon had agreed. The goose bumps rising on her arms confirmed his closeness. She glanced up. Gideon had dark circles under his eyes.

What's troubling him?

Lydia swallowed hard. Now wasn't the time to worry about such things.

A wooden bucket filled with fresh, clear water hung from Gideon's fist. Gideon lifted the bucket and poured it into Alton's cupped hands. She looked forward again and closed her eyes. The water was warm as it poured down over her head. Once, twice, three times.

"In the name of the Father, the Son, and the Holy Ghost," Alton said.

Lydia blinked and opened her eyes, water drops falling from her lashes. Gideon stepped forward again and extended his hand. Lydia placed her fingers in his, and he helped her rise.

Beside her Alton spoke. "In the name of the Lord and the Church, we extend to you the hand of fellowship. Rise up, and be a faithful member of the church."

Alton's wife, Katie, approached, placing a holy kiss on Lydia's lips. A thought flashed through Lydia's mind and heat rose to her cheeks. She wished it was Gideon she was kissing. She swallowed. Those thoughts weren't holy at all. She'd have to depend on God more than she ever had . . . and deep down she knew that's exactly where He wanted her.

She rose and turned, her eyes sweeping the congregation. Tears rimmed many eyes but flowed freely down her father's cheeks. He wiped them away with the back of his hand.

She looked around at their place packed with people.

I've come home, Mem. I've come home.

Gideon took a big bite of his bread slathered with butter and jam. His hand still tingled. It had been tingling since he'd held Lydia's an hour before. He told himself not to be foolish. She was a sister in Christ and nothing more. The knowing danced in his heart. She was staying. She'd become Amish and part of the church. Eve was right. It was more than he'd hoped for. With that knowing the memories of being lost on the mountain hadn't plagued him for the last few hours as they had for the previous weeks.

Yet as he watched her from where she stood in the kitchen with the other women, as they prepared lunch for after the church service, two thoughts battled for position within his mind. First, that God had brought her into his life for a reason. Maybe God had a plan for them — for a future together?

The first thought shined with hope, but the second darkened his thoughts with fear: if anyone could break his heart, Lydia could, and he couldn't handle that.

Was it just six weeks ago that she'd driven into town? She'd come in like a whirlwind. If he hadn't known better, he'd have thought she'd been *Englisch* her whole life. And now, looking at her, he'd have thought she'd never lived a day away from her Amish community.

He watched her working in the kitchen, chatting with the other women. Lydia took a spoon and tucked it under the lid of the pickled beets, lifting the rim and breaking the seal. Setting down the spoon, she quickly unscrewed the lid and set it out for Eve Peachy to take to one of the tables. She did the same with another jar, and then — as if feeling his eyes on her — turned and glanced over her shoulder.

Her gaze locked with his and brightened. He saw clear interest . . . but something else too. Worry? Shame? Maybe a bit of both. He swallowed hard, then took another bite of his bread. What was she not telling him?

Of course, she could ask the same question of him. Gideon lowered his head.

They hadn't talked since he'd chewed her out for giving Blue an apple. He should have told her then that he was going to the Peachys' house just to look at a horse Mr. Peachy was considering. He could tell from Lydia's gaze she believed it was something other than that. Something concerning Eve. He should have confessed that Mrs. Peachy had offered dinner in exchange for his advice.

An *Englisch* man had driven a horse up from Columbia Falls, and Mr. Peachy wanted Gideon's expert opinion.

The horse had been a great buy, but even though he'd chatted for a time with Eve and Hope, there was no attraction there. Why couldn't he risk telling Lydia how he felt? Maybe because it hurt too much. It was better just to be friends than to open up and have her back off again.

Lydia finished with the jars and set to work washing up dishes. Telling himself that he'd worry about her later, Gideon turned to welcome Amos, who had just taken a seat beside him.

I was just seeing things, Gideon told

himself. *That wasn't attraction, care, in her gaze. It must have been the sun coming through the window, distorting my view.*

Amos pointed to the jar sitting in front of Gideon. "Can you pass the pickles?"

"Oh, *ja*. Sorry about that."

Amos stuck a fork inside and pulled out a small pile, placing them on his plate. "Want some?" He held the jar up for Gideon.

"*Ne*. I'm not too hungry today." That was the truth.

"*Ja*, I heard that happens."

"What happens?"

"When you're in love . . . it's hard to eat."

"Who says I'm in love?"

Amos didn't answer his question. Instead he took a large bite of his bread, smothered in peanut butter. He swallowed, then pointed his fork at Lydia. "She cares for you, you know."

Gideon shook his head. "Yer just saying that."

"*Ne*. I wish. I've tried to talk to her at the store. Micah, too, but she hardly gives us the time of day. We've both seen the way she looks at you . . . like she's wishing you would ask her for a date."

"How can I do that? I don't have a buggy. There's no place to go. If I took her to dinner at the restaurant, everyone would see. It

242

would be like taking the whole town on a date."

"*Ja.*" Amos laughed. "That's the truth, it is." He scratched his head, causing his blond hair to stick up. "*Vell,* then, how about a walk."

"A walk?"

"*Ja,* a romantic walk."

Gideon ran a hand down the side of his face. He was already sweating at the thought. He'd asked to walk with her before. It still stung that she'd turned him down. He glanced over at Amos, narrowing his gaze. "What if she says no?"

Amos raised an eyebrow and leaned a bit closer. "Ah, friend, but what if she says yes?"

Gideon approached the Shelter house, and his brow furrowed. Numerous buggies were parked outside. What was this about? Surely not what he'd first thought.

Just as he was leaving the Wyse house after service today, Mr. Sommer had asked him if he could stop by the Shelter place tonight. He'd assumed that Will Shelter had also wanted to talk about a horse, but as he looked around he no longer thought that was the case. Through the front window Gideon saw that many Amish couples from the community had gathered. It looked like some type of meeting . . . but what about?

Children raced around the yard. The boys played tag, and the girls chased after them laughing. Gideon rubbed his forehead. When had things changed? When did things turn around and it become up to the men to pursue the women? It would be so much easier just to know who was truly interested in him — and who wasn't. Namely, if he knew about one person. Did Lydia care, or would she just push him away if he tried to get close to her again?

He walked up the front porch steps, and the front door opened before he had a chance to knock. Will Shelter opened the door. He was a tall man, as large as a bear, or so it seemed.

"Well, here he is," Will announced as Gideon stepped inside. "Here's someone else who could add to our conversation."

Gideon pulled off his hat and glanced around. Abe Sommer patted the empty chair beside him. Gideon placed his hat on one of the hooks on the wall by the door and hurried over to sit. "I'd love to give input . . . if I knew what this was about."

Laughter filled the room.

"*Ja,* that might help," Sallie Peachy called out.

Will Shelter cleared his throat. "The matter has to do with Lydia Wyse."

Heat rushed to Gideon's face, and he readjusted himself in his seat. From beside her husband, Deborah Shelter's face glowed. How did she know his feelings for Lydia? How did anyone know? He thought about his conversation with Amos at lunch. Had his friend mentioned something? He looked around, seeing some of the other deacons of the church. Did they call him here to warn him to give time and space to his feelings for Lydia? After all, she'd just been baptized today.

"We want to offer Lydia the teaching position at the school. In the last month or so many of us have spent time with her. She seems to be serious about her return to the Amish. Today was evidence of that," Will Shelter said.

"Still . . ." Mrs. Peachy used a clean paper plate to fan her face. "We know so little about this young woman. I mean, if we offer her this position we are setting her up to be an important example in the lives of our children. We are claiming that she is a spiritual example for our children to follow —"

"What we really want to know," Deborah Shelter cut in, "is what you know about her. We know you've spent time together."

"Not, much time, uh . . ." He paused to choose his words wisely. "What I'm trying to say is that I haven't spent every day with her — not even close — but I have seen Lydia enough to see a change. I saw her the first day she drove into town, and I didn't trust her. She'd left the Amish. We all knew that. We all saw the pain in the eyes of her parents, especially her mem."

He lowered his head, swallowed hard, and then lifted it again. "I didn't know what to think at first, because I was there, helping Jacob Wyse build his wife's coffin, and he had nothing but good things to say about his daughter. I didn't see it at first . . . mostly because all I saw was her *Englisch* car, her *Englisch* dress, her *Englisch* ways."

Gideon took a breath and continued, realizing he did know her — or at least was starting to. "But things started to change. Maybe it *vas* her mem's death, but maybe something else too." He looked around. "I think for the first time she's living the truth of who God made her to be. And only God working in one's heart can bring such transformation."

Many faces filled with smiles at his words — except for Mrs. Peachy. Gideon glanced past her. He didn't know why the woman had reservations about Lydia, but he

246

guessed her Mama Bear instincts for her daughters had something to do with it.

Ruth Sommer clapped her hands together. "Thank you. That does help."

Gideon nodded and then sat back and listened to them discuss Lydia. They discussed her strengths and he liked their logic: she edited books, so surely she knows a thing or two about teaching from them. She'd also been raised Amish and knew all about an Amish school.

Gideon decided to slip out. He grabbed his hat from the hook and waved his good-bye. This was their decision; he just hoped his words helped them.

His own comments — his defense of Lydia — put voice to all he'd been thinking. When had he come to admire her so? The change had come as silently as the chilling August nights, pointing to the autumn to come. As Gideon had shared with the Amish couples about Lydia's transformation, he'd realized he could no longer wait. His words had confirmed in his mind what his heart had been telling him for a while. She was not the same woman who'd driven into their community full of questions and doubts.

More than that, Gideon couldn't imagine his life changing for good without her.

CHAPTER 18

"Trust in the Lord with all thine heart; and lean not unto thine own understanding. In all thy ways acknowledge him, and he shall direct thy paths," Proverbs 3:5-6.

"Ask of me, and I shall give thee the heathen for thine inheritance, and the uttermost parts of the earth for thy possession," Psalm 2:8.

Lydia didn't know which she liked best — the short slips of Scripture that Mem had tucked into the Promise Box, the longer letters that she had written to Lydia, or the notes of Mem's own thoughts and doubts. Sometimes reading Mem's doubts helped her most — it helped Lydia know she wasn't the only one who had questions. She wasn't the only one who doubted God's promises at times.

She pulled out another letter and noticed

the date. Just two days after the day she was born. How had she not seen this before?

Lydia held her breath as she unfolded the letter. It wasn't folded as neatly as the others and there were spots on the page. Tears?

I don't think I can sleep tonight. I'm not sure I can ever sleep again. I don't want to close my eyes, unless I'm dreaming. All my attention is turned to one thing . . . one small person.

We arrived at the small village of Elk Run at noon and even though we'd come a week before the due date, Jacob's sister — the midwife — was waiting when we arrived. The smile on her face told us the news even before the words. She said the baby had come. Said she was healthy and beautiful.

"She?" My knees weakened at the word. A daughter. I'd always dreamed of a daughter to read stories to, to bake with, to sit in the garden and whisper secrets with.

"And the mem?" Jacob had asked. I knew he asked about her health, but so much more too.

"She is well. She is resting. She asked if you'd come yet."

I hoped then that she wanted to see

us, to share the joy, but my stomach clenched as the *Englisch* driver drove us there. Hopefully she didn't want to see us so she could tell us to our faces that she was keeping the child.

For as long as I live, I will never forget parking in front of the house. Three little boys wearing Amish clothes, with their blond hair cut straight across, watched us exit the van. I'd only taken two steps toward them when the oldest one — he must have been seven or eight — ran to me.

"Are you our sister's mem?" he asked.

I nodded and smiled. My joy was only tempered with their loss. With their mem's loss.

She asked to see me first. Her blonde hair was tucked under a sleeping scarf. She held the sweet baby curled under her neck. I entered, and her smile made me want to cry.

"She's beautiful, Ada Mae. I knew she was going to be. And look, red hair."

She held the sweet *boppli* out to me, and tears filled my eyes so much that it took me a minute to blink them away. Then — there she was. Small round face. Red hair. Lots of red hair. I looked to the woman in the bed and the question must have filled my gaze, for she answered it.

"The, uh, father . . . his hair was dark. But my mother's . . ." She covered her mouth with a quivering hand and relief filled her face. "My mem's hair was red. What a gut *Gott* to offer us this gift."

I slept on the couch the first night, and Jacob stayed at his sister's place. I felt helpless when the baby cried in the other room. She wasn't mine to tend to yet. I felt useless when I knew her mother was nursing her. I'd packed bottles and formula, but would I ever feel like her real mother?

Yesterday, though, I was dressed and sitting in the living room when she exited with the baby. A bag was packed, and she was already in a car seat for the ride in the *Englisch* driver's van that would take us back to the train station.

Sadness filled the new mother's face. So much sadness.

If only my embrace could heal her wounds.

"I do want to know one thing . . . before you leave." The woman's voice caught in her throat.

"*Ja?*" I held my breath. The car seat seemed light compared to the worth of the treasure inside.

"What . . . what is her name?"

"Lydia." The name released with a breath. "In the Bible she was the first one who believed Paul and who accepted the good news of Jesus. When thinking of names, what we wanted most is a daughter who believes."

Lydia moved to Mem's cupboard, pulling out the ingredients for cracker pudding. She'd been up early thinking about it. Even though nearly two months had passed since Mem's death, it was the strangest memories and longings that drew her. Mem had been her real mother — there was no doubt about that. She just wished she told her more often when she'd had the chance.

The note from Mem she'd read last night made her ache for her mother something fierce. In all her growing-up years, Lydia had never doubted Mem loved her, but as she closed her eyes tight, the weight of Mem's care pressed down on her even heavier than her thick quilt.

In addition to the cracker pudding, Lydia decided to make a pie. She cut the round for the crust, just as Mem always did, and her eyes teared up to see the long, thin bit of crust that remained.

"Our secret treat," Mem would tell her. They'd take the strip of dough, add butter and sugar, and then roll it into a small pinwheel and bake it just so.

"You got your daughter to bake with, Mem," she whispered to the empty kitchen, emotion heavy in her throat. And as the pie baked, dozens of other memories filtered through her mind. It would be impossible to be in Mem's kitchen without thinking of her . . . remembering.

"Koon essa," Mem used to call before dinner. Hearing those words, Lydia would run to the table. The words meant that the food would be *gut,* plentiful.

Lydia had gotten the idea to write a cookbook during her first trip to West Kootenai. She'd been away from home long enough to realize that while she knew how to cook and bake, there were dozens — a hundred more — of recipes she wanted for herself, and so she'd sit with Mem and write them down. She also asked Mem to write down her recipes as she cooked.

The hardest part was that Mem's manner of cooking was the same as most of the Amish women she knew. The recipes weren't written down, but were known from long experience. Lydia had tried to scribble down notes as Mem added flour and spice and lard, but the measurements didn't matter as much as "it jest feels right."

"Mem, how did you know to add an extra tablespoon of sugar?"

"I knew 'cause it vas jest so."

"And shortening, Mem — how much do you add?"

"The size of an egg."

That was the hard part too. Egg sized, handful, pinch, and sprinkling weren't easy to replicate.

And with the recipes, Lydia also jotted down familiar Amish sayings. Those had been easier to capture.

" 'Them that work hard, eat hearty,' " she mumbled to herself.

Looking back, collecting the recipes, was Lydia's way to keep close to Mem. It was her safe way of keeping a connection. It made her feel creative too, as she cooked the recipes. But had that cookbook actually hindered her real desire?

Now that her book — the story of her returning mixed with memories of her childhood — was well under way she wondered why she'd waited so long. Bonnie had known where the true story was. It simply took Lydia putting pen on paper to discover it.

This place, these people, Dat's home,

254

returning. There was a story in all of it — just not for the audience she first thought. The message wasn't what she thought either. She thought Mem had wanted a *gut* Amish daughter, but in truth she simply wanted one who believed.

When the pie was finished, Lydia cleaned up the scraps from all her cooking and baking, putting them into a bowl to take to the chickens.

"I believe You. I want to believe You more," Lydia whispered as she hugged the bowl of scraps next to her body, stepping outside and hurrying toward the garden. The ruts in the grass were evidence of the day's events with the church gathering, but her heart and soul felt as if they had been torn up even more — in a good way. Even though tears had flowed as she read Mem's letter, the words worked as a plow tip, breaking up the hard parts of her heart.

Reading about the moment that Mem saw her for the first time brought just as much hurt as healing. Mem could do nothing for the other woman's pain. Had her birth mother ever gotten past the trauma? The loss?

What about the boys — her brothers. *Brothers.* They most likely hadn't understood at the time what was happening. How

255

could a newly widowed woman explain such a thing to her sons? But did they understand now? Did anger fill them?

Lord, if the dear woman hadn't already faced enough with the loss of her husband. Why this?

Lydia entered the chicken coop and scattered the scraps at her feet. The small flock hurried around her, pecking at their dinner as she slipped out of the tall gate, locking it.

She told herself to focus on the good — celebrate Mem's joy, Mem's gift. But like two sides of a coin, the joy of one person — one couple — was another's pain.

She also didn't understand God's part in it all. For one woman to receive a promise, another had to face heartache. Yet she couldn't think of that. Evil ruled in the world, and it was only by God's grace that anything good came out of it. That's what she needed to focus on — focus on faith. On believing.

The air smelled of lilacs from the bush behind the house, heavy with flowers. Lydia paused and breathed in, considering how Mem and Dat had chosen her name. She'd never known she was named after a woman who'd believed. She knew it was a name from the Bible, but the meaning encouraged her now.

She plucked a lilac cluster from the bush and moved around the house to the front door. *Lord, help me to live up to my name.*

The empty bowl swinging in her hand hit her leg when Lydia rounded the house and stopped short. *Gideon.*

He walked toward her with a long stride. She hadn't seen him like that except when he was mad at her. Except this time she knew he wasn't, due to the big smile he wore on his face.

"Lydia!" he called to her and waved.

She paused and tilted her head. Gideon was even more handsome when he smiled than when he frowned.

"*Ja?* Where are you headed off to? It seems you're on a mission."

"I am. I've come to ask you something."

"Let me guess: did you want my apple pie recipe? Because that was what I was asked most today."

"*Ne.* I was wondering if you had time tomorrow for a walk?"

Emotion thickened her throat. "A walk? Like to the store?"

He removed his hat and ran a hand through his dark hair. Sweat beaded on his brow, and Lydia knew it wasn't from the heat. If anything, the air was a bit chilly as the sun set.

"No. A walk to the lake. I would like to spend time with you. I thought it would be nice to talk."

She took in a quick breath. "I, uh . . ."

His eyes widened, filled with worry. "I mean if you don't want to —"

"No, it's not that." She waved her hand. "It's my editor's mind. I was trying to figure out what word to use. I'd *love* to, or I'd be *honored* to. Either way, the answer is yes."

He nodded once, then placed a hand on her shoulder. "Ten o'clock?"

"Make it eleven o'clock, and I'll pack a lunch."

She didn't think it was possible, but his smile widened.

He licked his lips. "Will that include a piece of apple pie?"

Lydia nodded. "*Ja.* I'm sure there's an extra piece or two around here. I was saving it for something — someone — special. And you jest might fit the bill."

CHAPTER 19

It wasn't until she'd gotten out all the ingredients for cherry turnovers that Lydia realized she didn't have enough sugar. She stopped by both the Carash and Sommer houses to borrow a cup, but when neither were home she continued on to the West Kootenai Kraft and Grocery.

She glanced at the clock on the wall when she entered, hoping Edgar wasn't in a chatty mood. Sometimes he started in on one of his stories on how things used to be, and while she usually loved hearing his stories, today was not the day. She had a handsome bachelor to bake for.

The line was long, so Edgar rang her up quickly with a wink and a smile. Yet she'd only taken two steps out the door when a woman approached her. She knew the woman's name was Mrs. Shelter, but Lydia had only chatted with her for a few minutes once during their Saturday morning gatherings.

"Lydia! Yer jest the person I wanted to see. In fact, I was going to stop here to drop off a letter to be mailed, then I was walking down to yer place."

"Oh, well, I am heading home now, but I won't be there long . . ." Lydia didn't elaborate on why. News spread quickly in these parts, and if she were to mention Gideon, the folks in the community just might have them engaged and be planning their wedding by midnight.

"It'll jest take a moment of yer time, but there's something we'd like you to consider."

Lydia touched her *kapp,* making sure it was in place. "We?"

"*Ja,* us parents in the community."

Lydia nodded and stepped to the side to let other customers pass. Mrs. Shelter joined her, and they stood by the big ice cooler on the porch of the grocery.

"We had a meeting last week at my house to discuss the new teacher. We had one young woman who was supposed to come for an interview, but she cancelled. It was at church yesterday when someone brought up yer name, and we met again last night."

Tingles moved up Lydia's arms. *"Ja."*

"We know that there is much happening — the loss of yer mem, your returning — but we wondered if you'd consider teaching this year?"

"Me?" She placed her free hand over her heart and swallowed. Even though it's what she'd hoped for, she was honestly surprised. Did they see the changes? Did they trust her? She blinked back tears, thankful it was so.

"Are you all right, dear?"

"*Ja.*" Lydia nodded her head. "I'd love to be considered. If you'd like me to sit for an interview . . ."

"*Ne.*" The older woman smiled. "There were enough folks there to give you a good word — Ruth Sommer, Katie Plank, Sallie Peachy. Even one of the bachelors."

"One of the bachelors?"

"Oh, *ja.* Gideon is one of the most re-spected bachelors in the community. The men of the area are impressed with his work and his lifestyle. My husband asked him to come by so we could hear his thoughts. We've seen that you're friends."

Lydia nodded. Was that all they thought? "Yes, yes, we are friends."

"Gideon had wonderful things to say. He reminded us that only God working in one's heart could bring about such transformation as we've seen in your life."

Lightness filled Lydia. Her feet no longer felt connected to the ground, and she was certain if it wasn't for the heavy sack of sugar in the grocery basket in her hand, she'd just float away.

"This was last night?"

"Yesterday afternoon. That's why my mission today was to come to you."

"And Gideon knew that you'd be offering me this position?"

Mrs. Shelter pursed her lips. "Hmm, I'm not sure. Actually, I do believe he left before we made the decision, but he knew we were leaning that way."

Lydia nodded. No wonder Gideon had been in such a happy mood. No wonder he asked me to go on a walk. *He must have great hopes that I'll be teaching this year. That I'll be staying around.* That gave her hope that he'd stay longer, too, beyond hunting season this fall.

"Mrs. Shelter." She reached out and took the woman's hand, squeezing it. "I would be honored to teach. I know this was no small decision."

"Wonderful, dear. Ruth Sommer and I have been chosen to work with you — to help you prepare. I will contact you — and I know it's short notice. The school year starts in less than three weeks."

"*Ja.* I know, but . . ." She was about to tell the woman she'd already been thinking of lesson plans for the last month, jotting down notes in her journal, but changed her mind. "I — I don't mind. I do have one question, though. How many scholars will I have?"

"Fourteen — it's a big class."

Lydia smiled. "And I'm looking forward to knowing every one of them."

Fourteen little personalities. That would give her something to write about.

Gideon and Lydia strode along the dirt road side by side, walking to Lake Koocanusa, along the shore, and back up the road. Her breaths grew labored as they climbed the gentle, sloping hill to a spot where they could overlook the lake on one side and the houses that dotted the fields and woods on the other.

The more time Lydia spent in Montana, the more she was awed by the beauty. Today the lake sparkled topaz blue. A few speed-boats roared across the water, stirring up froth like ribbons of frosting. Great trees cloaked the hills like a prince's cape. Yet the image of Gideon, striding by her side — make that swaggering by her side — brought even more awe. Who knew a man like this existed? She was thankful for him . . . but even more thankful that she'd pursued God first, that she'd gotten her life right in His sight before she turned to the matters of her heart.

Even though their hands swung just inches apart as they walked, they didn't touch. Lydia shared her excitement over the school year to come, and Gideon spoke of his training with Blue. They talked as if they'd been friends for years, and Lydia liked that.

Gideon spread out the quilt they'd brought on the lush green grass at the top of the hill, and Lydia sat and pulled out sandwiches, canning jars filled with lemonade, and two kinds of dessert from the basket.

"I brought a piece of pie from yesterday, and I made cherry turnovers too."

Gideon's jaw dropped. "Turnovers? Really? That's my favorite dessert. My mem makes the best."

Lydia unwrapped the waxed paper and handed him one. "I'm worried now. I mean I think they're good, but how could they compare to your mem's?"

Gideon held it up, examining it. "It looks all right." The twinkle of humor lit his eyes. "But we'll have to taste."

He took a big bite, but the smile on his face faded.

"What? Is something wrong?"

Gideon held up one finger. "I'm not sure. I taste something . . ." He took another bite, chewing it slowly. Then another bite after that.

She held her breath as he swallowed.

"It's baking soda . . . maybe. There is a strange taste."

"What?" Lydia huffed. "I didn't taste anything wrong."

"Oh, you already had one?"

"*Ja,* I had to make sure they tasted good, and I liked it. Dat did too."

"*Ne.* I'm sure there is a problem. Here . . ." He reached for the wax-papered dessert again. "Let me try another one and see if I can figure it out." The corners of his lips twitched into a smile.

"Gideon!" Laughter burst from her lips. "You are such a joker."

"I'm sorry, ma'am, that you think so." He took another large bite from the second turnover, attempting to keep a serious look on his face. "I'm still trying to figure out what's wrong. It might take me the whole half dozen to come up with the answer."

"Well, you can eat all you want. I have an announcement."

Gideon took another bite and chewed. "Sounds serious."

"It is. I've been offered a job as teacher."

Gideon nodded and smiled. "And you're going to take it?"

"Of course. Don't you think I'd make a good teacher?"

"The best — and that's what I told everyone at the meeting. 'Hire her or all your horses will run wild!' "

Lydia laughed. "Seriously, it was what I'd hoped, but I didn't want to ask. Didn't want to assume —"

"You *hoped*? Like in the last few weeks when the interviewee fell through?"

She bit her lip, wondering how much to confess. Tension tightened her gut. "No, before that. That first morning at the Kraft and Grocery, when they mentioned it, I wanted the job. In a strange way I felt as if that's why I'd returned."

Gideon put down the pastry and wiped his hands on his pants. "But you were *Englisch* then . . ." He frowned.

Lydia's smile fell even as her heartbeat quickened. "But I was planning on returning. I'd already decided." Heat rose to her cheeks.

"That didn't weight your decision, did it? That or other things . . . ?"

Lydia immediately thought of the book. Of him. A part of her knew that those factors had weighed in, at least at first.

"Not really." Her words rushed out before Gideon could read the truth on her face. "After I found Mem's Promise Box, I started seeking God more. I knew He wanted me to give my whole life to Him."

Gideon nodded, but she read uncertainty in his gaze. "If you say so, Lydia."

Then a smile filled his face where a frown had been just a few minutes before. "But a new job like that is worth celebrating." He picked up another turnover and took a big bite.

They continued to joke as they ate lunch, and Lydia was pretty certain she'd never had a better day. She was glad he'd believed her about the teaching position too. Glad it hadn't caused a problem between them.

"Lydia, I was wondering . . ." He wiped the corner of his mouth with a cloth napkin. "I, uh, was wondering if we can do this again, often like."

Her whole chest warmed. Was it possible to start floating from the buoyancy within?

" 'Often like.' That sounds nice." She eyed him. "It'll give me a chance to know you better, Gideon. To hear about your life."

For the next thirty minutes they talked

about his family back in Bird-in-Hand. His father's farm. His brothers and sisters and the time he broke his arm when he fell out of a farm wagon.

"My younger brother and I were trying to see who could stand on one foot longer as Dat drove through the rutty field. We both fell when the wheel hit an especially large hole, but I landed wrong."

She told him about sneaking a piece of pie Mem had prepared to take to a neighbor who was ill.

"I covered it with a cloth and Mem didn't know until we got there. The neighbor acted as if I'd spit in her tea, but Mem couldn't stop chuckling for the rest of the day."

They chatted some more and then a blue jay joined in, filling in any empty space between their words with a song. Lydia glanced at the world around them, trying to remember every detail. Every word.

"So is this your first time in Montana?" She packed up their lunch.

The smile faded from Gideon's face.

"No, I've been here once before, but I was just a kid." The color in his cheeks faded to gray. Gideon grabbed the picnic blanket and basket, and they headed down the hill. Lydia quickened her steps to keep up, a tightness growing in her chest as she waited for him to say something more, but Gideon continued on silently.

When she couldn't bear the quiet any longer, Lydia glanced up at him. "Did I say something wrong? Do something? You seem lost in thought. I mean you're here with me . . . but not here."

He glanced at her. Worry tinged his gaze. "Are you sure you're going to stay?" The words seemed to come out without him meaning them to.

"In Montana? *Ja,* there is my dat to care for. And now I'll be teaching during the school year."

"I mean stay Amish."

Lydia paused her steps, unsure of where this was coming from. "You saw me get baptized yesterday." She studied his eyes and noted concern, but for some reason she felt there was something else he wasn't saying. She tried to again think of what she could have said to trigger his sour mood. Nothing came to mind.

He stopped beside her. "*Ja,* I know you got baptized." He shrugged. "I just got the image of you in the car. It fit you so natural like. I was thinking how great it would be to have more days like this. Many more. But I was wondering if there would ever come a time when you'd start to miss things."

"Like what?"

"Like editing. Like driving. Like . . . electricity."

Lydia chuckled. "Well, electricity is nice. Driving is more convenient. But the closeness I feel to God, my dat, and friends — I appreciate that so much more. And instead of editing, I'll be grading papers. That should satisfy. And . . ." Lydia paused. She wanted to tell Gideon about the book she was writing — a book just for her — but she couldn't yet. She didn't want him to think or act in a certain way because he thought she would be writing it down.

"And what?"

Lydia twirled her *kapp* string around her finger. "And I was just going to say that if I get more days like *this* for giving up days like *that,* then it's completely worth it."

A smile glowed on Gideon's face. "*Ja,* totally worth it." He reached out and took her hand. Her stomach flipped.

They were nearly to Lydia's house when their date was interrupted by a gelding happy to see them. Blue trotted to the fence and eyed the picnic basket.

"Sorry, no apples for you today, boy." Lydia giggled. "But next time I walk to the store I'll make sure I get enough to bake a pie . . . and bring you some apples too."

They petted Blue until he backed away and returned to the pasture, nibbling on the clusters of grass.

"You seem to be a natural at training. Is it something you've always wanted to do?"

Gideon's shoulders straightened, and she could tell he took her words to heart. "I started out as a farrier, actually."

"A farrier?" Lydia searched her memory, trying to remember what that was.

"One of the neighbors down the road needed an assistant. He trained me to take care of the horses' hooves, doing the trimming and balancing and placing of shoes. Dat told me once, 'Son, if you learn how to shoe a horse and ride 'im, you'll be able to eat.' He was proud I listened. I remember jest being sixteen and Dat telling everyone I was part blacksmith, part veterinarian — because a farrier is a bit of both. I enjoy making sure the hooves are trimmed so they have proper footing. But my greatest joy is training, especially when I can take a wild horse — one that a person's considering putting down — and turn him around."

Lydia gasped. "Were they thinking of that for Blue?"

Gideon looked away, lifting his head to watch an eagle's slow, sweeping circle over the pasture. He didn't have to say the words. She understood.

He then pointed to Blue. "I'm sure Blue doesn't understand. There are times he runs from me. He doesn't want to submit to the training. He fights against the halters and ropes, yet I don't back down. I can't. The pressure and small amounts of discomfort I offer him are like a gift compared to what's in store if I leave him to his own wild devices."

Gideon's words reminded Lydia of something she'd read just this morning. "I 'will refine them as silver is refined, and will try them as gold is tried,' " she said.

"Excuse me?"

Lydia stepped forward and placed her forearms on the wooden rail of the fence post, leaning on it for support. "It's a Scripture verse that I read this morning. I'm not sure if you knew, but Mem had health issues for most of her married years. They diagnosed a heart problem years ago. She lived far longer than the doctors expected her to. Dat —" Lydia's voice caught in her throat. "Dat said her will to see me grown was greater than any heart problem." A sad chuckle escaped her lips. "She was stubborn like that."

She reached down and plucked a tall stalk of wild grass from around the fence post.

"But I liked what Mem wrote me once: God wanted her so purified that she shone. Her desire was that through her shining God could look down and see His reflection."

Gideon tilted his head and smiled. "I like that, *ja.*"

"It's been helping me — Mem's words and the way she looked at things. It seems she not only read God's Word, she turned to Him in prayer, and she waited to hear how what she read applied to her life." Lydia leaned forward and rested her chin on the fence post.

Gideon sighed. "I heard it said once you cannot train a horse with shouts and expect it to obey a whisper."

"I love that. And the amazing thing is that those whispers echo — because I can hear them too, through her pen to my heart."

Gideon nodded. "My *oma* used to say, 'We get too soon *oldt, undt* too late *schmart.*' But I'm proud of you, Lydia. You're listening. Understanding."

"Now . . . now I am. But all those years wasted . . ."

"I understand, Lydia." He looked at her. "It's almost like this gelding here and other challenging cases. They think they need to save themselves. Protect themselves."

The intensity of his gaze overwhelmed

her, and then he quickly glanced away.

"Looking back, I wish I'd made different choices."

"Don't we all." A mournful look darkened Gideon's face — one she didn't understand. She was about to ask him about it, but then Gideon turned to her. "It's a way of maturing, I suppose. You wouldn't make the same choices now as you did then, would you?"

"Ne."

He crossed his broad arms over his chest. "I suppose the thing that surprises me the most isn't that we — as humans — make stupid choices, but that we are allowed to make choices at all. If Blue realized his strength, he wouldn't listen to me. He has the ability to overpower me every time. It's amazing to think that God gave us that same power too — our free will."

"*Ja.* Wow. I never thought of it that way." The words released with her breath. "But you're right."

They sat there for a while, taking in the sight of Blue nibbling on the grass, watching the eagle's invisible path, and following the dip of the sun to the west. A contented peace came over Lydia, and she remembered something she and Bonnie had shared long ago. Lydia had told Bonnie that she'd know the right man for her when she was just as comfortable with him in moments of silence as she was in moments of talking. The only thing was up until a few months ago she'd never figured that man would be Amish.

Gideon made a clicking sound with his mouth, and Blue pricked his ears and trotted over.

Lydia's eyes widened. "Did you teach him that?"

"*Ja.*"

Gideon tried to hold back the smile, but he wasn't doing a very good job. The lightness of his heart reflected in his eyes.

"You must be proud when you see a difficult horse come so far."

"It's not about pride, Lydia — it's about stewardship. We're supposed to take care of what God puts into our possession. Going forth and subduing the earth isn't about forcing yourself. It's *tending to.*"

"Do you train horses for buggies too?"

"I have."

"There's a buggy shop near our old home in Sugarcreek. Mem and I used to walk down there and watch them work. I remember what a big problem it was when the police asked them to start installing reflectors because of all the accidents. You'd think our friends and neighbors were asked to start flying spaceships for all the commotion."

"I wondered if the buggies are similar to the ones we have in Pennsylvania. I'm always amazed how almost each area has different styles and standards."

"Do you want to see photos?"

"Photos?"

Lydia lifted her chin. "You say that word as if I'd just confessed to wearing *Englisch* clothes under my dress and apron."

"I'm sorry. I guess I shouldn't be so surprised." He chuckled. "If that's the worst thing you have to hide, Lydia . . . if that's the worst thing, I think we'll be all right."

An uneasiness stirred inside her. She thought of the small stack of notebooks tucked under her bed. They were filled with all that had happened since she'd returned to West Kootenai. The book of memories she was writing was just something she was doing for herself — at least she was pretty sure it was only for her. Her plan was to go back to those notebooks and pull out sections for a book for Bonnie. Sections that wouldn't reveal too much, but that would interest readers who weren't familiar with Amish ways. Her returning would be a good story . . . without her spilling all her heart and emotions into the printed page.

She was writing it as a testimony to what God was doing in her life, and maybe a testimony to her future children and grand-children too. But she wasn't hiding those notebooks, not really. She'd tell Gideon when the time was right . . . when she was sure he felt settled with her and would not be spooked away as easily as an untrained horse.

She didn't respond with her words, but instead Lydia placed her hand in his and tugged on it, taking two steps toward her house.

"I'll show you a few photos. Bonnie — my friend — rented out my condo in Seattle for me, and she was kind enough to pack up my personal things and send them. But after the photos I must get dinner started. Dat is used to eating early and going to bed early, and he's like a bear. If I don't provide something, he'll start foraging around for himself."

Gideon tugged back on her hand slightly, and she paused to look at him.

"Does that mean I'm invited for dinner?"

"*Ja,* of course, but I've talked enough for both of us today. After dinner it's your turn. I want to hear more about your life. I want to hear about what it was like growing up."

Her mind was already trying to decide if

277

she wanted to make the potpie like she'd planned or come up with something easier. But as she turned back toward the house, something other than her dinner menu was even more worrisome. The briefest flash of fear crossed Gideon's gaze. Lydia didn't understand it.

Maybe I'm just seeing things.

What about his childhood was so painful to share?

CHAPTER 20

Lydia made chicken potpie. As soon as the table was cleared Dat excused himself for the night — even earlier than normal — and Lydia knew the truth. He wanted her and Gideon to have as much time together as possible.

Gideon sat in her mem's log rocking chair. Where Mem had been engulfed in the chair, Gideon's tall frame made it look as if it were a child's chair.

His eyes followed her as she washed the dishes and cleaned the kitchen. A soft smile touched his face. She looked back every now and then. Did he pretend the same thing she did? That this was their house, that she was his wife. The last glance back he winked at her, and she guessed he was thinking that. Her stomach tingled as she lit the candles lined up on the table.

"So what brought you to Montana?" she asked as she moved to make both of them a cup of tea. "Is the hunting as big of a draw as everyone says it is?"

He took the mug of tea and spoon from her and nodded when she offered him sugar.

"I do like to hunt, but I came because my parents visited here when I was a boy." He added sugar to his hot tea and stirred it slowly.

"I bet they miss you . . . being so far."

"There are thirteen children in my family, and the older six are all married with little ones. Family gatherings involve half the town and . . ." He glanced down and placed his spoon on a napkin on the side table. "With one hundred people there, what does it matter when one's gone?"

Lydia's lips opened slightly. She'd struck a nerve. "Thirteen children?" It was all she could say.

"It's a lot, *ja,* but not unusual in our community. It was hard, though. I felt like the invisible child — the middle of thirteen. Six older than me, six younger. I'm surprised sometimes when people notice me."

She wrinkled her nose. "I had no trouble noticing you."

The sadness on his face brightened, and he laughed. "You really didn't have a chance to ignore me, did you?"

She shook her head. "How could I ignore

the stranger stomping toward me and telling me to put away the camera or he'd take it?"

"I'm sorry about that. I have a problem with tourists. That's what I thought you were. Living in Bird-in-Hand, well, millions of folks come through there every year. They take photographs, even though we ask that they ought not be taken. They stare at us. Follow us. Treat us like animals in a zoo, when we're just trying to live our normal lives."

"That happened some in Sugarcreek, but I guess I never thought of it much." Lydia smiled at him. "Mem told me that everyone wanted to take photos of me because they liked my red hair. I didn't realize until later that the color of my hair had little to do with it. The style of my dress and the life my parents and I lived mattered far more."

Gideon shrugged. "Maybe other people aren't as bothered by it. I talked to my brother once, and he said he didn't mind the stares. He didn't mind being different. He always felt like we had something better than everyone else, and that's why they were drawn to us. But I do think it's wrong when *Englischers* try to make money off our ordinary lives. How would they like it if we rented tour buses and drove up and down

281

their streets gawking?"

"I suppose I never thought of it like that." Lydia took a sip from her tea. "I'm from a smaller community that not many know about — nor talk about much. I did have photos taken of me when I was younger, but when I got older no one paid much attention to a plain-looking, freckle-nosed Amish girl."

"Lydia. You're anything but plain." From the look in his eye she could see Gideon meant it.

"That's kind of you to say." They sat for a while, Gideon rocking in the chair and she sitting on the sofa. She felt close to him — this day had built that closeness. She could picture a future with him.

Lydia pressed her lips together. "Want to know a secret?" She sucked in a breath as soon as she released them. The words splashed a cold dread on her face. What she had to share was special. Did she really want to invite Gideon in?

"*Ja.* Yes, of course." He smiled and leaned forward. He looked so happy, so hopeful. How could she not share?

"All right. I'll be right back."

Lydia hurried into her bedroom and picked up her Promise Box from the bedside table. She took off the letter from the top

— the one that she'd read over and over. The one in which Mem talked about meeting her birth mom and claiming Lydia as her own. She wasn't ready to share that with Gideon. Not yet. She hadn't even told him she was adopted. She hadn't told anyone here in West Kootenai. The people she grew up with in Sugarcreek knew, but even then they didn't know the whole story. A cold shiver ran down her spine over telling anyone that, even Gideon.

She entered the living room with the box in hand. "This is something special, and I wanted to tell you about it. My mem, you see, had a bishop promise her that God was going to give her a child, and that day she wrote down the promise. In the months and years to come she wrote down more promises — mostly from God's Word." Lydia's voice caught in her throat.

"That's amazing, Lydia. The promise . . . how beautiful, *ja.*" Gideon's eyes were on her as he said those words, and then he held out his hands, and she placed the box in them. He caressed the wood as if she'd just handed him priceless jewels. "It's amazing, don't you think, how something so simple can mean so much? I can imagine how much this means to you. Did you always know about it?"

"Ne." She shook her head. "Only recently. Dat knew. But it wasn't until Mem's death . . ." She let her voice trail off. "I'm glad, though. I wouldn't have appreciated it before. It's like water in a desert. The most refreshing water comes after you've been thirsty for so long."

Gideon reached up and fingered a red curl that had slipped from her *kapp.* "You do have a way with words."

"Do you want to read one of the promises?" she asked. "There are some Scripture verses near the bottom I haven't opened yet." There were more letters, too, that she hadn't read, but she didn't tell him that. She needed to wait on those. She needed to read them first.

She opened the Promise Box and reached her hand near the bottom. She pulled out a scrap of paper that was folded in half and handed it to Gideon. He opened it and leaned closer to the candlelight on the side table. He cleared his throat.

" *'And they that know thy name will put their trust in thee: for thou, Lord, hast not forsaken them that seek thee.'* " He paused and looked at her. "I'm not sure if I've ever read that Scripture. I like it."

He read it again, silently.

Hope swelled in her heart, pushing worry

to the edges.

He looked to her. "Focusing on God's promises. It seems we don't do that enough, do we?"

"I know. And the more I read it, the more I realized it's just what Mem would do." Lydia was about to ask Gideon about his parents — did they have a similar faith? But she could see something in his eyes. That underlying sorrow. She wouldn't ask. At least not tonight. Hopefully they had days, and weeks, and much longer than that together. For now she wanted to focus on this moment . . . on the promises in Mem's box and the unspoken promise of their growing relationship that this day had brought to her heart.

Gideon stood in misery as he leaned against the doorframe, preparing to leave. He'd tried to pretend that he was just enjoying the conversation, but all he could think about was if he could pull it off. If he could leave everything in Pennsylvania and come here . . . because he didn't want to live a day without Lydia. A lump the size of a pinecone filled his throat.

"I had a wonderful evening — a wonderful day," Lydia said. "And I wanted to tell you that if I'm busy over the next couple of

weeks it's only because school will be starting soon, and it will take a lot of work to
get things ready. I wanted you to know that.
I didn't want you to think that if I didn't
have time . . . that I, uh, didn't care."

"I understand." Gideon gazed into her
green eyes. "I know you care. More than
that, I can see it in your eyes."

"*Gut.* I'm glad. I, uh, feel the same."

He walked home then, with a lightness to
his step. The night air was cold, but a large,
full moon lit his path. When he reached his
small cabin, light flowed out the windows.
Caleb was inside with Micah. They were
playing a game of checkers when he entered.
Caleb glanced up only briefly, but Micah's
gaze lingered, as if he'd been waiting to tell
Gideon something important.

"You've been gone all day," Caleb commented. "Some of us had target practice.
We went looking for you but couldn't find
you. You weren't at the store . . . weren't at
the Carash place."

"I was with Lydia." Gideon couldn't help
but smile as he said her name.

"The *Englisch* girl?" Micah asked.

"She's not *Englisch* anymore. She was
baptized into the church. If you had been
there yesterday, you might have seen that."
He spat the words.

"King me." Micah placed his red checker in the home spot. Then he shrugged. "I was tired. It's been a long week over at Log Works."

"There are many excuses for not following the Lord." Gideon couldn't help but say it. Like many Amish bachelors, there was pride in the set of Micah's jaw when he was around *Englischers.* A pride that came by following the rules of the Amish lifestyle since childhood. But dressing Amish and showing up to church when it was convenient wasn't enough. Lydia was helping him see that.

Micah scoffed. "*Ja,* well, I live a good life. And if I was like you, I might go to church often if I needed to do lots of confessing. For turning my heart to a woman who has been tainted by *Englisch* ways. More than that, if I was guilty of killing someone."

Hearing his words, Gideon sunk down on his cot. His lower gut ached as if someone had just punched him. His breaths came shallow and ragged.

Caleb jumped to his feet, taking a step toward Micah. "Who do you think you are? There is no need for that. You need to apologize for saying such a thing. As if Gideon could be capable. I've seen a horse rear up and gash his cheek, and my cousin didn't even raise his voice."

Micah leaned back in his chair and folded his arms over his chest. He didn't argue with Caleb. He didn't have to. He sat there with a smirk, waiting for Gideon to tell the truth.

"He's right." *But how did Micah know?*

Gideon leaned his elbows on knees. "I didn't kill someone, but I caused the death of a man." He then went on to explain about getting lost. About the search parties — those things he'd already known his whole life. Then, in a low voice, he explained what Edgar had told him.

Caleb's eyes widened as he listened. He pushed the checker game to the side, and his face paled to an ashy gray as Gideon finished.

"So you see . . . it's my fault."

"*Ne.* Not really. I mean getting lost doesn't mean you meant anyone any harm. You were just a kid." Caleb shook his head.

"My mind knows that. But tell it to my heart."

Micah jutted out his chin. "Does Lydia know? Have you told her yet?"

"That's between us, isn't it? What I want to know is how you know."

Micah stood and reached into his pants pocket. He pulled out a white envelope and waved it in the air. "I'm sorry, but Edgar stuck this letter in my mail. Yer mem's handwriting looks jest like my mem's. I didn't even realize until I started reading that it wasn't for me."

Gideon didn't have to ask if Micah had read the whole thing. It was clear he had. Not that he blamed him. Who wouldn't read such a thing? It was like racing to an accident to see who'd been hurt and how bad.

Micah rose and placed the letter in Gideon's hands. Then — as if sensing he needed time alone — the two men rose and left. Caleb's face was a mask of sadness, confusion. But Micah seemed almost glad to see Gideon brought low. Why? Did he honestly think he could get a chance at Lydia's heart by kicking Gideon to the ground?

Their checker game sat half finished on the table. Looking at it, Gideon let out a low sigh. So many things in his life also seemed undone.

After such a wonderful day with Lydia, why this? Why now?

Dear Son,
    We weren't surprised when we received your last letter. You said you were going to talk to a man, to discover the truth. I am sorry you didn't hear it from us first.

When I read your letter, your sadness was evident, which is one reason Dat asked me not to tell you all these years. We didn't want to see your sadness. Even though a man died because of your actions doesn't mean you are to blame. You didn't know when you headed out into those woods what would come of it. You were just a boy, but it does go to show that disobedience to one's parents brings unjust results. That is why we worked even harder to raise our children to obey.

We cannot ask God, "Why did this happen?" He most likely will say, "You did not choose to listen to those put in charge of you." You have seen the results of leaving the path. Your dat and I pray that this lesson will be one you heed your entire life.

We say this because Caleb wrote and told his mem that you were fancy on an *Englisch* girl. Even if she chooses to become Amish again — as Caleb hopes — there are years of influence that have tainted her. We trust you will be wary of this. We know how wolves try to mix within the crowd in sheep's clothing. Seek the advice of the bishop and trusted leaders.

The death of our friend reminded us all what happens when we choose to follow worldly things. God says, *Vie Gottlofen haben jein jrierlen, wider mit Gott, oder ihr gewissen.* The ungodly have no peace with God or their conscience. Just know that what happens from your life now matters in eternity.

Even though you are far from home, remember that God watches all. We have heard about that community from Caleb and others. He wrote of one young woman who left the Amish to marry a musician. We know you were brought up knowing that music leads to *der bose Gheist,* a prideful spirit. As far as we are concerned, we cannot wait until the months pass and you return home.

Sincerely,
Dat and Mem

He turned the letter over in his hands. If he could have chosen any letter for Micah to read, this would not have been it. His parents spoke to him as if he were a child, even though he was nearly twenty-four. There was no news about the family. There were no words of hope. His parents meant well, but their message was clear: we are worried about you, worried about your soul, until you return.

In their eyes he was still the irresponsible child who'd wandered off and caused much pain. The thought ripped at his gut, especially at having to tell them he had full intentions of pursuing Lydia as his future bride. And he had every intention of moving to this community for good.

As he read the letter again he couldn't help but contrast it with the slip of paper he'd read by Lydia's mem's hand. Both his parents and Lydia's parents were Amish, yet while his family offered warnings, hers spoke of promises. Could he cling to those promises? Were they meant for sons who'd attempted to live right and good, as much as they were for wayward daughters?

CHAPTER 21

The cold Montana air bit at Lydia's nose as she arrived at school. *Six forty-five a.m.*

September had barely made her arrival when cold winter winds fought for position. She pulled her coat tight under her chin as she hurried up the steps of the small log schoolhouse. Arriving at such a time was expected by the teacher. Her students would arrive by seven-thirty, walking the quiet country roads.

Her flashlight's beam had lit the way. Unlocking the door, Lydia hurried inside and moved to the pressurized white-gas lamp. Even though she'd been switching on electric light switches for the last six years, lighting the lantern was as natural to her as bringing a spoon to her lips. She turned on the lower knob, followed by the upper knob. When she heard the hiss, Lydia struck a match near the mantel. Poof, in a second, the gas exploded with light, and she then

293

hung it on the hook over her desk and hurried to light the two other lanterns around the room.

She'd spent the last few weeks getting everything ready, working on lesson plans, decorating the classroom. A smile touched her lips remembering Gideon sitting cross-legged on the floor helping her cut out white construction paper clouds to pin across the room. On them she'd written Scripture verses and one of her favorite sayings as a child:

"When you talk you only repeat what you already know, but if you listen you may learn something."

She'd also found a poem she liked in a book of Christmas poems and plays written by an Amish woman for an Amish classroom. She considered using the full poem for Christmas, but before then she pulled out the "Be" phrases and made a nice poster:

Be REVERENT in spirit low
Be GENEROUS, give all you can, then give
    a little more;
Be THOUGHTFUL of the people who are
    lonely, old, or sad;
Be READY quickly to respond to special
    appeals;

Be UNSELFISH — all self-seeking with
    abandon cast aside;
Be HOPEFUL for the best in life, for hope
    has wondrous worth;
Be APPRECIATIVE for great riches of
    Christ and of His love,

It was easier to memorize these sayings than to live by them, but Lydia hoped that as God allowed her to work with the children, He'd mold her too.

She also decorated the room with alphabet letters, books from her collection, and a world globe she'd found in Kalispell. Gideon had helped her pin a large paper map just over the hooks where the scholars would hang their coats and lunch pails.

Lydia considered lighting the fire. Would the children need someplace to warm up after their long walk in the chilly morning air? She looked at the wood and paper and matches, wishing she'd taken time to practice at home. Pushing a button on the heating and air conditioning unit was so much easier. Lighting the fire wouldn't be the problem, but staying clean while doing so might prove to be a challenge. She decided against the fire, just in case any of the parents stopped by. It wouldn't do to see the new teacher a rumpled mess.

And that was the least of her concerns. The Amish people in this community knew she had been living an *Englisch* life for many years. She'd be watched closely. The work she gave would be evaluated — her dress, her talk — they would all take note to see if anything appeared too worldly. She patted her *kapp,* ensuring it was in place.

What amazed Lydia was how easily and quickly the specifics of her Amish lifestyle came back. The rules, down to the smallest detail, including how many folds were in one's *kapp,* came back to her as if she'd never left. These trivial things had seemed silly to her when she entered the *Englisch* world. Yet, being here again, she knew it was for a good cause. To dress the same meant no one could be prideful. To live a simple life meant trusting in family and community instead of worldly conveniences.

What mother wouldn't do all she could to protect her children, to keep them on the straight and narrow path — even if that meant measuring hems and counting folds in a *kapp?* Lydia's lip quivered when she remembered Mem sewing Lydia's school dresses and using a ruler to measure the length of the hem from the ground.

Lydia placed newly sharpened pencils on each desk. How proud Mem would be to see her here. Yet as she wrote the first lesson on the board, Lydia also chuckled, imagining what her neighbors in Seattle would think of how differently things were done.

In Seattle the children caught a school bus right at the front entrance of the condos. Even though they could see their children from their windows, parents didn't let the children stand at the curb and wait. Instead they waited with them. Or drove their children to school. Her closest neighbor Megan walked her young son to his first grade classroom every day. What would she think of five- and six-year-olds walking two miles to school just as dawn broke over the high mountain peaks? Of course the dangers of Seattle and those of West Kootenai, Montana, were quite different.

Lydia glanced at the clock on the wall. Did she have time to jot down a few notes in her notebook before finishing up preparations for the day? She'd already filled two notebooks with her "book." At least a quarter of that was devoted to her interactions with Gideon, whom she looked forward to seeing each day.

The children barely cast a glance at the pine-studded granite mountains on their way to school. To them the pointed peaks are as common as the golden orb that rises each day. Girls in dresses, aprons, and *kapps,* and boys in homemade shirts and pants, appear like any other Amish youth except a fleece jacket covers their Plain clothes. With temperatures dropping into the thirties even in fall, red-tipped noses glow almost as brightly as the children's smiles. Curious eyes look upon me and then glance at each other as their knowing looks pass questions about the new teacher. I read the inquiry in their gazes: *is it true Miss Wyse lived for a time in the* Englisch *world*?

Lydia set down her pen, then looked over the short description. True, the children hadn't arrived yet, but she'd attended school herself in an Amish schoolhouse and could imagine the scene.

She pulled out her notes and wrote the arithmetic assignments for the sixth, seventh, and eighth grades on the blackboard. Then the door opened. The Sommer children arrived first. Three older boys — David, Charlie, and Josiah — were followed by little Ellie with rosy cheeks and grayish-brown eyes. Ellie's fine hair was neatly pinned up under her white prayer *kapp*. She moved to the front of the room and sat in one of the smallest desks. The boys moved to various desks around the room, and Lydia assumed they were slipping into the spots they had last year. Lydia had planned on designing a seating chart, but it was Mrs. Shelter who'd changed her mind.

"There's enough change this year with a new teacher," Mrs. Shelter had said. "Let the children relax by having some things be the same, familiar, like where they sit."

Lydia had thanked her for her advice; the older woman was right. After stepping back into her old way of life, Lydia had found small measures of comfort in simple things like a familiar mixing bowl or cookbook. Through them, memories had a way of bringing pleasant times of the past into the present.

The other children arrived until all fourteen sat in their desks.

Andy Shelter, tall and blond, looked to be the oldest of the group. Lydia knew him because she'd spent last Saturday at the restaurant. Nearly every scholar had come in that day, and with each one who'd entered, Annie, the owner of the store, had told her each child's name and a little about him or her. Andy had many older siblings, including a sister Sarah who'd been Annie's best baker until she moved to Ohio, following an Amish bachelor she'd taken a fancy to.

The next oldest was David Sommer. Even though the three Sommer boys had different coloring, they had a similar appearance with thin frames and wide smiles. The middle one, Charlie, walked with a slight limp. What had happened to him? She'd have to ask Annie.

The two youngest students were girls, Ellie Sommer and Evelyn Shelter, and it was clear by their wide-eyed gazes that this was their first year of school. Both sat in the front two desks, clutching each other with firm grips.

"I'm Miss Wyse, and we're going to start with the Lord's Prayer."

Only small Ellie looked confused as if she didn't understand the directions. Ellie clutched the hand of her friend Evelyn, and Lydia squatted before them.

"I can help you with the words if you'd like."

"*Ja.*" Both girls nodded.

On other days Lydia planned to have a student lead in prayer, but today she couldn't think of anything more special than leading these young souls in prayer herself.

Our Father in heaven,
hallowed be your name.
Your kingdom come,
your will be done,
on earth as it is in heaven.

Lydia led the words slowly, purposefully, and was happy to see the young girls attempting to say the words with her. She smiled as they continued.

Give us this day our daily bread,
and forgive us our debts,
as we also have forgiven our debtors.
And lead us not into temptation,
but deliver us from evil.

They sang a few hymns next, and Lydia hoped the children didn't mind that she was slightly off key. She got the older boys busy in their science text *God's Orderly World,* and then had the rest of the children write out their Scripture verse for the week while she worked on reciting the alphabet with the young ones.

" 'And as ye would that men should do unto you, do ye also to them likewise.' Luke 6:31," the middle grades recited to each other.

When she'd finished working on the letters A and B with Ellie and Evelyn, Lydia stood and looked around. The children were happily at work — each grade in their own way — and Lydia knew more than she'd ever known that this was where she was supposed to be.

She got out her measuring stick to use as a pointer and was about to move to their geography lesson when movement outside the window caught Lydia's attention. "Keep working, class. I'll be right back."

When she hurried to the door, Mrs. Shelter stood on the porch, her back to the door.

Lydia opened the door. A cool breeze hit her face. "Can I help you?"

Mrs. Shelter turned quickly, her eyes wide with surprise. "Oh, I'm so sorry, Lydia. I didn't want to disturb you." She pressed her lips together. "It's jest that . . ."

Tears filled Lydia's eyes as she remembered the letter from her mem. "It's Evelyn's first day of school, isn't it?"

"Ja." Mrs. Shelter clutched her arms around herself. "I wasna this way with the others. Maybe it's because Evelyn is the youngest, but the house seems especially empty today."

"Tell you what . . ." Lydia reached a hand to the woman. "We were just going to get started in geography, and I have some coloring sheets for the little ones. Would you like to sit and help them while I teach the continents to the older kids?"

"You don't mind?"

Lydia shook her head. "*Ne,* I understand. Loving mothers sometimes have a hard time letting go. I'm sure Evelyn will be happy to see you. And I don't mind help on my first day either."

With a smile, Lydia stepped aside and welcomed the woman in.

CHAPTER 22

"Come unto me, all ye that labour and are heavy laden, and I will give you rest," Matthew 11:28.

"As one whom his mother comforteth, so will I comfort you; and ye shall be comforted in Jerusalem," Isaiah 66:13.

I told Lydia the truth today. Did I make a mistake? Dear daughter, when you read this someday, know it's the hardest thing I've ever done. The truth came from my love. I wanted you to focus on the fact that you were a gift to your father and me, but instead you focused on the sin. The sin of a man. The sin against your birth mother.

I tried to comfort you, but you stiffened in my arms. Do I look different in your eyes? Since you were a child, you knew that another woman carried you, but for the first time I saw it. You looked into my face, and you longed to see the face of another.

You couldn't be my daughter any more than you are. Many nights I woke to your cry, fed you, changed you, swaddled you, and sang your favorite lullabies.

When you had colic, I bounced you — pressing your stomach over my arm — until the gas bubbles eased. When you skinned your knees, you'd come to me first to kiss them. When you burned your first pie crust, I helped you roll out another. Have you not seen the joy in my eyes reflected a thousand times, Lydia, when I looked upon you? I know you didn't see the pain when you stalked out of the room tonight.

Of course this isn't about me, as much as my heart hurts. I hurt even more for the pain the truth caused. I considered giving you the name and address of your birth mother. Maybe it would be the best thing . . . for you to talk to her. To hear her part of the story. But fear grips me. If you meet her, will you still need me?

Friday afternoon, Lydia wished the last student a good-bye and "Have a happy weekend" and then hurried to the chalk-board to put up some of Monday's lessons.

She'd just written a few words of next week's memory verse when footsteps sounded behind her.

"Did you forget something?" Lydia turned expecting Andy or one of the older boys. Instead Gideon stood there with a handful of wildflowers.

A gasp escaped her lips, and the heaviness that she'd carried since last night lifted — not completely, but some. Enough to make a difference.

"They say you're supposed to bring apples for the teacher, but Blue ate them all." Gideon extended the flowers to her — wild roses and daisies mostly. "So I brought these instead."

"Thank you." She reached out and took them in her hands, breathing deeply. "They're beautiful."

He straightened the collar of his clean work shirt and offered her a wink. "I also made reservations for the finest dining establishment in town."

Even though they'd spent every day together since that picnic at the lake, she still wanted to pinch herself. This had to be a dream, didn't it? It was hard to imagine that someone so wonderful had chosen her. And yet from the words he used and the care he offered, Gideon had made his intentions known. He saw a future for them . . . just as she saw it.

Lydia gazed up at him, weariness creeping up her bones. "So Annie's saving us the table in the back corner with a view of the mountains out of two windows?" She needed to sit. To put her feet up. To have a moment of silence, but from the eagerness in Gideon's face she couldn't tell him that.

He stroked his chin and grinned. "*Ja,* how did you know?"

She winked. "That is the best table in town. It sounds like the perfect evening. I'll just have to tell Dat —"

"Already got that covered yet," he commented. "I stopped by earlier and talked to Annie. She's going to deliver a meal to him herself."

She rubbed her tight neck. "That's sweet of her, and sweet of you for thinking about it."

"I'm glad you think so, but . . ." Gideon took a step closer, looking into her face. "Are you all right?" Concern filled his gaze.

Lydia shrugged. "It's been a long week. A *gut* one, but long. The kids are bright, but those boys . . . It's hard to get them to settle down at times."

Gideon reached up and cupped a hand on her cheek. She leaned into it.

307

"I can come whip them into shape if you'd like. You don't mind me bringing in a few ropes and halters, do you?"

Lydia laughed and then blew out a deep breath. She closed her eyes and took another step toward Gideon. He dropped his hand from her cheek and wrapped both arms around her, pulling her close. She gripped the front of his shirt, drawing from his strength.

"It's more than that. But yer the only one I can share this with. I've been reading more of Mem's notes, and it's so hard. To read her words, to know her heart." She shook her head.

"*Ja,* I can only imagine. They say that grief goes through stages. The missing isn't going to go away anytime soon."

"I wish . . ." Lydia let the words drop. What she really wished was that she hadn't been so self-focused when she was a teen. Lydia had only considered her feelings, her pain. Not once could she remember ever thinking about how hard it was for Mem to tell her the truth.

But it was more than that. Lydia gripped Gideon's shirt more tightly and pressed against one of the buttons with her thumb. She was also mad at Mem. Mem had written everything down in letters, but why hadn't she talked to Lydia about some of these things? Mem could have said, *"Lydia, it's hard for me to tell you the truth"* or *"I'm afraid you'll love your birth mother more than me . . . but I have loved you every day of your life."* It might have made a difference. Lydia released a shuddering breath. She didn't understand why parents had to hide their pain. It's not like their kids believed them to have their whole act together. Or believed them to be perfect. These same kids lived with them, after all. A bit of truth from Mem might have gone a long way.

Lydia soaked up Gideon's embrace, and when she felt strengthened, she stepped back. Her stomach rumbled, and she placed a hand over it. "Did you say something about dinner?" She forced a smile. "I shared my lunch with Eli Yoder, who forgot his."

"Ja." He turned and offered his arm. "I believe this is how the *Englisch* do it."

Lydia slipped her hand into his arm. "I think so, but it's possible for us Plain folks to be jest as romantic."

"Do you think so?" Gideon paused his steps, looking down at her. "Because I've never done this before."

"Done what?" She gazed up at him, noticing his hair rumpled under his hat.

"I've never taken a woman on a date in a

restaurant. I've never opened my heart." And then his eyes softened. "I've never done this." With his free hand he ran a finger down her cheek. The touch warmed her, soothed her soul, reminding her that the pain of the past did not have to ruin today — this moment with this man.

"Or this." He slid his finger under her chin and tilted it up toward him.

Lydia swallowed, anticipating what was to come.

"Or this." He bent closer, and her hand went to the nape of his neck, holding the place where his dark hair met the warm skin of his neck.

She closed her eyes, accepting his kiss. His lips were soft, but the passion behind the kiss could not be denied.

They stood in the middle of the classroom, yet they could have been in the middle of the Kraft and Grocery for all it mattered to her. Gideon was the only thing on her mind. His taste, his touch. Since their first picnic three weeks ago she'd wondered when — not if — this was going to happen. Their first kiss.

After a moment he leaned back, and her eyes fluttered open. "Flowers for the teacher, um-hum. You offered more than flowers, Gideon." She smiled, feeling more of the tension she'd been carrying ease.

"*Ja,* well." His voice was husky. "How did I do?"

She released his nape, ran her hand down his neck, and then squeezed his arm. *"Gut, real gut."* She winked. "This teacher gives you an *A.*"

CHAPTER 23

Friday nights at the West Kootenai Kraft and Grocery were a gathering of sorts as those from the community came to relax after a long week and enjoy the once-a-week buffet. Chicken, ham, potatoes, vegetables. Just a little of each filled Lydia's plate. She could only eat half of what she got, though. Partly because her eyes were bigger than her stomach, but mostly because her attention was on the handsome man across from her. Gideon's thoughtfulness and humor brightened her day. She believed more each day that God had a good plan for her life with him, and could only imagine good things for them from this point on.

Lydia was thankful that they had dined early, because by the time six o'clock rolled around, the restaurant was filled with folks coming for the Friday-night buffet. It was great seeing the members of the community — and finally feeling a part of it — but every time she and Gideon started a new topic, without fail someone would approach. Either a parent of a student with compliments or one of the men of the community who had a horse question for Gideon.

When Mr. Peachy showed up and pulled up a chair next to Gideon, Lydia knew it was the perfect time for a bathroom break. She rose.

"Lydia, wait . . ." Gideon reached a hand to her.

"I'm just using the ladies' room, but when I get back, why don't we head back to my place and check on my dat? I feel so bad leaving him all alone."

Gideon nodded. "*Ja.* I like that idea. I'll get us some cobbler to go?"

"Perfect."

She'd only gotten halfway to the bathroom when a familiar blonde woman in the dry goods aisle caught her attention. The woman's smile caused her to pause.

"Lydia, I'm so sorry I haven't been down in a while to check on you." Susan Carash — her closest neighbor — took Lydia's hands. "Both kids have started sports practice all the way down in Eureka. My littlest one, Sally, has piano practice down there too. Is everything all right with you, yer dat?" Susan eyed Lydia's *kapp.* "We heard from the Sommers about your baptism. I am thankful God drew your heart — isn't He amazing like that?"

"*Ja,* yes, I agree . . . and we're doing fine, Dat and I." She pointed to the table in the back corner. "Gideon comes often." She couldn't help but smile. "He's another blessing God has gifted me during this time."

Susan squeezed her hands. "I'm so glad. And I wanted to tell you, too, we have a prayer meeting every Monday at our house. I would love for you — for Gideon — to come any time. There are many who attend, and we come together to lift up our requests."

"I have heard about that." Lydia nodded, even though she didn't know how she'd be able to attend. She'd heard the meetings were attended by Amish and *Englisch* alike, and even though she personally didn't mind the idea of Amish and *Englisch* praying together out loud — something the Amish never did — she was the Amish teacher now. She couldn't do anything that would cause parents to question her example as an Amish woman. She couldn't do anything to lift even one eyebrow of disapproval.

"Well, if you can come . . ." Susan released

her grip.

"Not this week, for certain, but I'd love to have you down to our house for tea. I'd love to hear your memories of Mem . . . being her closest neighbor and all."

"Yes, of course. I would love that. Your mem was a wonderful woman, and Dave and I pray every day for you and your dat. But I best get home." Susan reached over to the grocery shelf she was standing by and grabbed a package of spaghetti. "I didn't realize until I had the spaghetti sauce made that I didn't have any noodles." She offered Lydia a quick hug. "I'll see you around, dear."

Lydia was slightly jealous to watch Susan pay for her spaghetti and then run out and jump in her car, driving away. She was slightly jealous she couldn't join the prayer meeting either.

I have chosen the better way, she told herself as she hurried on. *God has me here for a reason . . . and being Amish is part of that.*

Five minutes later she exited the bathroom. Two of the bachelors, Micah and Amos, stood by the front counter. She smiled, waved, and was just about to move past when Micah came toward her.

"Lydia, do you have a second?"

She frowned and paused, looking over at Gideon. He was still talking to Mr. Peachy. She turned back, offering a half smile to Micah. "*Ja,* I suppose, but not too long. We were just heading out."

"Oh, I was just wondering how Gideon is doing."

"How he's doing?" She shrugged. "Fine, I suppose. I didn't know anything was wrong." She swallowed. Had she missed something important?

Micah steepled his fingers and placed them against his lips while he studied Lydia with a faint frown. "You mean he didn't tell you?"

"Tell me what?"

"Well, he found out something really horrible. I was talking to Edgar and the older man filled in bits and pieces of the story."

Outside a large diesel truck pulled up. The rumble of its engine made Lydia unsure if she'd heard Micah correctly.

"Did you say he found out something horrible?" She thought of Gideon earlier and the way a romantic smile had tipped up the corners of his lips. He sure didn't seem like he'd just heard something horrible. Unless it was something he'd known for a while. Unless it was something he was trying to hide from her.

Lydia crossed her arms and shook her head. "I'm sorry. I don't know what you're talking about. Can you fill me in?"

"I'm not sure . . ." Micah touched the back of his hat brim, tilting it forward. The look in his eyes said he wished he hadn't said anything, but she wasn't going to let him get off this easy.

She let out a sigh. "You can't just say something like that and back down. I mean if it has you worried . . ."

"Well, I could tell you, but I have a feeling Gideon doesn't want you to know. He might not want your sympathy."

"Stop." Lydia raised her hand. "Would you just tell me?"

"I'm not sure where to start. It seems to be that little Gideon was from a large family. It must be easy to lose one with so many heads to count. Sort of like Jesus in the Bible. There were two or three Amish couples who came here with all their kids for vacation many years ago."

Micah let out a sigh and shook his head. "There were so many kids running around that Gideon's parents thought he was with everyone else. It wasn't until the evening that his parents asked around. No one had seen their four-year-old since that morning."

Lydia gasped. "Oh, that's just awful."

"They started a search party right away," Micah continued. "The fathers and mothers and some locals headed out. It was already almost dark, but no one wanted to think what could happen to a little one."

"Did someone find him?" Worry tightened her chest. Not only to overhear what had happened, but worry over the relationship she thought they had. She and Gideon had talked about their childhood many times — why hadn't he told her before?

Maybe for the same reason you've held onto your secrets. The thought filtered in, but she quickly pushed it away.

"*Ja,* they found him. The next day. He'd wandered about two miles up into the mountain. Edgar told me all the details. Little Gideon was sleeping under a tree when they spotted him, as peaceful as if he was at home curled into his own bed."

Lydia placed a hand over her heart. Why she hadn't heard this before? Why Gideon hadn't told her? "It sounds like the story ended up well."

"Not at all."

"What do you mean?"

Micah lowered his head. "Two men spotted him. They also saw a bear —"

"Stop!" Gideon's voice called over her

shoulder, causing Lydia to jump. Her knees grew weak, and she thought her heart was trying to escape.

"Gideon." She turned and slugged his arm. "What are you trying to do to me? I'm going to have a heart attack." Not only had he scared her, he obviously didn't trust her. She could tell from his response that this story — this event — was true. Anger caused the hairs on the back of her neck to rise.

Gideon stepped forward toe-to-toe with Micah. He pushed a finger into Micah's chest. "It's not what I'm trying to do. It's what *he's* trying to do."

"Micah's trying to help. Micah's telling the truth. You should have told me. If I'm that important to you, you should have . . ."

Lydia pinched her lips together. Instead of stirring her anger toward Gideon, the words pointed a finger her direction.

It's different. I have reasons for keeping my secrets.

Gideon pressed a hand into Micah's chest.

Micah leaned back, arching his body over the top of the counter. "What? Are you full of the *diebel*? I just was asking how you were feeling . . . now that you know the truth."

The truth. The two words quickened her

heartbeat again. Gideon had hid the truth from her . . . whatever it was. She looked into Gideon's eyes. Pain, betrayal, darkened them. Then she looked to Micah. What was that she saw? Humor. Anger coursed through her, but not at Gideon.

"Gideon." She grabbed his arm gently. "I've seen you control yourself with a foolish horse. I'm sure Micah is a bit more thick skulled, but he's not worth your anger."

Her words seemed to move from the top of Gideon's head and down his body, physically calming him. He took a step back. "You're right. You're exactly right, Lydia." He blew out a heavy breath. Then he took her arm and guided her to the door. She followed, noticing his hand trembling. With quick steps they hurried from the store into the cool night. The light was fading and she knew the sun would set before they were halfway home.

They stepped down the wooden-planked walkway, and just as they got to the end of it — to where the wood met the gravel of the parking lot — Gideon paused. He turned to her, gently grasping both of her shoulders. "I'm so sorry. I should have told you. I —"

"Stop." Lydia reached up and placed a finger on his lips. "I shouldn't have let

320

Micah prod me on like that. I should have waited. I should have talked to you about it. I should have trusted you — trusted your heart."

His eyes widened at her words, and he pulled her into his embrace. This afternoon he'd given her strength and now — even though he was holding her — Lydia knew their closeness was giving Gideon the ability to go on.

After a minute, Gideon pulled back. He looked down into her face and lowered his head slightly. And just when Lydia was certain he was going to place another kiss on her lips, his mouth parted, and he whispered one word. "Tonight."

She trembled at the pain in his gaze.

"Lydia, I want to tell you the truth tonight."

Chapter 24

They walked hand in hand, watching the setting sun dip behind the western mountain range, rimming the mountains with pink. With a low voice Gideon told her the rest of the story. About the two men who came upon the bear. About how they distracted the bear and got the creature to run after them to save Gideon, and how the one Amish man — a friend of his family — died after sustaining a fall.

Lydia's tears came easily, not only from thinking about the man's wife and children, but also when Gideon shared how his parents had hidden the truth from him. The pain was clear on his face — to have felt the burden all these years and then discover it was worse than he imagined.

"You'd think that they'd be more sensitive toward me," he said. "After what happened you'd think they'd want to keep a watchful eye on me, that they'd want to keep me close. But that's not what happened. It's almost as if they were in so much pain for thoughts of losing me that they didn't want to go through that again. It's as if my parents — Dat especially — put a wall around their hearts."

He pulled something from his pocket and handed it to her.

"What's this?"

"It's a letter . . . from my parents."

Lydia paused her steps. "Do you want me to read it?"

"I think you should. I've tried not to let the words bother me, but even as I've been in the pasture, working with Blue, their words played over in my mind."

Lydia tipped the paper to the dimming sunlight, and her heart ached as she read the letter. His parents said the accident wasn't Gideon's fault, but the tone of the rest of the note spoke otherwise. Instead of offering grace, they delivered warnings. She sucked in a breath as she read what they said about her.

Caleb wrote and told his mem that you were fancy on an *Englisch* girl. Even if she chooses to become Amish again — as Caleb hopes — there are years of influence that have tainted her. We trust you will be wary of this. We know how wolves try to mix within the crowd in sheep's clothing. Seek the advice of the bishop and trusted leaders.

Her heart clenched in her chest, as if someone had grabbed it with a large fist.

Gideon must have read the pain on her face. "Don't hate them for what they said, Lydia. They're worried, that's all. Their greatest fear is that one of their children will stray from following the Amish way." He squatted down and picked up a pinecone in his hand, turning it over. Then he stood and hurled it into the empty pasture. "The thing is I'm not sure what they're most afraid of: one of their children going off the narrow path or how they would look to the community if they had a child like that."

She spotted an acorn on the road, amazed that something so small could transform into something so powerful — so useful. Instead of throwing it, she tucked it into her pocket.

They turned on the road in front of the Carash house, and she spotted Blue within the corral. The electric lights were on inside the house, and she could see the family gathered around the table for dinner. A television flickered in the corner and it looked like they were watching a movie as they ate their spaghetti. Since the Carashes were *Englisch,* the children attended a public school in Eureka instead of the Amish school where she taught. Every time she talked to Susan Carash the woman shared something wonderful about what God was doing in her family. And she'd been so kind and warm as she invited Lydia to their Monday night prayer meetings.

Lydia ran a hand down her throat, realizing how outward appearances mattered little. Amish folks could look at the *Englisch* Carash family and point to the numerous ways they'd succumbed to the world, yet their love for the Lord was clear. Then there were folks like Gideon's parents, who had generations of children and grandchildren who've stayed Amish, yet who lived their lives focused on laws and fear instead of grace.

No wonder Gideon didn't feel as if he were missed at home.

He placed a hand on her shoulder. "If anything, you point me to God. You remind me that He's a God of grace, and not of rules and orders only." Gideon took a step closer. "But not that it matters to them. What will matter is that you were baptized. I haven't written to tell them yet, but they'll warm up. You'll see."

"I'm not going to hold a grudge." She shrugged. "I don't take your parents' words to heart." She winked at him. "I'd be worried if they didn't warn you about a young woman who was *Englisch* so recently." She sighed. "It's the other words in their letter that bother me more: *'We are eager to have you at home.'* Because that's the last thing I want — for you to leave."

"I think, *ja,* they're saying that because they want to keep an eye on me. Not that they miss me."

"Maybe so, but what about you? Do you have plans, Gideon? After hunting season?"

"It depends, Lydia." He took her hand as they continued on, and grasped it as if not wanting to let go.

"On what?"

"If you think we have a future together. Because if we do —"

"*Ja,*" she interrupted.

He opened his mouth slightly as if not hearing her correctly.

"*Ja,* I do see a future . . . with an amazing man. A man who cares. A man who has chosen to love God and do good. A strong man."

Gideon glanced away. Why did her words make him uncomfortable?

Lydia stood firm, knowing that even though he'd told her the truth, he needed to know some truth too. "Have you read about Gideon lately?"

"Excuse me?"

"Not about yourself, but in the Bible. You were named after the man in the Bible, right?"

"*Ja,* but what does that have to do with us now?"

"Dad and Mem used to read Bible stories to me when I was young," she said, "and the story of Gideon has always stuck in my mind. I'm not sure why. Maybe for this moment. Maybe for now." She glanced up at him. His strength was obvious, but she could tell from his eyes that Gideon still felt like that scared little boy inside.

"Gideon knew how the Lord cared for his ancestors," she continued. "He knew that God had saved his people from Egypt, but that was ancient history to him. He questioned if God still cared for him, for his family *today.* In that day that he lived.

"But what God wanted to show him was that He was the same God in Gideon's day who achieved all the wonders for Gideon's ancestors. Yet Gideon was too busy looking at his own weaknesses to trust God's strength."

He raised an eyebrow and waited. His hand tightened around hers even more, but his steps did not slow.

"It's easy to try to figure out what others could have done differently," she said. "We can look back in history and point out their failures and successes, but we forget that we're making history in this moment. I mean, sometime my descendants — yours — might be reading about our faith jest as I'm reading about Mem's."

Gideon nodded. "I know you mean to encourage me with your words, but so far the one biggest impact I've had on others has led to their pain."

"That's only if you blame yourself. God knew the day of that man's death, Gideon, even before the day he was born, yet we always like to point a finger. It's human nature."

Up ahead, lights were on in their small log house too — kerosene lights. And in the window a lone figure stood. Dat. Tall, thin. He waited for them. She guessed the house was too quiet, and she was again glad she'd stayed — not only for her new job and for Gideon, but also for her father.

She slowed her steps. "One of the books I edited for my work was about how major events in history could have been changed by one person — how ordinary people do matter in the big picture. Like Fredrick Fleet."

"Who?"

"He was one of the two men in the crow's nest of the *Titanic.* Due to a mix up in the last-minute shift of the officers' assignments, the lookout crew was without binoculars. He was hired for the job of being a lookout but was never issued binoculars.

"I remember out of all the stories, that one stuck out to me the most. His father was unknown. His mother abandoned him to run away with a boyfriend, and Fredrick was raised in foster homes. He was one of the men who manned the life-boats, so he survived, but from what I read guilt plagued him his whole life. He survived when so many others didn't."

"It wasn't his fault." The words shot from Gideon's lips. And then he lowered his head. "It wasn't his fault." The words appeared to wrap around him like a warm blanket. "This might have been different with binoculars, but we'll never know."

"Fredrick did the best he could with what he had available to him. He still saw the berg, he just saw it too late to make a difference."

"*Ja,* but my situation is different. I caused

the trouble. If I had just stayed put . . ."

"True, but we'll never know how things would have been different. We can't change history. And when I think of Gideon in the Bible, the one thing that stands out is that God saw the truth. God saw him as a mighty warrior even when he couldn't see it himself."

"How come you're able to see the good in everyone else?"

"Everyone else?" She peered up at him.

"Everyone but yourself?"

Lydia stopped short at those words. "I — I don't know what you're talking about."

"There's something in your eyes, something you're not telling me. I have a feeling, Lydia, that I'm not the only one with a secret or two."

"Yes." Lydia released a sigh. "There are things. And . . ." She reached for his arm. She wanted to tell him, but not this way. Not like this. "I —"

"It's all right." Gideon studied her face. "I'm sorry. I shouldn't have brought it up."

"No, you should have. If I'm going to give you a hard time, then . . ." She raised a trembling hand to her forehead. "I just need to sit for a bit."

"*Ja, ja,* of course." He placed an arm around her and led her home. The moon made its presence known as the last rays of sunlight slipped away. The biscuits, chicken, and peas that Lydia had eaten at dinner turned into rocks in her stomach. Yes, it was easy for someone to hold a mirror up for another. It was harder when the mirror was turned, and the reflection was one's own.

CHAPTER 25

Dat opened the door as they mounted the porch steps, and a smile filled his face. "Your Aunt Millie wrote. Annie brought the letter by with dinner." He held it up. "Your aunts and uncles from Sugarcreek had a small gathering in memory of Mem." He stepped aside, allowing them to enter.

The room was warm, inviting. She paused and offered her dat a hug. "I'm so glad she wrote and told us. Are they doing well?"

"They planted a rose bush for Ada Mae," he said. "Yellow roses were her favorite."

Lydia nodded and the tightness in her throat grew. She and Gideon sat on the couch side by side, and Dat settled into his favorite recliner, telling them about his day. He'd gotten the rest of the vegetables out of the garden. He'd had a nap. Lydia smiled softly and rejoiced inside over the simple things that made up her dat's day.

Gideon asked about Sugarcreek, their

home and family there, and Lydia was glad. It gave her time to consider how she'd tell Gideon the truth — what she'd say.

"We loved Sugarcreek. It's pretty there." Excitement caused Dat's voice to rise in volume. "Not like this, but pretty with rolling hills. It's much bigger than West Kootenai — four thousand people or so. The first people there were Swiss and German settlers. Some folks call Sugarcreek 'Little Switzerland' of Ohio yet. We had a really nice farm there. A young couple bought it from us back a few years ago."

Gideon's face brightened to see Dat's excitement. "Sounds as if you liked it. Why did you move?"

Dat's eyes widened. "Didn't you know?" He pointed to Lydia. "Didn't you tell him yet?"

"Tell him? I'm not sure myself." She forced a chuckle. "All Mem said is that she heard about West Kootenai, and it sounded like a real nice place."

Dat's forehead folded into wrinkles. "That's what she told you?"

Lydia leaned forward. "*Ja,* was that not the truth?"

"*Vell,* this place is nice, but the truth, Lydia, is that you were in Seattle. This was the closest Amish community to you."

"Of course." She glanced to Gideon. "And yet I was too busy with deadlines and meetings, and manuscripts to visit." Her voice trailed off. "I was running . . . running from the truth."

"I know, Lydia."

She almost seemed to melt into the couch cushion to hear his words. If she'd ever wanted to open her heart — her past — to anyone, it was Gideon. She felt a closeness with him she hadn't felt before, even after the kiss. She understood. It was easy to share a kiss. It was harder to share one's pain and heartache. The same openness she sensed was reflected in Gideon's gaze.

"I best git to bed." Dat rose. Was there more going on between them than talk of farms and moves to Montana? He bid them good night, then shuffled into his bedroom.

A few minutes passed, and Lydia's mind focused on the ticking of the clock. It had been a long week, and as she sat there her eyes grew heavy. Yet she couldn't let another day pass without talking to Gideon. He'd already shared so much.

"See this?" She pulled the acorn from her pocket and held it up. "My heart is encased by something like this. It's like there's a shell around me."

"Is it because of the secret?"

"*Ja.*" She placed the acorn on the side table and then looked at him. "I'm adopted, Gideon."

He furrowed his brow. "*Ja,* I knew that."

"What?" Lydia's head jerked backward.

"Yer dat told me — the day I was helping to build your mem's, uh, coffin."

"He did?"

Gideon nodded. "He shared how much you meant to them. He said they never expected to have a child. I didn't think much of it. I didn't realize it bothered you so."

"Oh, I'm not bothered too much." She fiddled with the sleeve of her dress. "I jest wanted to be honest with you . . . after hearing your story."

Lydia shifted in her seat. Could she stop there? She knew she should tell him more, but how?

"There is more than that, Lydia. I can see it."

"How could you? How could you know?"

"Because I've seen the same look in my mother's eyes — my father's eyes — a hundred times."

Gideon made her a cup of tea, and Lydia took a long deep breath. She'd never told another soul about her birth mom. Never shared how the truth made her feel . . .

335

■ ■ ■ ■

"There were tears in my eyes when she told me." Lydia fingered the edge of her apron. "I'd known for as long as I could remember that I was adopted, but Mem sat me down and told me there were *circumstances.*" She dared to glance up to Gideon. "I still cringe whenever I hear that word."

"Was there a reason why she told you?"

"I had just turned sixteen. I told her I was old enough to know the truth." Lydia shook her head. "I don't think there's anyone, any age, who wants to know a truth like that."

Gideon's eyes narrowed. "Does it have to do with your birth mom?"

Lydia nodded. "I'd always known I was adopted. I look nothing like my parents. Strangers would always ask, 'Where did you get that red hair?' But even when I got old enough for my parents to explain adoption, I knew they weren't telling the whole story. They'd stumble with their words and pass a knowing look between them. Finally, after months of prodding and fussing, Mem told me my birth mother's name was Grace. She was an Amish woman, and I had three older brothers. That didn't settle anything in my mind."

Gideon studied her face. Hung on her every word.

"As a young girl, one of my friend's older sisters got pregnant by an *Englisch* boy during her *rumspringa.* I always thought my birth mother's story would be more like that. But why would a woman with three boys already not want her fourth child? Why wouldn't she want a girl? After three boys, anyone would want a girl, right?"

Pain filled Gideon's eyes, and she knew his heart ached. Maybe it was simply a reflection of the pain in her gaze. Her shoulders tensed, and her legs twitched as if urging her to get up and run — run from the story as she'd been doing for the last five years. Run from the truth. Run from the look of horror that was sure to come in Gideon's gaze.

Would he look at her differently when he knew?

"There's no easy way to say it, Gideon. Mem told me that Grace's husband died of cancer. It wasn't long after her third son was born. The community helped to care for her. She'd taught school —" Lydia paused for a moment. She'd forgotten that. "She'd taught school before she was married. So many in the community cared for her. After a year or so Grace started giving away her husband's things. There was this traveler . . ." The words caught in Lydia's throat. "She saw the man sitting on the bench in front of the general store. She told him her husband had died — that she had some clothes. Would he like some?" Lydia lowered her head. "The man seemed eager. She told him she'd get some things and return." Lydia covered her face with her hands. "But Mem told me he must have followed her home. Grace was in shock . . . after . . . She didn't know who to talk to or how to tell. And then she found out about . . . me."

"Oh, Lydia." Gideon's arms wrapped around her and he pulled her to his chest. She closed her eyes and focused on the cotton of his shirt. He smelled of the mountains and the tall grass that Blue trotted through. It was easier to focus on Gideon's arms around her rather than on the story she'd just confessed.

"No woman should ever have to go through such a thing." His words filled the quiet room. "But although my heart aches for her, I'm thankful . . . for you. For your life."

She tilted her head back and looked up in his face. "That's *gut* of you to say, but after hearing the truth from Mem, I understood why she didn't want to keep me. How could one face such a painful memory every single day?"

"But you were innocent. It wasn't anything you did that had caused Grace's pain."

"*Ne,* but my life — my birth — added to it." She pushed against him, sitting up. "I suppose that's why I was mad at God for so long. Why would a loving God do that? Grace had already faced enough. How could God have allowed even more pain to happen to a sweet woman like that?"

Gideon didn't stay much longer. She could tell their conversations weighed heavily on him, and she understood.

Lydia walked him to the door, gave him her flashlight to use, and sent him off with a wave. As she closed the front door she thought about one of Mem's Scripture verses that she'd read a month ago. It said, *"The truth shall make you free."* Ever since then she'd been trying to understand those words. The truth had not freed her. Not one little bit. And even though sharing with Gideon made her feel closer to him, she had a feeling of disconnect within herself once again. She was thankful that Mem's letter said the red hair was from Grace's side of the family, but what about the rest of her?

What traits did she have from . . . him?

She turned out all the lanterns and blew out all the candles but one. The lone flame lit the way to her room, and she walked down the wooden floor with stockinged feet. She changed into her bed clothes, but didn't put on her sleeping handkerchief. That was one thing she hadn't gotten used to since returning. She'd been use to combing out her hair and letting it splay on her pillow as she slept.

Lydia ran her fingers through her hair and then picked up the Promise Box. She didn't have enough energy to read one of Mem's longer notes. Instead, she pulled out a small, pink slip of paper with a Scripture verse:

"Know therefore that the Lord thy God, he is God, the faithful God, which keepeth covenant and mercy with them that love him and keep his commandments to a thousand generations," Deuteronomy 7:9.

Under the verse Mem had written two sentences: *Write the story. Share His loving kindness for a thousand generations.*

Goosebumps raced up Lydia's arms and the tiredness of a moment before disappeared.

Write the story. She picked up the Promise

Box again. Mem had done just that. She hadn't typed a manuscript or sought a publisher, but she'd shared her life — her story — in pieces of paper folded up in a box.

Lydia was returning the slip of paper when she noticed another pink slip. She paused. Why had Mem written those on pink paper? On the outside of that slip there were the same words: *Write the story.*

Lydia opened it.

"Be not afraid of their terror, neither be troubled; but sanctify the Lord God in your hearts: and be ready always to give an answer to every man that asketh you a reason of the hope that is in you," 1 Peter 3:14–15.

Dear Lydia,

When I started writing down the promises of God, I did it for me. I wanted to remember. The first thing I wanted to remember was the promise of God bringing you to us. Then I wanted to remember the moments in yer growing-up years when I felt God do something special. It was only as you got older that I thought my notes might be something that you'd want to read.

I thought about this more when I read this Scripture verse this morning. It was something I read, and something I'm eager to share with Annie when she stops by later. There are promises I feel God whispering in my heart. First, not to fear. This speaks to me because of the fears that like to creep in: What if Lydia does not return to her faith? What if my heart continues to turn for the worse? Who will care for Jacob when I'm gone?

Dear Lord, take my fears. You are Lord. You ARE Lord. More than that, I want to thank You for putting it on my heart to write these notes. And I pray that someday my daughter will be able to read of the hope that I had. I pray she will not only accept the faith — the hope — but that she too will share it.

For as long as she was a young girl she's been making up stories. Her creativity never surprises me, and after I've read those books she's edited, her talent is clear. I keep thinking, though, about what could happen when Lydia returns to the faith. How could her words impact others . . . those she cares about most?

Lydia, as the Word says, be prepared to give an answer for the hope that you have. I'm writing this in faith. If you've been impacted by my words at all, then think of how you can use your own words. Your own story.

Love, Mem

She sat there a minute, thinking of her mem's words. Lydia had been writing the story of her return, but she'd considered her words only for herself. But what if her words were for someone else too? Or more than one person?

Lydia hurried to the dresser and pulled out her small stack of notebooks. Sitting under them was her cell phone, still turned off, still with half a battery. Three of the notebooks were already full, and she'd just started the fourth. She wrote in them every day. The only thing was Lydia wasn't collecting promises. She was recording God's faithfulness in one woman's life in a way that could be shared with generations coming after her.

As she flipped through the pages, she was amazed at how much was captured. Her emotions on the day of Mem's funeral. Her attraction to Gideon, nearly right from the start. Her friendships with Amish and *Englisch*.

And as Lydia looked at the record of God's faithfulness, she knew what she had to do. She picked up her cell phone and turned it on. How many weeks had it been since she'd used it?

She saw that she had five messages, but Lydia ignored those. Instead, she typed out a text to Bonnie.

Sending u 3 notebooks. Have them typed & edited (spelling). Make two copies & send back to me . . . bill me cost. Will pay out of substantial teacher's salary. Haha.

Lydia smiled as she turned off the phone. She could almost picture Dat and Gideon's faces as they read God's story in her life — the parts they knew — and the parts that might surprise them.

Then she hurried back to bed and pushed her pillow against the wall, leaning against it. There was a lot to capture today in her words. School, the visit from Gideon, the kiss, and the sharing of her heart with another. It was a day of highs and lows, but wasn't everyone's story?

Lydia took the cap off the top of the pen and began to write.

CHAPTER 26

A gentle rain plunked against the metal roof of the schoolhouse, and Lydia's soul felt as if it, too, were being washed by rain from the heavens. She lit the lanterns and wood-stove and soon the small building radiated with warmth.

At first, after hearing Gideon's story — and sharing hers — the truth had stung. It reminded Lydia of the time when she was a little girl and skinned her knee by falling off the concrete steps at the grocery. Bits of dirt and rocks had embedded themselves into the wound.

At home Mem had taken soap, water, and a clean cloth to the cut. The cleaning had stung, and it was only when she stopped crying and looked up that she saw tears had been in Mem's eyes too.

"I'm so sorry, dear one," Mem had said. "But you can't heal unless the junk is cleaned out. If I were to let it be, an infection would surely come, *ja.*"

Had God said the same thing yesterday? Lydia's lower lip trembled as she pictured tears in His eyes. Thinking of that warmed her even more than the woodstove.

By letting so much of her past go unattended, the wounds had only gotten worse. Yesterday was just the first step of getting the junk out, but she trusted that God would continue to work from there.

She pulled corrected papers from her satchel and laid them out on the students' desks, humming as she did. It was only as she returned to her desk to spend a few minutes writing in her journal that Lydia realized the song she'd been humming. It was the hymn that the congregation had read together at Mem's funeral.

Just over yonder, beyond the river,
There is a City of pure delight,
Where many loved ones are congregating
With palms of vict'ry in robes of white.
Just over yonder, there'll be no heartaches,
No lonely days will ever come.
There'll be no crying, there'll be no dying,
Oh, what rejoicing when we get home.
Just over yonder, I'll soon be going
To see my Savior upon His throne;
And hear a welcome ring out through

heaven,
Oh, weary pilgrim, this is your home.

The words resonated in her heart, and she was struck again by how far God had brought her. Not only here to Montana, but steps closer to a healed heart too.

Lydia sat down with her notebook and pen.

The sound of rain on the metal roof of our house did not hinder my mood as I woke. God's grace falling. That's what it sounded like: *plunk, plunk, plunk.*

I rolled over and looked at the Promise Box, and a smile filled my face. If Mem had not been faithful to write down God's promises, where would I be now? *Ja,* God could have used someone else — something else — to get my attention, but I'm thankful for Mem's faithfulness. The words are ink on paper, but they're also linking spirit to spirit — with God's truth as the white dove that carries them to my heart.

One of the things I prayed for is that I will learn to be faithful with my story. I think doing so would make Mem happy. Memories fade, but our testimonies — our stories — can live on. Mem's words have not only eased my return home . . . to my father's house. They point me to eternity . . . my forever home. And carrying that truth on my heart makes every day more precious.

This morning I made Dat pancakes, and he started the coffee. He offered to hitch up the buggy and give me a ride to school, but I told him that wouldn't be necessary. It's less than two miles and the quiet path has become a prayer walk.

Lodgepole pines hug the road I walk on, as if trying to reclaim the property taken from them. They also sway and lean in, as if they're listening in to my whispered prayers.

A weathered cowgirl drives her truck down the muddy dirt road. I believe her name is Millie, and when she gets to me she asks if I need a ride. I tell her I'm almost there, and I point to the school. She tells me she's glad they found a new teacher and reaches out of her truck window. I give her my hand and she shakes it, squeezing tight.

The umbrella did fine, and though my shoes are muddy they will get cleaned, and my feet will soon be dry and warm.

One of my favorite things about walking is to see the light filling the windows of my friends' homes. *Ja,* it's only a few months since I've been in West Kootenai, but the friendships I've made are blooming. This Saturday I'm invited to a quilting bee at the Yoders' place. It's been over six years since I quilted, but I have a feeling the women will be patient with me. They're gut in that way. Their eyes reflect the goodness of our Lord on ordinary days during ordinary tasks.

Lydia wrote for a few minutes more and then thought of a quote her teacher Miss Yoder had taught her once. It seemed to summarize what she'd been feeling.

She wrote the new quote on the blackboard: *"Friendship is a lamp which shines most brightly when all else is dark."*

Maybe the relationships she experienced now — with Dat, with Gideon, with her neighbors — shined brighter because of the dark times she'd walked through. Lydia had a feeling they did.

She held her breath in eager anticipation as the students began to arrive. Yet before the first hour was through, she was already counting the minutes until the first recess break.

The newness of their teacher had worn off, and while all the kids wiggled in their seats, it was the oldest boys who caused the most trouble. Part men — mostly boys — Andy and David whispered about hunting season to come while Lydia was trying to read a story aloud. They sketched pictures of guns and bullets on their math homework. Lydia knew their influence was rubbing off on the other kids when the younger boys broke off their erasers into the shape of guns and started chasing each other around the room with them during their indoor recess.

At lunch, Lydia was just about to raise her voice and ban all talk of hunting when Gideon walked through the door.

"You've come to rescue me." She hurried to him with her lunch pail swinging at her side. "I'll pay you in chocolate chip cookies if you go back and get your ropes and halters for these boys."

"That bad?"

She shrugged. "I suppose they aren't horrible, but I can't imagine two more months of this until hunting season starts."

Gideon's eyes twinkled. "I imagine that would get them excited, especially since 'hunter safety' starts tonight."

"Is that it? I was blaming the rain." Lydia placed an open palm on her forehead. "It makes sense. But the whole room has been disrupted this morning."

Gideon scanned the room. "Which one is the problem?"

"Well, all of the boys are caught up in the act, but . . ." Lydia looked around the room at the children eating at their desks. "I'd have to say that David Sommer is the one who gets the others started."

"Him?" Gideon pointed to the tall boy with blond hair and hazel eyes.

"Ja."

Before she knew what was happening, Gideon strode across the room to David.

"Son, can I talk to you for a minute?"

The boy paused with the sandwich halfway to his mouth. "Uh, yessir."

They moved to the front covered porch, leaving the door cracked open. Lydia hung around the back, straightening up the kids' boots and backpacks, trying to hear what Gideon was going to say.

Gideon squatted before David. "David, that was a full classroom back there, wasn't it?" Gideon's voice mixed with the sound of rain as it carried through the doorway.

"Ja."

"Full of what?"

"Books, desks, kids."

Lydia could imagine him shrugging.

"Big kids or little kids?"

"Little. All smaller than me. 'Cept for

351

Andy. We're the same age."

The rain let up some, and the plinking on the metal roof lessened, making it easier for Lydia to hear. "Do they look up to you like I'm looking up to you now?"

"Yessir."

"Do you think they respect you?"

"Uh, yessir."

She glanced out the window. Gideon's back was to her, but Lydia could see David's nose wrinkled up. He eyed Gideon and wiggled from side to side as if worry scampered up his spine like a rogue lizard.

"Do you think that if you climbed to the top of the roof and wanted to jump, they'd want to try it too?"

"Yessir, some of them."

"But you wouldn't do that because you know that some would get hurt."

"No, sir, of course I wouldn't do that."

"Well, your attitude is just as interesting to them. Those kids in there are looking up to you. You can bet they're watching how you treat Miss Wyse. You're leading them, son, and they'll be sure to follow too."

"I never thought of it like that."

Lydia stepped closer to the window, curious as to where the conversation was going.

"So are you going to be a *gut* example, David?"

"Yessir."

"*Danki.* I knew I could count on you."

There was movement, and Lydia stepped away from the window so Gideon wouldn't see her spying on them. She couldn't see what was happening, but she imagined Gideon standing and patting the young man's shoulder.

"Sir, is Miss Wyse your sweetheart?"

A smile filled Lydia's face at the question, and she covered her mouth with her hand to halt her laughter.

"*Vell,* I guess you can say that. She is pretty special."

"My sister Marianna was right. She said she saw you looking at Miss Wyse the other day at church and your eyes were as big as Mrs. Carash's prize tomatoes."

Gideon chuckled. "That must be big, all right, and you can tell your sister she's pretty smart."

Lydia heard footsteps. She turned and hurried to the front of the room toward the chalkboard, but it was too late. The door swung open and Gideon and David entered. Behind her, Gideon cleared his throat. She paused her steps and looked back over her shoulder.

"Caught you!" David laughed and pointed, then hurried back to be with his friends. He wore a soft smile as he passed her. Lydia knew David would probably try to be kinder and more respectful, and his trying would be helpful indeed.

"Finish up your lunch, children. Start cleaning up your board games. Your lunch break is over in five minutes."

With hesitant steps she approached Gideon. "*Ja,* as large as tomatoes." She placed a hand over her heart and then swallowed hard. "A *gut* description."

"I didn't think you were listening."

"I'm glad I was."

"Really, why's that?"

"Because it's *gut* to know I'm not the only one feeling jest so. I'm glad to know you have a sweetheart, and it's me. Now . . ." She placed her hand on her hips. "I know you just made my day easier, but what did you really come for?"

"I wanted to see if you'd like to go on a short hike — maybe Saturday? Edgar claims it'll be our last good day before the cold days of fall claim their place."

Lydia's lips pursed. "I'd love to, but I already promised to go to a quilting bee."

"Sunday afternoon, then?"

"*Ja,* that sounds like a plan, but after listening to these boys' stories, I'm not sure if I want to venture out in those woods. And look at this." She moved to her desk and Gideon followed. Lydia smiled as she picked up Josiah Sommer's multiplication sheet. He had written on the top: *If you do hike bring bear spray, make nose, and don't go alone.*

Gideon chuckled and lowered his voice. " 'Make nose'?"

"I'm sure he meant 'noise' but I think they're trying to scare me."

Gideon scanned the youngsters who chatted as they cleaned up their board games. "And why would they do that?"

"Maybe because they know I'm not from around here and they think it'll be funny to scare the teacher."

"There is that." Gideon winked. "Or I could have paid them to scare you . . . so that when we do go on a hike, you'll stay right by my side and cling to me the whole way up the mountain."

Lydia laughed and shook her head. "I wouldn't be surprised, Gideon. I wouldn't be surprised."

CHAPTER 27

Only two days had passed and Lydia was already wishing that Gideon would return. But it wasn't the boys who were causing trouble this time. Instead it was the littlest ones in the group. It had started when Lydia began working with the two youngest girls, teaching them to write complete sentences. They'd mastered their letters. Wasn't this a good next step?

Ellie stared at the paper. Instead of writing with her pencil, she put it down and watched it roll off her desk. Behind her one of the boys snickered.

Lydia turned and glared at Josiah. "Please don't encourage your sister."

"Sorry, Miss Wyse."

"Ellie, can you pick up the pencil, please?"

Ellie shook her head. *"Ne."*

"Can you speak English, please?"

Ellie folded her arms and lowered her head onto them. *"Ne."*

"Is there a reason you don't want to do your work?"

Ellie shrugged. *"Wonnernaus."*

" 'Wonnernaus'?" Lydia cocked an eyebrow. Silence echoed in the room. She didn't hear the sound of one pencil writing on paper. Lydia cleared her throat. "Yes, it is my business. I'm yer teacher."

Ellie didn't budge, and Lydia closed her eyes, praying for wisdom. After a minute passed she came up with an idea.

Lydia rose and went to the supply cupboard. Inside there was a half-used bag of rice. She guessed the other part of it had been used for a craft. Lydia tore off a large piece of waxed paper and took the paper and the rice to the desks where Ellie and Evelyn sat. With all eyes on her, she placed the paper on the floor and proceeded to pour the rice onto it. Small gasps erupted around the room. It was only then that Ellie lifted her head to see what her teacher was up to.

Lydia sat on the floor, and with her hands she spread the rice into an even layer over the waxed paper. Satisfied with the result, she picked up the pencil and lifted it toward Ellie.

"Girls, how would you like to write your sentences in the rice?"

Evelyn's eyes widened and she jumped to her feet. *"Ja!"* But Ellie seemed unmoved.

Evelyn sat down with her pencil. A large smile filled her face as she wrote her name.

"Are you sure you don't want to try, Ellie?" Lydia didn't push. She didn't scold. She just waited.

After a moment Ellie shrugged, and Lydia handed her the pencil. With slow movements Ellie rose from her desk and sat next to Evelyn. As if seeing their world was in order again, the rest of the students went back to work.

Lydia rose and returned to her desk. She sat. Her hands trembled, and a sinking feeling overcame her. What had she been thinking to want this job — to accept this job? The future of these children was in her hands. Their parents expected them to learn, not only about school subjects, but about respect and working as part of a community.

She pulled out a pile of papers and shuffled through them, not knowing what she was looking for. What if Ellie's defiance continued? What if the boys started to act up again? Suddenly the weight of responsibility seemed too much to bear.

"Class, get out your spelling sheets and look over your words. I'll be testing you in ten minutes."

Julia Yoder raised her hand. "Miss Wyse, today is Thursday. We always do our spelling tests on Friday."

"Yes, Julia, I know, but . . . I've decided to change things today." Her throat grew tight. "Ten minutes should be enough time to review your words. You've had three days already to practice them at home. Don't you think that's fair?"

"Yes, Miss Wyse." Julia lowered her head. Her shoulders shook slightly.

Seeing the girl's reaction made matters even worse.

"Who trusted me with this job?" Lydia mumbled to herself. She thought of her birth mother, Grace. How had she done it? Had teaching school been different almost thirty years ago? Lydia guessed not. Things didn't change much in an Amish community. Grace would have had the same struggles and problems. Had she turned to the community for support? Had she turned to God for help?

Deep down Lydia knew becoming the teacher wasn't just about the children, it was about her. It was as if God tapped her on the shoulder, "See, you're gonna need others — need Me to pull this off." Lydia thought back to the first few weeks of school. She'd poured everything into teaching and had done a good job, but . . .

God's Spirit spoke to her heart: *Don't make this about them versus you, Lydia. Remind them that you're all in this — the walk of faith — together.*

As if a fog lifted, Lydia knew what to do. She moved to the chalkboard. "Actually, class, Julia is right. We will do our spelling test tomorrow. Instead I want to talk about challenges. My challenges as a teacher, and yours as a student. The year is just getting started, and things won't always be easy, but I want to talk about this quote we have up here. Julia, can you read it?"

Dark-haired Julia sat straighter in her seat. " 'Friendship is a lamp which shines most brightly when all else is dark.' "

"Very good." Lydia smiled at her class. "I'm not sure if you know it, but when we grow and interact with the world, we'll find enemies as well as friends. Not always those who want to hurt us physically, but those who consider our path foolish. Or who think our God is not real."

She looked around the room. Children's eyes widened. "*Ja,* it's true. That's why it's so important to know what we believe and to trust God." Lydia placed a hand over her heart.

Charlie Sommer's hand shot into the air. "Yes, Charlie."

"Is it true that you used to live in the *Englisch* world?"

"*Ja,* I did."

"My uncle says that you shouldn't be teaching . . . because your mind is too full of knowledge and prideful thoughts." It was Andy Shelter who said those words, and they were like a jab to Lydia's heart. "But my mem told him that yer a great teacher, and she was going to smack his head hoping he'd get some smarts," Andy continued. Laughter spilled from his lips.

"That's a perfect example, Andy," Lydia said, trying not to allow the words of that boy's uncle to bother her. "It would have meant a lot to me for your mem to tell me I was a great teacher, but her words mean even more because of the dark opinion told to her." She looked around. "Does that make sense, class?"

Students' heads nodded, and even the youngest girls seemed to be paying attention.

Well done. She felt — more than heard — the soft whisper to her soul.

"All right, class. Now everyone get out your papers with leaf photos. We're going to discuss the upcoming leaf collections." All the children, even little Ellie, obeyed without question, and there was a special sense of unity in the room that hadn't been there before. They'd walked through a struggle together and had come to the other side.

Lydia smiled as she walked over to the leaf poster, hoping this day's impromptu lesson would be remembered long after these students learned to multiply and spell. She just hoped that during the school days to come there would be more moments of light — and that not too many dark days loomed ahead.

CHAPTER 28

Dear Gideon,

I know I haven't written much since you've been gone. Things are always busy here. Your sister Susie had a baby boy, and they named him Elam. Dat had been bugging me for days to see how you're doing. Now that you know 'bout what happened up on that mountain, he wonders if you shouldn't come home. Maybe you've had enough of the mountain air?

Dat has tossed and turned for days, and I know you're the reason. He wonders if people will still treat you well when they discover who you are. Personally, I doubt very many are around who were there at the time. Do many people know that you are the little boy lost, or jest that one man? If anyone else asks, jest tell them you don't know about the occurrences of that day. That's the truth, as the good Lord knows. Dat made sure you didn't know as a way of protecting you. And his father heart longs to protect you still — even from this distance.

Write soon and tell us when you'll be able to come,

Mem

Gideon crumpled up the letter and tossed it on the ground of the corral. He couldn't believe his parents. First his dat for being worried about what people thought, and then his mem for writing the letter. He was twenty-four years old — an adult. He didn't know if any of the other folks had figured it out, but he had nothing to be ashamed of. He'd been just a little kid, right?

He bent over and picked up the letter, tucking it into his pants pocket. Just then he heard whistling behind him. Gideon turned to see Lydia strolling toward him.

"Hey, there!" She waved. "I was hoping you'd be out here."

She neared, and Gideon opened his arms. He was surprised that she stepped into his embrace. But just as quickly she backed up again. For an Amish woman he wouldn't expect any less.

"Did you have a *gut* day at school?"

Lydia let out a heavy sigh and shrugged.

"That good, huh?" He forced a menacing glare. "Do I need to come and have a talk with someone again?"

"Oh, dear no!" Lydia giggled. "I think she'd try to hide under my apron if she saw your stern face."

"She?"

"*Ja,* Ellie Sommer. She's six, I believe . . . and something got into her today." Lydia shook her head. "But thankfully we all made it through the day." She stepped forward and reached a hand toward Blue, patiently waiting. "I don't want to spend all our time on my day. I want to know how your day was."

"It was *gut.* I put a harness on Blue — to prepare him for pulling a buggy next — and we walked down the road a bit."

"Really?" Lydia clapped her hands together. *"Ja!"* Her face glowed with excitement, warming Gideon's heart.

She reached up and softly patted his cheek, looking deep into his eyes. "This is great news, don't you think?"

Gideon ran a finger under his shirt collar, unsure of why he felt so warm, so happy. Yet looking deeper into Lydia's gaze, he saw something. Respect. He hadn't seen that much before — not directed to him, anyway.

"Well, if you want to see, we can take Blue back to the barn."

Gideon led the way. The barn was spotless and the items he needed were hanging on the wall just as he'd left them. The letter in his pocket made a crinkling sound as he walked, but Gideon didn't want to think about that. He could get used to being with a woman who respected him. A woman who didn't point a finger at his past. A woman he could trust.

Lydia glanced around the barn. It looked new, as if it had just been built in the last few years. She thought about asking Gideon why they'd chosen to teach Blue how to pull a buggy, since the Carashes weren't Amish, but she'd save that conversation for another time — she didn't want to take away the horse's focus from his new job.

"This thing here is a collar." Instead of talking to Lydia, Gideon turned his attention to the horse. He held the leather oval up for Blue to see. Lydia couldn't believe how patient Gideon was in showing Blue the leather oval before placing it on him. Even though she shouldn't let her mind wander, she couldn't help but think what Gideon would be like with a child — their child.

With gentle motions Gideon buckled the collar beneath Blue's neck. He pressed it against the horse's wide shoulders, talking to him the whole time in a low tone, like a father would talk to his toddler.

"Snug, but not too tight to cut off oxygen," he said. Lydia wasn't sure if he was talking to her or the horse.

Knowing what he needed next, Lydia moved to the hooks on the wall of Mr. Carash's new barn and took down the harness.

"You're familiar in the barn," Gideon commented.

"I'd follow Dat often. He didn't have a son and didn't mind me hanging around."

"I can tell. Blue can tell. He doesn't seem the least bit nervous that you're in here with us."

With slow, gentle movements Gideon seated the hames on the collar, buckled the strap, walked to the horse's flank, and adjusted the breaching seat. Then he walked forward again to connect the breast strap to the hames. He ran his hand ahead of him along the horse's muscles, speaking with low words as he did. Lydia stood silent, motionless as he worked. She didn't want to be a distraction — to Blue or to Gideon. She had the same awe watching him work as she used to have for her neighbor who was a carver. Gideon was like an artist as he worked with Blue — it was a gift indeed.

"I can't believe this is the same animal they considered putting down," she dared to whisper.

"I like to hear you say that, Lydia. It makes me feel as if what I do matters."

"It does matter . . . very much." Her words weren't more than a whisper, but you'd think she'd shouted them by the way Gideon's head swung around. His eyes locked with hers, and his focus was intense, as if he was drawing strength from whatever he saw in her gaze.

Not more than ten seconds later, Gideon turned back around and adjusted the belly band. The horse had been perfectly still the whole time, yet Blue blinked one slow blink when Gideon put the bit into the horse's mouth and fed the reins through the cheek rings.

When he finished, he led the way out of the barn. Blue matched Gideon's steady stride. "Do you want to go for a short walk with us, Lydia?"

"*Ja.*" The air had a light chill to it. She pulled her sweater tighter around her, wishing she'd brought a scarf too. Yet being in this beautiful place was worth the cold.

Pine-shrouded hills stretched in every

direction. In one of the nearby trees, two birds carried on a conversation and then stopped. Gideon and Lydia walked along, neither speaking. The silence was broken only by the dull thump of hooves.

They crested the hill as they neared the Sommer place, and Gideon paused his steps. *Lydia Wyse,* his gaze seemed to say, *what do you want from me?*

"Just yer love," she found herself muttering.

"What was that?"

"I was just responding, Gideon."

"But I didn't ask anything."

"I know, but I'm a teacher. I can read things. I know which student really did tug on Julia's *kapp* string. I know who studied his spelling words and who was just guessing . . . even before I grade the papers."

"You can, eh? Okay, what am I saying now?"

He leaned close so his face was only six inches from hers. She looked up from beneath her lashes and felt his breath on her forehead.

"You're not saying anything. You're asking." Lydia lifted to her toes. "And yes, sir, you may kiss me."

Gideon blew out a low breath. "Well, I'll be . . . You *are* a mind reader."

As Gideon kissed her, the playfulness of a moment before disappeared, lifting like vapors of dew under the sun. Warmth, eagerness, pressed against her lips. It was more than attraction. It was validation. She took a step closer, opening her palm and pressing it against his chest. Blue whinnied and Lydia pulled back. Then she heard it. The sound of a truck coming down the roadway.

Gideon stepped back and held the reins tightly as the truck passed. She read worry on his face. How would Blue perform? The truck rumbled by, and they waved to their neighbor from down the road, yet Blue didn't move.

"Do you see?" She pointed. "That was amazing. Blue didn't budge."

Gideon shook his head and scratched his cheek. "Unlike when you first drove into town."

She glanced around at the dirt road, high mountain pastures, and trees. "You call this a town?"

"Well, the area." He shook his head.

"Back then, did you ever think it would come to this: me and you stealing kisses on this very road?"

"*Ja.*" He nodded.

Lydia playfully slugged his shoulder. "You

did not!"

"All right. I maybe didn't think of this, but there was something about you then that I was attracted to. There was a spark, Lydia. I don't want you to lose that spark." He patted Blue's side. "It's like horse training. There are those who train a horse by beating it down. The horse will obey but it is like a robot."

"So you are saying you don't want me to be an Amish robot?" She couldn't help but chuckle.

"What's so funny?" he asked.

"It's funny because I never thought I'd use those words together in a sentence."

"No, I don't want you to be an Amish robot. I want you to be the woman God created you to be. One who happens to look beautiful in a *kapp.*"

She bent over and picked a wild daisy — the last one lining the road this season. "But the more time we spend together, the more we seem to complement each other. I like to write, you like to read."

He nodded. "I like to eat, you like to cook."

She considered the verse she'd read this morning from the Promise Box: *"Delight thyself also in the Lord: and he shall give thee the desires of thine heart."*

"It wonders me how a woman like you could care for someone like me," Gideon said, interrupting her thoughts. "Yer more than I ever dreamed of, Lydia. It's like having two dollars for one slice of Annie's pie and then realizing you get the whole thing for that price."

"*Chust* a minute now." She tucked her chin and made her Pennsylvania Dutch stronger than normal. "Are you comparing me to pie?"

"*Ja.*" He reached out and touched her shoulder, running his palm down her arm like he did when he was calming a horse — only it was his wild emotions he was trying to calm. "What is it about you, Lydia?"

"Excuse me?"

"I've — I've never felt this way about anyone before."

"I understand. It's . . ." A dozen words flashed through her mind, too quickly to pick just one.

"What?" he asked.

"Never mind. It's silly."

"No, tell me," he insisted.

"Well, it's like when I'm working on a paragraph. My mind tries to capture what I'm thinking and feeling. I try to put into black letters on a white page a glimpse of a moment — a part of me. And then the words file into place, and I finally can stop holding my breath." Heat rose to her cheeks as butterflies spun and danced in her stomach. "You — you walking into my life made sense to a story that was just a jumble of words before."

He lifted an eyebrow. "Your story?"

She couldn't help but smile. "Our story."

They stood on the side of a road that smelled of sun and rain, and the patient gelding stood by. One of Lydia's stockings had pooled around her ankle and the wild grass from the side of the roadway, blown by the warm breeze, tickled her skin.

Since the first moment he'd taken her hand in his during their walk she knew this would happen. The emotions had bottled up like baking soda and vinegar, and they had no way to escape except through her confession. "I want my story to be *our story* from now on, Gideon. Listen to me. I sound so desperate, don't I?"

He glanced down at her and smiled, as if the words gave life to his soul.

She searched his face, waiting for him to say something — anything. "Aren't you going to respond?"

He shrugged. "I — I . . ."

"Mem always said my words were prettier than Bev Troyer's garden at times, but don't feel you have to, well, be all eloquent," she said. "Just say something . . . anything."

"Do I have to?"

He stepped closer until his dirty work boots touched the toes of her brown shoes.

He lifted her chin, his touch so gentle she almost wasn't sure if he touched her at all, and then he bent to her.

Lydia reached a hand and cupped it around the nape of his neck. Her eyes fluttered closed and his lips were on hers. More forceful, yet gentle too — as if it took everything inside to restrain his emotion.

Her breaths grew short, and his arm circled around her back, lifting her inches off the ground. Then, just as quickly, he released his grip.

Lydia slid back to the earth. Well, her feet touched down, but the emotions in her chest soared like the hawk doing a lazy circle around the field.

"Wait . . . we . . . I . . . ," he said.

"Are you trying to use the English language, sir?" She winked at him, feeling the heat again rise on her cheeks.

"*Trying* is a good word. Not succeeding." He lifted his brimmed straw hat and rubbed his forehead. "What I am needing to say is we — I — need to talk to yer dat. I don't want you to think that I will steal your kisses only to return to Ohio and break your heart."

"You better not." But then, realizing further what he was saying, Lydia crossed her arms over her chest. Was he really going to talk to Dat about the next step in their relationship — courting with plans to marry?

"How could I ever leave after I've had a taste of something so wonderful?" Gideon grinned.

"*Ja,* well, I've seen you and that pie." She touched her fingertips to her lips and took a step back. "And I have to warn you: don't try to eat yourself full. Two kisses are enough for tonight."

A chuckle burst from his lips. "Oh, you don't have to worry about that, Lydia. I have a feeling I couldn't get enough of you — I couldn't ever git my fill."

"*Ja,* well, before I get too caught up in all your fancy, romantic talk, I need to head home and fix dinner for Dat." She turned and moved in the direction of her house. The emotions between them were strong, and she thought of what Mem had told her more than once: *"Many things have been opened by mistake, but none so frequently as the mouth."*

If she stayed here, they'd just continue

with their sweet talking . . . and that would lead to even more kissing. It was wonderful, *ja,* and that was the problem. A prudent woman knew better than to indulge in a God-given gift before it was time to open it.

She waved. "Tomorrow, then."

"*Ja,* tomorrow. Hopefully I'll see you after school."

"Or you can stop by for lunch."

He winked. "Are you suggesting a lunch date with the teacher?"

"*Ja.*" She smiled. "I'd like that. I'll pack a lot, just in case someone's a *wutz.* Maybe even a whole pie."

Gideon chuckled, but instead of waving good-bye, he reached out and gently grasped her arm. "I have a feeling when I'm with you Lydia — a feeling of fullness."

"Like you've eaten too much pie?" She chuckled.

"Sort of, but it's my heart that's all filled up." His gaze turned serious. "We've been talking about all the holes — the pain — in our past, but the more I'm with you, the more the present seeps in and fills up those spots, like a healing balm."

"I like that, Gideon," she said, thankful that God had used them to bring healing to each other. Lydia thought of her birth mother, but then she pushed thoughts of

Grace out of her mind. Couldn't she be content with what she had? With what God had given her? "What a *gut* God to bring us on this healing path . . . together."

CHAPTER 29

The children had been so well behaved that Lydia decided to give them an extra five minutes of morning recess. The sounds of their laughter filled the air, and she smiled as she got out the modeling clay, eager to show them how to make imprints with leaves.

A minute before she was about to call the children in, the school door opened and a young woman walked in. She was petite with brown hair and a soft smile. Instead of a *kapp,* the woman wore a scarf over her head. Her clothes were plain but not Amish.

Lydia approached. "Hi, Marianna. Can I help you with something?"

"*Ja,* I came to talk to you about Ellie, my sister. I was visiting my parents last night and Charlie mentioned to me that Ellie's having a difficult time."

"I suppose. I mean, I'm trying my best. I don't know what I can do to help her."

"I am sure you're doing a *gut* job. Ellie was the youngest for many years until little Joy came along. I'm afraid we've all been easier on her than we should." Marianna glanced around. "But if you'd like I can stay today — to help with her. My husband and I don't have a *boppli* yet." A smile filled Marianna's face as she said the word 'husband,' as if that word still brought her great joy. "Ellie will not act up with me here — at least I hope she won't."

Lydia's brow furrowed; she was unsure of what to think. "I would love to have you, Marianna, but is it all right? I mean, I hate to say this, but I know they only allow Amish teachers and . . ."

"Oh, I see what you're saying. Because I'm not Amish you think the families won't want me here." Marianna touched her scarf. "I should explain. I live in this community, too, and these families are my friends. I don't attend the Amish church, but I believe much of the same. I'm married to an *Englisch* man, Ben."

"And your family doesn't shun you?" It was a question Lydia had wanted to ask.

Marianna crossed her arms. "If I was in Indiana, things would be different. For many years my parents wanted me to stay Amish more than anything. Yet they respect

Ben. He has a great love for God. My dat hasn't left his Amish heritage, but he agrees a love for God is most important. I feel the same."

Lydia enjoyed the gentle way Marianna spoke. It wasn't false humility, but a gentle peace that lit her face over knowing she'd done the right thing. Lydia hadn't seen such joy often, which seemed strange since she lived among a people who turned their backs on the ways of the world to do exactly what they believe God required.

"But I understand if you don't want me here, or if you need to ask."

"No," the word rushed from Lydia's lips. She touched her *kapp.* What did Marianna think of her returning to the Amish? Did Marianna believe you could love God with your whole heart within the Amish community too? She hoped Marianna could see the hope in her eyes.

"I would love to have you here. Ellie's a sweet girl. There has to be a problem with the way I'm handling things because she doesn't seem to have problems in other areas at all. In fact," Lydia hurriedly continued, "I'd like her to sing a small solo part in the Thanksgiving production next month."

Marianna cleared her throat. "I don't

think that's a good idea."

"Why not? She has such a sweet voice, and maybe if I can highlight her strengths —"

"*Ja,* but that would make her stand out. It would be prideful, don't you think, for her to be treated in a different and special way?" Marianna bit her lip. "Or at least that's what Mem would say. She wouldn't allow it, so it shouldn't even be brought up."

The peace that had been on Marianna's face before folded into wrinkles on her forehead, like ripples that circled out from a stone thrown into a still pond. A tendon tightened in her neck. Even though Marianna wasn't dressed Amish, perhaps she still struggled with what to believe — what to accept and what to walk away from. Maybe it was easier for Lydia to see since she'd walked away from it all for a time.

"I understand what you're saying, Marianna. Do you think you could talk to your parents about Ellie's solo? I grew up just like you, and I understand how we don't want to do anything that would lead someone to be prideful. I do have a friend, Bonnie — my boss, actually — who invited me to an *Englisch* church many times. I went three or four times, and once when I was there a woman sang. Her voice was amazing. I remember staying fixed in my seat. The strange thing is when I watched I wasn't thinking so much about the woman, but of God. I had a feeling in that moment that God had made her as she was to point to how amazing He is. Do you find that strange?"

"Not at all." Heat rose to Marianna's cheeks, and she glanced to the side and then back to Lydia again. "My husband — he is a musician. Just last year he was traveling the country and performing concerts. He has some music CDs . . ." Marianna seemed to struggle for words and the ripples in her forehead deepened into trenches. "And we're both praying about next steps. If Ben should do concerts or . . ."

"I know who he is, Marianna. Who isn't familiar with Ben Stone?"

Marianna didn't answer, but from the look in her eyes, Lydia saw that she still found it hard to believe her husband was so popular in the outside world.

"I know that story," Lydia continued. "I saw him on television. I watched the press conference after he was arrested. And I read an article in *People* magazine that he fell in love with an Amish girl."

Marianna gasped and covered her mouth with her hand.

"I'm sorry. I didn't know it bothers you."

"It doesn't bother me. I'm just always surprised to hear that people know." Marianna folded her hands, and brushed her thumbs over each other. "I jest wonder what people think of me. I mean, I'm the reason he's not doing concerts. I wonder too, if like that woman singer you spoke of, Ben needs to be using his talents to glorify God. It's something that I struggle with every day."

"God will give you the best answer, Marianna." Lydia reached forward and grasped Marianna's hands. "You might have never thought that you'd leave the Amish. And the truth is I never thought I'd return. But for some reason over the last few weeks, I've realized that God doesn't have one life path for all of us — even if yer Amish. It would be too easy to find it and set off on it without Him. Instead He has a unique path for each of us, and the only way we'll find it is by seeking Him, reading His word, and being open to His still, small voice."

Marianna nodded, and Lydia could tell she was listening and trying to figure out what that meant for herself, her husband.

Even after she said those words, Lydia knew it was something she needed to write down later. Sometimes she discovered a truth and it took a while to sink in, but other times she didn't realize she'd already embraced a truth until she spoke the words and felt the conviction radiate through her soul.

Lydia knew that for her, returning to the Amish was the right thing. Not because it was the only path to God. Not because she would be damned to hell if she chose a different way. But maybe because God knew she'd find Him better here than in the *Englisch* world.

" 'A dead fish can float downstream, but it takes a live one to swim upstream,' " she found herself saying.

"Excuse me?"

"It's a strange thought, I know, but even a dead fish can follow the easy way, the comfortable and known path. But it seems when we leave what's most comfortable to us, that's where we need God most. And when we need Him, and cry out to Him, then He comes to us, and it's in the coming there's life."

"You're a wise woman, Lydia."

"I don't think so." She chuckled. "But the words sound *gut* to me. Maybe they're something God's speaking to me too."

Lydia squeezed Marianna's hands. "I'm glad yer here. Thank you for coming in today and offering to sit with Ellie."

Marianna chuckled. "*Ja,* I offered, and I'm the one receiving your help. *Danki.*" She smiled. "I can tell we're going to have a special friendship . . . if you don't mind having an *Englisch* woman as a friend, that is."

"Mind? I don't think I'd mind at all." Lydia winked. "In fact, I have a feeling I can teach you a thing or two about being *Englisch.*"

The school door slammed open. Little Julia raced in, her dark eyes wide.

"Miss Wyse, we have a problem," Julia gasped, trying to catch her breath. "It's Ellie. She was there just a minute ago on the swing, but now she's gone!"

Chapter 30

"Ellie's gone?" Lydia tried to comprehend what Julia was saying. "Is she in the out-house? Or maybe playing hide and seek?"

Tears filled Julia's eyes as her lower lip trembled. "*Ne*, Miss Wyse. We checked the outhouse and all the kids have been lookin'."

Lydia and Marianna rushed outside. Lydia's eyes made a quick scan of the playground. "I should have been watching them. I'm usually out here."

David ran up to his sister. "Last thing she said to anyone, Mari, is that she was going to be first to get all her leaves for our collection."

Marianna grasped Lydia's arms, and they both looked down the dirt road to the rolling hills in the distance. The hills filled with trees.

Lydia's mind filled with thoughts of Gideon . . . and the danger of a child wandering off. "Do you think she went out there, by herself?"

Dear Lord, please don't let this happen again.

Charlie ran up too. "I can run home and tell Dat and Mem."

"No!" The word shot from Lydia's mouth. "We can't have any of the other children taking off."

Marianna's face was gray. "Lydia — Miss Wyse is right. It's not a *gut* idea."

Lydia hurried into the schoolyard. "In fact, everyone, please get up on the porch. *Danki.* I need to make sure no one else is missing. We'll send for help."

David stepped forward, straightening his frame so he stood the same height as Lydia. "I'm almost an adult. This is my last year of school. I can't just sit here —"

"*Ne,* David," Lydia interrupted, sending up another prayer for wisdom. "Marianna, can you run to the store and —"

"My phone!" Marianna reached into the pocket of her dress. "I didn't want this phone, but Ben insisted . . . in case of an emergency." Tears filled her eyes. "I'll call Ben, and I'll call the store too. Ben and Annie can round up people to come help search. I'll have him tell my parents."

"Yes, good idea." Lydia placed a hand over her pounding heart. "And have him call the

Carash house. Have Ben tell Gideon to come. I need Gideon to come."

Mrs. Sommer showed up first. She'd been at the store grocery shopping when Marianna got ahold of Annie. Someone called the Log Works too — the small factory right behind the store. Within ten minutes the schoolyard was filled with men and women trying to figure out what had happened, but Lydia didn't feel peace until she saw Gideon running up the road. He entered the schoolyard, and she hurried to him, resisting the urge to fall into his embrace.

"Are you okay, Lydia?" Gideon placed a hand on her shoulder. "I was on my way here for our lunch date when I heard what happened."

Lydia nodded. "Ellie is . . . gone. Someone called the sheriff. He is on his way. Mrs. Sommer is here. Ben went to go get Mr. Sommer, Abe, who's working on a house not far away." She covered her face with her hands. "This is all my fault. I was talking to Marianna. I wasn't paying attention."

Gideon's hands gripped her upper arms. "Listen, Lydia. She's in God's hands. He's watching over her, just like He was watching over me. You have to trust that."

She nodded and lowered her hands, and

then glanced around. "But a few guys from the Log Works have already headed down the road. Anything could happen."

Gideon's jaw clenched. "It's not. Do you hear? Nothing bad is going to happen today." He swallowed hard and looked past her to the children on the porch. "You need to remain calm. Those kids are counting on you. They need your faith, Lydia. You need to be strong for them." He released his grasp on her arm.

Lydia nodded. She prepared to turn but then paused. She took his hand. "Are you going out there — going to look for her?"

Gideon nodded. "*Ja.* You know I have to."

Lydia swallowed hard. "Yes, I know. But be careful, *ja*?"

"Yes, Lydia. I'll be careful."

Lydia turned and hurried to the porch. Some of the children — the girls — were crying. She forced a smile. "All these folks have come to help, but we have a big job to do too."

Josiah's dark hair tumbled in the wind and his eyes grew wide. "What's that?"

"We're going to gather around inside and pray. Pray that Ellie is safe and that those searching for her will be safe too."

Inside, they sat in a circle, holding hands, with their heads bowed in silent prayer.

Lydia sat closest to the open window so she could see what was happening, so she could know that something was being done.

A few sniffles here and there broke Lydia's heart, but her attention was on the sounds from outside.

"Everyone gather around!" It was Gideon's voice. "It's important that we search for Ellie, but we need to be safe."

"I'm not going to wait. That's my niece out there." Lydia recognized the voice of Ike Sommer, Abe's brother.

"I know, Ike. I know your fear. But we need to set perimeters. We need a system for checking on each other."

"I can't just stand here," another man said. Lydia lifted her head, noticing a dozen bachelors standing there, Micah and Amos among them. They turned and stalked off.

"Stop!" Gideon called to them.

They didn't listen, but continued with quickened steps.

"Stop!" Gideon called, his voice full of authority. "Because the worst thing you can do is save Ellie but die yerself!"

The two bachelors stopped and turned. "It's not going to happen," Micah spouted. "Who put you in charge anyway? Just because it's yer girlfriend who let her be lost in the first place."

"Not only can it happen. It did." Gideon strode over to them. "Twenty years ago. And you know it."

Amos scowled. "How do you know what happened twenty years ago?"

"I know because I was here. I was a little boy lost in these woods — and a man died looking for me. I —" Gideon's voice caught in his throat. "Can you guess how that makes me feel?" Silence fell over the group.

Amos's jaw dropped. "I had no idea." He turned to Micah, but Micah's face showed no surprise. Instead it showed regret. Did Micah finally understand how Gideon's past made him feel?

Gideon continued. "We will find Ellie. We will. We just need to do it as safely as possible. Understand?"

Micah and Amos nodded.

"Now gather up. It'll only take a few minutes and we'll get this figured out, but first . . ." Gideon looked back over his shoulder. His eyes met Lydia's through the open window. "But first," he continued, "we're going to pray."

Gideon scanned the crowd of those gathered. To his left Mrs. Sommer's hands covered her face. The shaking of her shoulders told him she was trying her hardest to hold in the wails. Annie stood beside her, as did a few of the other women from the community — Amish and *Englisch* alike.

The Amish around Gideon lowered their heads. All his life he'd only known silent prayer, but as he stood there, the words couldn't be contained.

"Dear Lord!" Gideon prayed out loud. Even though his eyes were closed he felt the other bachelors standing beside him shuffle uncomfortably. "I don't know how to pray. I'm not sure what words to use, *gut* God. But I do know that You know where Ellie is. Please, Lord, keep her safe. And keep all of us safe." A low moan escaped him. "And thank You for saving me. Amen."

Somber faces focused on Gideon. Men shuffled from side to side, and he knew they were eager to get started. A truck pulled up, parked, and two men jumped out — Abe Sommer, Ellie's father, and Ben Stone, Marianna's husband.

"Has anyone found her yet?" The words rushed from Abe's mouth.

"Ne." Ruth shook her head. "We're getting organized now." She looked to Gideon.

"We need someone to check yer house. She might have gone home," Annie commented.

"We stopped," Ben said. "We didn't see her."

Gideon nodded. "Take the older boys and check again. Have them look in every spot Ellie uses in her play. And a few of you . . ." He pointed to the bachelors. "Check the woods just to the side of the roads on the path from the school to Ellie's home. She's only six. You'd think she'd walk the way she'd be more familiar with."

Edgar walked into the schoolyard. He still had on his cashier's apron from the store. Dave Carash pulled in next, parking his car, and the two men approached the school together.

"The rest of you men — I'd like us to circle around Edgar and Dave. These two know this place better than anyone. I'd like them to tell us how to split up and let us know how to check in. Edgar, you don't mind, do you?"

Edgar's shoulders straightened and a slight smile brightened his face. "Gideon's right. I've seen what works and what doesn't." He looked to Dave. "We're going to break up the search into four quadrants — consider the crossroad here as the boundary. We'll do a one-mile sweep while we're waiting for Search and Rescue, calling her name, and looking for any sign of a little girl. Then we're going to meet back here in thirty minutes." Edgar glanced back at Gideon, then pointed a finger at all the men one by one. "If yer not familiar with an area, do not go into it, do you hear? We don't want anyone else in danger. No loss of life today, gentlemen. No loss of life."

CHAPTER 31

Lydia watched the clock, scanning the roadway for the sheriff's vehicle. It had been forty minutes already. She knew he had to drive up from Eureka, and she wished there was more that she could do than just wait. As she looked around, the other women and older men had the same look — a mix of anxiousness and helplessness.

Thankfully, all the parents had come to be with their children. Other women came from the community, too, and they huddled in small groups talking in low tones. Some mothers asked the children what they remembered — hoping to find another clue — but all said the same thing: one minute they'd seen Ellie on the swing, and a few minutes later she was nowhere to be found.

An *Englisch* woman approached. Lydia had only seen her around the store one or two times. "I knew something like this would happen." She narrowed her gaze and focused it on Lydia. "This is why Amish schools should be regulated. I don't understand how the government lets you people get away with this. One teacher — no helpers." The woman looked around. "There isn't even running water or an indoor bathroom in this place. And they claim to educate children here? It should be illegal."

Tears filled Lydia's eyes as she saw it from the woman's point of view. She didn't have a doubt that some of her Seattle friends would be saying the same thing. Instead of responding, Lydia only nodded. This wasn't the time to discuss it, but that didn't keep the words from adding another jab of pain to her heart.

Another *Englisch* woman, this one with cropped brown hair, approached Lydia, butting in. "Do we know why she left?" she asked. "Or could it be possible that someone took her?"

"I — Uh . . . I don't know. I suppose . . ." She hugged herself. "I hope not."

Why hadn't she thought of that? If she'd still been in Seattle, that would have been the first thing she thought of. But here?

"Actually, I do think she left." It was Marianna's voice. She approached and stopped next to Lydia, placing a hand on her arm. "I stopped by to talked to Lydia

— Miss Wyse — which is why she wasn't outside. I also think my showing up is what triggered Ellie's leaving."

Lydia studied Marianna's face. "What do you mean?"

"I bet Ellie saw me and assumed she was in trouble. After all, she has been acting up."

Lydia nodded, running a hand down her neck. "*Ja,* I bet you're right. Oh, poor Ellie." She stepped closer and put an arm around Marianna's shoulders. "Children do these things. They have so much to learn. We'll just keep trusting that God is with her, and that He'll lead the right person to her."

Marianna sighed. "*Ja,* we'll just keep trusting that."

Gideon climbed over the fence and strode across the pasture. He looked behind him, and there was the school. Straight ahead — less than a mile away — he could see the Sommer house and the Carash and Wyse places beyond that. He'd never seen any children in the pasture before — Blue's wild nature had made sure of that.

He resisted the urge to jog through the pasture. Instead Gideon walked with slow, even steps as his eyes swept from side to side. "Ellie! Ellie!"

Tension tightened his shoulders, grasped his throat. The fall day was warm — warmer than it had been in a few days. The air smelled of sunshine and pasture grass, but Gideon had to push away the feelings of darkness that threatened to creep over him.

His stomach ached and he wrapped his arms around himself as a shiver ran up his spine.

"Ellie!" Suddenly he wasn't Gideon the grown man. Inside he felt like Gideon the little boy. It had been dark, cold. He'd cried and cried, but no one had come. No one had been there. He'd wandered off. It was his fault. He deserved to be lost.

Gideon walked on, calling Ellie's name. He searched the high mountain pasture, but in his mind's eye he pictured himself alone.

Another prayer slipped from his lips. "Lord, be with this child. Watch over this child. Protect this child."

Even as he prayed for Ellie, his mind took him back to another group of men, women, and children — families that no doubt had been praying for him.

Gideon stopped short. In his thoughts he still saw himself, but for the first time he saw another there too. He pictured Jesus, with eyes of compassion, looking down at him. Jesus didn't point a finger or blame him for walking away. Instead He stood there, watching over Gideon, answering the prayers of the people of West Kootenai in unseen ways.

"You were with me." A burden of pain released from Gideon's shoulders as he said those words. "Jesus, You are with Ellie." His steps felt lighter and hope radiated through his heart. "You are with me still."

Something ahead caught Gideon's attention. A spot of red in the brown wild grass. At first he thought it was a small red shoe, but when he bent down and picked it up, he saw it was a red handkerchief. One that he used to wipe his sweaty brow when he was in this pasture training Blue. He must have dropped it.

"Blue." Gideon scanned the pasture. Where was the horse? He'd let him loose out here before heading to the school. Gideon looked toward the Carash house. Had someone put him in the corral? He wasn't there. Fear leapt to Gideon's throat again. Had Blue somehow gotten out?

Typically, Gideon couldn't take one step into the pasture without the horse seeing him and heading his direction.

Gideon turned in a slow circle again, his eyes searching the trees at the far edge of the pasture. *There.* He spotted the horse standing about twenty feet back in the trees.

What in the world? Blue was looking his direction, but he didn't budge. Gideon put two fingers to his mouth and whistled, but still the horse didn't move. The horse's ears were perked, but instead of coming to Gideon, Blue gently pawed the ground.

Gideon's heartbeat quickened again, but this time from excitement. He broke into a full run across the pasture, hoping Ellie was indeed there at Blue's feet. Hoping she was all right.

When he neared the horse, Gideon slowed his pace a little. A white *kapp* caught his attention. He wanted to whoop, but settled for a smile.

Ellie sat behind a tree stump. She motioned for Blue to go away. The horse paid her no mind. He stood patiently by her side.

Gideon approached with slow steps. "Ellie."

The young girl's eyes were wide as she turned to him.

"What are you doing?" he asked.

She lowered her head and shrugged.

"Did you run away?"

Ellie didn't look at him, but she did nod slowly.

"Do you know you have many people worried? Your dat, mem, your brothers. Marianna and Miss Wyse."

Ellie pouted. "Mari is mad at me. She's gonna tell Mem."

"Tell Mem that you weren't listening to Miss Wyse?"

Ellie nodded again.

Gideon opened up his arms, stretching them toward the young girl. "Tell you what: if you come back with me, I'll talk to Marianna, Miss Wyse, and yer mem for you. I'll make sure they don't get mad. In fact, I think they're going to be happy to see you. Would you like that?"

Ellie nodded again before standing and hurrying into his arms. Gideon picked her up, hugging her to his chest.

"Thank You," he whispered. "Thank You, God, for protecting this child. Thank You for watching over us both."

CHAPTER 32

Lydia looked at the piece of paper from Mem's Promise Box and smiled as she read the words:

"I will never leave thee, nor forsake thee," Hebrews 13:5. It had been the verse she'd pulled from the box last night, and it couldn't be more appropriate. God hadn't left Ellie. God had protected the girl — protected all of them. God had even allowed Gideon to be the one to find the girl. His face had glowed when he'd carried her on one arm into the schoolyard. The healing had begun — deep healing. She saw it in his eyes.

The community had gathered again to rejoice at the school. Everyone had been safe. God had taken care of them. They all decided to take the next day off — just for families to be together. Many women also stepped up and offered to come and help Lydia during the day. It had been their fault, they said, for expecting one woman to do so much. They didn't blame her. Rather they blamed themselves and were ready to make a difference. Lydia was thankful. Not only for the help, but for God's reminder that she couldn't do it all alone — and that He didn't expect her to.

Then, just as she and Gideon were heading out of the schoolyard to go home and tell her dat of the excitement, Dave Carash stopped them. He'd asked them to give him some time the next day. Said he needed to talk to them both. Lydia would have been worried if she hadn't seen deep compassion in the man's gaze.

Morning had come, and her heart was still full of thankfulness. Lydia had pulled Mem's rocking chair onto the porch and rocked as she waited for Gideon. When she saw him ahead she tucked the Scripture verse back into the Promise Box and set it just inside the door. "I'll be back in a little while," she called to Dat.

"*Ja,* have a *gut* time."

She couldn't help but jog down the steps and rush to Gideon. He wore a soft smile, but his eyes looked weary.

"Hey, you." She offered him a quick hug. "Looks like you haven't slept a wink."

He chuckled. "That obvious?"

"*Ja.* Are you worried? Do you think there is a reason Dave wants to talk to you?"

Gideon shrugged and they headed back the direction he'd just come. "I don't know. I've been wondering . . . into the wee hours. I suppose we'll find out."

Lydia slid her hand into his. "You know what?"

"Hmm?" he responded, but she could tell his mind was someplace else. "What's that?"

"I've decided that by your side is my favorite place to be."

His steps slowed slightly. "*Vell,* that's *gut.*"

"I wouldn't rather be anyplace else. Doing anything else."

"Nothing?"

"Nothing."

"Not even writing that book you've been wanting to write?" Lydia's spine straightened like one of the tall pine trees outside the window. Should she tell him of the notebooks she'd been filling up? Bonnie had texted that her notebooks made it and the manuscript was in capable hands. She had nothing for him to read. He'd have too many questions. Her heart beat against her rib cage, and though truth pushed against her lips, fear kept them corked. If he knew everything would he still love her?

She'd tell him — she would. She needed

the right words first.

An invisible wall rose between them. One she knew too well. A wall of shame that God's love and light were just starting to penetrate. She needed more time. Soon enough he could discover everything — her whole heart — for himself.

"No." She shook her head. "I like being with you even more than that. And," she hurriedly continued, changing the subject, "I've been thinking about something else too."

"What's that?"

"After the experience with Ellie, I've decided I don't want to live anywhere else. Everyone — well, almost everyone — was so *gut.* Amish and *Englisch* alike. It's as if the dividing line isn't as thick or long here. The Amish people here are different. I like that."

"*Ja,* they're good people." Gideon nodded. His eyes glanced over, and the worry eased. "They shed a few pounds of rules when they come to Montana, I think."

"What do you mean?"

"*Vell,* folks do not end up in Montana by accident. It takes a lot of work to transplant to a new place, even for a season. It takes boldness to walk away from a safe community into an unsafe one — and when I say unsafe I'm not talking about the rugged peaks or the dangerous animals like bears and such. I'm talking about the dangerous *people.* The Amish who attend prayer meetings. The *Englisch* who run to their Amish neighbor's side whenever there is a need."

Gideon softly chuckled. "And then there's that Amish woman who left the Amish to marry a singer who loves God. Marianna is such a rebel. Or even the parents who allow a recently *Englisch* woman to teach their children."

"I see what you're saying."

"It's as if, when the winds blow through the mountain passes, stretching down to the log homes, it's not just the wind. It's more like the Spirit of God that jest can't leave things be. He brings winds of change."

As if highlighting his words, a light, cool wind blew from the south, brushing Lydia's cheek and causing a collection of dry leaves to dance over her shoe tops as they scurried across the road.

Gideon watched them. "It's like when one removes the chaff from the wheat. Moving to Montana is like taking a pitch-fork to all yer thoughts and ideas, and as you toss them up the wind carries away the meaningless until only the wheat — the substance — remains."

"It sounds as if you've been thinking about this for a while."

"I have been thinking about it — even before this incident with Ellie — and over the last few days, I've talked to Caleb about it too. It seems only a special sort of people move here for good. Ones who are willing to face the wind and be sifted."

They neared the Carash house, and Gideon slowed his steps. The look in his eye told her he had more to say before he met with Dave.

"Sifted as wheat." She muttered those words, sure they were in the Bible somewhere. She was sure she'd just read it recently. That was one thing about Mem's Promise Box: the Scripture passages were good, but not enough. It was like nibbling on snacks when her soul wanted dinner. Because of that she'd asked Dat for Mem's Bible, deciding she needed to read it for herself. Discover more of God's promises for herself.

Gideon blew out a breath. "The sifting doesn't leave the wheat still and unharmed. It rips it apart. And I've been thinking, Lydia, what if the pain we all face is for a purpose?"

"What do you mean?"

"My parents always say," he continued,

" 'God's ways are best. We need to trust Him.' But that always put a bitter taste in my mouth. If He is a good God, a loving God, why do bad things have to happen? Why does a sweet Amish woman who just lost her husband have to deal with being raped?" Gideon squeezed her hand tighter. "Why does a *gut* Amish man who was trying to help a lost boy have to die and his wife and children suffer?"

Gideon sighed. "Yet, from the horrible act your birth mother faced, you were born — a gift to your parents and something I'm thankful for."

"And about that man — that Amish man that saved your life? Has God spoken to your heart about that?" Lydia softly bit her lower lip, hoping God had.

Gideon lowered his head but didn't answer.

Dear Lord, please help Gideon find peace for his soul.

Finding Ellie had only been the beginning of God at work. Lydia knew God wanted to do more. He always wanted to do more.

Dave Carash drove them to the last place Lydia expected: the small cemetery where many of the faithful citizens of the West Kootenai area were buried. Gideon placed a hand on Lydia's back as they walked through the simple metal gate. Her eyes moved to the grave where Mem had been laid to rest. A simple stone marker gave Mem's name and dates of her birth and death. Unlike the *Englisch,* the Amish she knew never wrote more than that. They never wrote things like *Mother, Sister, Friend* or even sweet sayings like *Forever in Our Hearts.* Maybe it was because the Amish believed it was God alone who saw the soul — who knew what was deep in a person's heart.

The last time Lydia had been there, Dat's neighbors had just started filling in a gaping hole in the ground where Mem's coffin lay. Months later, the grass hadn't completely grown over the spot, but some had. Time had passed and things had changed. But she had changed most during that time.

Lydia expected Dave to say something about Mem, but instead he turned to Gideon.

Dave cleared his throat. "There's one thing unique about this cemetery. My guess is that it's one of the few places where Amish and *Englisch* are buried side by side."

Gideon nodded and looked to Lydia. "As they live in life, so are they buried in death." Then his gaze left hers and focused again on Dave.

"Another thing: there are some folks buried here who lived here their whole life — like Edgar's parents. They were some of the first settlers to the area and rarely left these mountains." He strode over to a grave closer to the back corner.

"Then there are those who were only here for a few days."

Lydia's gaze moved to the headstone — the old weathered one from twenty years prior — and her heartbeat moved to her throat. She glanced from the simple head-stone to Gideon's eyes, a gasp escaping her lips. "Mose Umble. Is that him? Is that the man who saved you?"

She didn't need Gideon to answer. From the shocked look on his face, she knew that it was.

Gideon's legs felt like water. The world around him darkened to shades of gray. He heard Lydia's voice, but he couldn't make out her words. Dave was saying something too.

Focus, focus. He turned to Dave. "What did you say?"

"I was saying that, as you know, most Amish don't write anything but names and dates on headstones, but Mose's wife . . .

she insisted."

A thousand needles moved up and down Gideon's arms, and he was thankful for Lydia's hand in his. Thankful he could focus on the warmth and strength of her presence.

Gideon read the words again, his stomach clenching:

"Some things are worth dying for."

"It's, uh, a nice saying." He forced the words from his mouth.

"Yes, yes, it is. But it's more than that." Dave stepped forward. "If I would have known you were *the* Gideon, I would have told you the story sooner. I didn't know, didn't realize you were that boy. I didn't know until Ellie got lost. Hadn't put two and two together."

Gideon nodded, not knowing what to say. What to do.

"I'm not talking about the story of Mose finding you and coming upon that bear," Dave said. "I'm not even talking about the fall. I'm talking about what happened afterward."

Lydia stepped closer. "Maybe we should go to the restaurant, get a cup of coffee. Gideon, you're looking pale."

"Ne." He shook his head. "I want to hear at this place. I need to . . ."

Dave crossed his arms and looked up to the mountains. Then he pointed. "See those hills over there — where they sweep down and meet over? That's about where we found you."

"We?" Gideon asked.

"*Ja.* I was Mose's search partner. We were the ones that came upon you."

"But I thought — Edgar told me it was two Amish men who found me."

Dave shook his head. "Edgar has a good memory, but not perfect. I was the other one, but at the time I'd only lived here for six months. I wasn't even married to Susan yet. We saw you first in the distance. Then, only seconds later, we saw the bear lumbering your direction. Neither of us talked about what to do. It was like instinct. We started throwing rocks at that bear and shouting."

"And then you started running." Gideon pictured it in his mind's eye. The young *Englisch* man and the older Amish man, father of twelve. Of course the bear went after the slower one.

"We got separated," Dave continued. "It took us awhile to find him."

"Us?" Lydia asked.

"Yes, there were some other searchers who'd heard the yelling and had come. They found you still asleep. Two men carried you down the hill, while three others and myself went looking for Mose."

Gideon shook his head. He glanced to the grave again and then back to Dave. It was easier to look at Dave.

"I remember being lost, but I don't remember being found," he said. "You'd think I'd remember that. How was he . . . when you found him?"

"He was alive, conscious, but not doing good at all. We could tell right away that his neck was broke. We knew better than to move him, so one guy went down for Search and Rescue." Dave pinched his lips together and lowered his head, then looked up to Gideon. "Mose didn't have strength to say much. He started going in and out of consciousness then. He did tell me to tell his wife and children that he loved them. He also asked about you."

Tears threatened to fill Gideon's eyes. He nodded.

"I told him, *'Mose, the boy is fine. Not a scratch. But it doesn't look as if you're doing too good.'* Mose smiled then. It was a big, happy smile. Then he whispered, *'Some things are worth dying for.'* "

The tears came now. Gideon couldn't hold them back. He didn't want to. He released Lydia's fingers, and then his hands covered his face. Yet with the tears came peace.

Dave stepped forward and placed a hand on Gideon's shoulder. "I wanted you to realize that, Gideon. Mose knew, and he was thankful he was able to make the sacrifice. He was a father. He would have picked the same thing again if he had the choice. I know it. I told his wife, Myrna, what he said, and she insisted that it be put on his gravestone, no matter what the bishop said. She said people needed to know. Needed to remember."

"Some things are worth dying for," Gideon whispered the words. "I was worth dying for."

CHAPTER 33

More than anything, Gideon wished he could spend the day with Lydia. After leaving the cemetery with Dave yesterday they'd spent the whole day together . . . and he hadn't gotten enough of her. She'd been by his side as he worked with Blue. She'd watched him hitch the horse up to her dat's buggy for practice.

Gideon took a sip of his coffee and smiled at his own surprise. Lydia had fallen in love with Blue, almost as much as she'd fallen for him. She'd be overjoyed to discover he'd bought the horse for her as a special wedding gift. But first he needed to figure out the best way to ask for her hand. Last night, instead of his thoughts dwelling on the past, he'd been thinking about the future. A future with Lydia. Was she considering him as she stitched a quilt with some of the other ladies from the area? As she shared news of the community, did she plan a wedding quilt for them in her mind?

He glanced at the clock, wishing the hours would move faster. Lydia asked him to come that afternoon. He couldn't wait to see her, hug her, and maybe even sneak a kiss.

It was nearly lunch at the restaurant, and Gideon was about to order a piece of pie to go when he saw a woman park a red convertible outside the front door and stride up the porch steps in bright-red leather boots. She had straight black hair and an outfit that looked like something you'd find in the city. The woman didn't fit in. Not even close. Gideon ordered another cup of coffee and settled back in. What was this about?

She walked into the store. Edgar welcomed her with a howdy, but she barely glanced his direction. Instead she headed straight to the restaurant area. A group of women were seated there — both Amish and *Englisch.* She scanned the crowd, frowned, and then set her eyes on Marianna Stone and hurried toward her.

"Excuse me, I was looking for Lydia Wyse."

"*Ja,* I know Lydia." Marianna glanced around. "We all know Lydia. How can we help you?"

"I need to talk to her. It's very urgent. I

have an offer . . . Well, it's one she won't refuse."

"An offer? Like for another teaching job?"

"A job . . . of sorts." The woman's words trailed off. Then she glanced around. "Wow, it's amazing. This place is just as she described. I haven't been here for two minutes, but I already feel as familiar and comfortable here as my grandmother's living room."

Then she scanned the faces of the women and pointed a finger. "I'd guess you to be Marianna. So pretty, and you're not wearing a *kapp*. She turned her attention to Mrs. Sommer next. "And I'd guess you to be Ruth. Your daughter has your lovely features. And with your gray eyes — both of you — I'd recognize you anywhere."

"Wait a minute." Millie Arnold stood, brow furrowed. "What's going on here? How do you know my friends?"

Laughter spilled from the woman's mouth. "You have to be Millie — an older Calamity Jane if I've ever seen one. Not my words, of course, but Lydia's."

Gideon couldn't sit back and watch any longer. The tension was evident on his friends' faces. Seeing the women's anxiety tightened his own chest. He stood and approached the woman.

"Excuse me, ma'am. Can I help you?"

She was already smiling as she turned. And . . . were those tears in her eyes? "Oh, Gideon." A hand covered her mouth. "Dear sweet man. I am so sorry you feel that man's death is your fault."

Her words felt like a physical slap.

"Excuse me. How did you know about that? What's going on? Where did you come from?"

"How silly of me. Laura Fletcher from New York. I'm here to acquire Lydia's book. I've never done this — in all my life I've never traveled to meet an author. I've never gone out of my way like this, but I had to come. I had to discover if the place Lydia talked about was real."

"Book? What book?"

"She's calling it *The Promise Box,* but I thought a more catchy title would be *Amish Homecoming.* Anything with 'Amish' in the title brings bigger sales."

"Lydia is writing a book? She's writing about . . . us?" It was Marianna's voice. Gideon looked to her. Color had drained from her face. It looked the color of a cloudy Montana sky. Marianna glanced around. "All of us?"

"Oh." The woman's lips circled up. "I didn't think of this." She pulled out a log chair and sat. "I just assumed she would have talked to all of you. You mean she hasn't asked permission?"

"*Ne.* No one has asked permission." Mrs. Shelter stood and turned to the door as if she were going to stalk off and find Lydia herself.

"This must be some mistake." Gideon took a step toward the woman, towering over her. "Lydia would have talked to me."

"She should have, that's for certain. But I can see now why she didn't. It would have ruined everything." The woman pressed her hand to her forehead.

"Everything?"

"Oh, yes." She twisted a strand of silky black hair around her finger. "Everything would be different — you would have acted differently — if you knew Lydia was writing down your every word. If you knew that her sole purpose for being in this community was research for a book she's always wanted to write."

Pain hammered into Gideon's heart. *Her sole purpose?*

The woman peered down her nose at them. "If you knew that she had no intention of staying Amish, then you wouldn't have welcomed her into your lives so easily."

The woman's words were like a fist to his

gut. Gideon had never wanted to harm a female before, but this woman was different. It took all his restraint not to lift her to her feet, to turn her toward the women seated there, and to point out the obvious pain she was causing with her thoughtless words. Then again . . . why was he blaming this stranger? She didn't know any better. She'd assumed Lydia had gotten permission. Any decent writer would have.

No. It can't be the truth. Lydia's smiling face came to mind. He thought of the woman with wild red hair that had driven into town and how — in just a few weeks' time — she had returned to her Amish ways. She'd once again dressed in her Amish clothes. In two weeks' time she'd gone from driving a car to acting as if she'd been Amish every day of her life.

Gideon thought of a phrase he'd heard one *Englisch* man say to another once: "If it seems too good to be true, it probably is."

He sank into the chair and lowered his face into his hands. Voices rose around him, but he couldn't make out their words. He had come to Montana for the truth . . . and he thought he'd found love in the process. Now he knew it was a lie. Not only Lydia's love, but all she claimed to be.

Her mem's kitchen smelled like apples and cinnamon, just like it used to when Mem was feeling well and making Dat's favorite desserts. Lydia hummed along to one of her favorite *Civil War* songs playing through her head. Out of all the things she'd given up in returning to the Amish, her radio — her favorite bands — was the thing she missed most. That and flipping a light switch instead of having to light kerosene lanterns.

She had a good time at the quilting bee and had arrived home eager to see Gideon. She'd started baking right away. Was the saying "The way to a man's heart is through his stomach" true? Lydia already had his heart, but some tasty food would never hurt.

She pulled the second apple pie out of the oven and a smile filled her face. The crust looked perfect and in the center of the dough she'd used a cookie cutter to cut out the shape of a heart. She hoped her message was clear. He had her whole heart.

She heard the *clip clop* of a horse's hooves. Gideon approaching on Blue. She thought about setting the pie on the hot pad on the counter, but she couldn't wait to show him — couldn't wait to see him.

Lydia rushed out the door. "Look at you!" she called. "You're riding Blue! You've come so far!"

His head was lowered, but she still held out the pie. "Look, Gideon, I made this for you. There's a message in this pie. Can you see it?"

He halted the horse and swung his leg over, dismounting. He dropped the reins and strode forward with quickened steps. When he pulled off his hat and lifted his head, Lydia expected a smile. But instead anger flashed in his gaze.

"Gideon, is something wrong?" Lydia took a step back and placed the pie on the wooden bench by the front door. "Did something happen? You look . . . mad."

"Mad is an understatement, Lydia." He paused before her, gazing up to where she stood on the steps. "How could you do it?"

"What are you talking about? What do you mean?"

He ran a hand through his hair, then shook his head. "I should have known better. I knew you were up to no good the first moment I saw you driving down the road. It was too good to be true when you decided to become Amish again. Now I know it was just a lie."

"A lie? How could you say that? You were

422

there when I took my oath and was baptized into the church. It wasn't something I took lightly."

"I thought that," he spat, "but now I know the truth. Out of all people . . ."

He paused and turned.

"What? Out of all people, what?"

"Out of all people, you should know how much it hurts me when people withhold the truth."

She touched her fingertips to her forehead, trying to make sense of his words. There was nothing she'd hidden from him. Nothing, unless . . . her book had gotten into the wrong hands. *Dear Lord, no.*

"Gideon, please, you aren't making any sense." She hurried after him. Her stomach lurched, and she was sure she was going to be sick. "I don't know what you're talking about. Can you please just tell me what's going on?"

"There was a woman, a publisher from New York, who came into the restaurant today. She told me you were writing a book about the Amish in West Kootenai. She said you'd returned to the Amish to get the inside scoop. She knew things about us — all of us, Lydia. Things only you knew. Things I never wanted to tell a soul outside of the folks in West Kootenai. To hear a stranger talk about things — secret things."

"Bonnie, how could you?" Tears sprang to Lydia's eyes. "My boss. She must have shared. I sent her my story to have it typed up. I hate the computer. I told her to make two copies. One copy was supposed to be for you and the other for Dat. I never dreamed she would send it on to a publisher."

"If that was the truth, why didn't you tell me? You told me before your greatest dream was to have a book published. And yesterday when I asked you if you'd rather be with me or have a book published, you paused — as if you were uncertain. Now I know why."

"I was pausing because I was trying to decide if I should tell you then about what I'd written. But I didn't. I wanted it to be a surprise." Her lower lip quivered and her knees felt as if they were made of jelly. She took a step toward Blue, but even he snorted and took a step back. "I made a mistake, a big one. I should have told you about the book. I should have talked to my friends about it — the parents about it — but honestly it's not the reason why I returned and got baptized into the church."

Gideon cocked his head. Did he believe her?

"I mean, I did love writing about my returning, but it was my own journey. One I only wanted to share with a few people. Besides, we wouldn't even be standing here if I hadn't become Amish. My love for God is true, Gideon, and . . ."

"And?"

"And I knew it was the only way a good Amish man would look twice at me. I knew even if I loved God and chose to live for Him it wouldn't matter to you. You wouldn't have even gotten to know me unless I was Amish."

"So you were trying to lure me with lies?"

"I didn't think of it like that." Her heart felt crushed. "I honestly had good motives."

"I tried to believe that. I really did. I forced myself to believe that. But when you told me about the teaching job — how you had wanted it while you were still *Englisch* — I struggled. I wanted to believe you, but I could tell from your eyes that you weren't being completely honest. I pushed away the doubts that told me your change had more to do with what you *wanted* than what you *believed*."

Lydia's jaw dropped. "I don't believe you just said that."

"So no part of your returning had to do with making a name for yourself as a writer?

About holding a book with your name in your hands? When were you going to tell them, Lydia? When their names were in print and you had yer books in a fancy bookshop?"

She covered her mouth with her hand, attempting to hold back the sobs. "It was never about that. That was never my plan."

"I love you, Lydia, I really do. But I've spent too many years living with pain from my parents holding back the truth. Can you imagine making a commitment to each other but saying, 'I promise to tell you everything. Well, almost everything.' Every time I brought up your writing you changed the subject. You could have told me you were writing about your journey — you were keeping a journal or something. Would that have been so hard? Isn't hiding the truth just as bad as lying?"

Gideon lowered his head, pain evident on his face.

"I can't think anything worse than coming home and looking into my wife's eyes and wondering what she's keeping back from me that day — whether it's a big deal, or if it's just something small like she spent more at the grocery store than she'd planned on."

"It wouldn't be like that. I usually tell the truth. I've told you . . ."

"I know you didn't mean to hurt me, but you did. I also think before you can be truthful, you need to discover the truth — the truth of your mem."

"I don't think that's fair to her, to bring up that." Lydia swiped at her eyes. "Why would I want to do that to her, go to her and demand to know more? It's better to just let her forget."

"Do you think she's forgotten? How could she ever forget?" Gideon's voice softened.

"And how could you say you love me and not believe me? To believe some stranger over me?"

Gideon didn't say anything. He didn't turn to face her. His head remained lowered, his shoulders slumped. He just stood there stroking Blue's neck as if the horse was his only friend in the world.

CHAPTER 34

Lydia pushed Bonnie's phone number for the tenth time and groaned as the message came on again: "This is Bonnie. I'm out of the country on a work project. Leave a message, and I'll get back to you as soon as I can. *Adios!*"

She hung up. She'd left nine messages already. Mostly angry ones. How could her boss do that to her? How could she ruin everything?

The cell phone battery was getting low but the small pixel envelope reminded her messages waited. When she'd sent the text, telling Bonnie she was sending her notebooks and asking her to type up copies, she'd had five messages waiting. Now she had seven. Lydia dialed voicemail and waited.

Lydia, this is Bonnie. Have you thought any more about writing the book? I have a pub-

lisher in New York that's interested.

Lydia, this is Bonnie. It's been two weeks since your mother passed. I just wanted to let you know I was thinking of you. Call me if you get a chance.

Lydia, this is Bonnie. I got the last two books you finished editing. Thanks, friend! As always, you did a stellar job. Let me know when you're ready for more work. You know you'll always have a place with us.

Lydia, I hope you're checking your messages. Laura, the publisher, called me again. If you have anything — anything — she can read, please send it. She knows your work and is talking a six-figure advance. Just think about how that could help your dat.

Lydia, please, will you call? If you even have a notebook, scraps of thoughts on paper, just send it to me. I'll write up a proposal. I promise this will be worth your while.

Lydia gasped realizing that that fifth message was left just days before she'd sent her notebooks to Bonnie. *Of course. Bonnie must have assumed I was writing a book.* Lydia stood, knowing she had to talk to Gideon. She had proof now. She could explain. Or could she? It was still her word against . . . well, against everything.

Her phone flashed "Low battery." She listened to the next message.

Lydia, this is Bonnie. Your writing is beautiful. I know I shouldn't do this, but I have a friend who has been questioning her faith. I let her read about your mem's promise of a child. She was in tears. I was in tears. I'll let you know what Laura in New York says.

Then Lydia listened to the last message.

Lydia, I'm in Cancun with an author and we're brainstorming a book idea . . . and enjoying a little sun. There was a phone message from Laura. She's coming to West Kootenai. She wants to publish your book. She's your new biggest fan. I've got to go.

Lydia hung up the phone and saw the last of her battery was done. She put the cell phone back into the drawer, realizing her heart felt as drained.

A car pulled up and parked outside and then came a knock on the front door. Dat answered. It was a woman's voice. The woman's excitement was clear.

Dat came to her room and knocked.

"Come in." She could barely force herself to say the words.

Dat opened the door and looked in. "Lydia. Someone is here to see you. From New York?" His eyebrows arched in question.

Lydia had no strength to rise. Her whole body felt numb, including her heart. She'd ruined . . . everything. Hurt everyone. Her friends. The man she loved. She'd forsaken the community. They would never believe her. Never accept her. The words from her teen years echoed in her thoughts. *You will never, never fit in. You don't belong with them. You're not worthy.*

"Dat, can you get her number and tell her I'll call her in a few weeks. I need time. Time to think."

Dat stroked his long beard. "Are you sure?"

"*Ja,* Dat."

"But she says that she has something you'll want to hear. Something you won't want to turn down."

"I'm sorry." She rose and moved to the

door. "There are some things worth more than money and fame. I know that now, and I need to know what God wants me to do . . . next."

With a resigned sigh, Lydia leaned back against the wall and dropped her head. Her eyes slid shut and the tears came. Fresh, hot tears.

Gideon's words pierced her heart — harsh, accusing. He hadn't even listened when she'd tried to tell him the truth.

I don't belong. They were the same words that had replayed in her mind for so many years. She thought she could come back — that she could fit in. She'd done her best, but now? No one would ever accept her.

How many people had been in the restaurant? What had the woman said? She'd said enough for Gideon to know that she'd put his deepest secrets on paper. That she'd hidden the truth. Foolish, foolish. She should never have sent the book to Bonnie. She should have been like Mem and kept her most precious memories stored up, in a box, for herself . . . and maybe for her child someday.

Not that it would ever happen. Her heart ached over hurting him. Just when he was starting to heal.

Why do I stay? Her dat was the only

reason she could think of, yet she knew it wouldn't be too hard to convince him to go with her. Maybe to another Amish community as far away from this one as she could find?

Yet another question pounded through her temples even stronger: *But where can I go? Where do I belong?*

Lydia must have fallen asleep because when she awoke the last fading light filtered through the window. She could hear Dat in the kitchen, scrounging up something for dinner. She knew she should get in there and help him find something. Then again, pie for dinner never hurt. There was plenty of that.

Before Lydia could face the world — face Dat and tell him what had happened — she needed something. Needed hope. Lydia looked to the nightstand and was surprised to find Mem's Promise Box there. Dat must have brought it in while she slept.

She picked it up, feeling the smooth texture of the wood, and fresh tears trickled down her cheeks.

"Lord, I need something," she whispered the prayer. "I need direction. I need help. I don't know where to go or what to do. Please, Lord."

Lydia opened the box and unfolded the next slip of paper, and the words jumped off the page. A gasp escaped her lips and then the paper fluttered to the polished wood floor. She leaned down and picked it up.

She sat there for a minute, rereading the words in the gentlest of whispers: *"Can a woman forget her sucking child, that she should not have compassion on the son of her womb? yea, they may forget, yet will I not forget thee. Behold, I have graven thee upon the palms of my hands; thy walls are continually before me,"* Isaiah 49:15-16.

Could a mother forget her child? Wasn't Gideon talking about that very thing — that her mother would never forget?

Did her mother think of her? Remember her? Surely she must. But what did those thoughts bring? Pain? Hate? After all, her mother not only had to deal with being raped, but carrying the man's baby too.

Go to her. The words were the softest stirring within her heart and mind. *Find her. Go to her.*

"God?" Lydia looked over her shoulder at her bedroom door, almost expecting her dat to be there, but it wasn't her dat.

This was how God spoke, she was learning. Not with an audible voice, but with a gentle stirring in her mind that she knew wasn't from her own thoughts.

No. She couldn't do it. She wasn't strong enough to do it. Instead, she straightened her clothes and her *kapp* and hurried to the kitchen. She'd cook something up for Dat. It was the only thing she could think of to get her mind off the worst day of her life.

Dat stared at her over dinner. "Yer awful quiet tonight."

"Sorry. I have a lot on my mind."

He pushed his mashed potatoes around on his plate. "I heard what happened. A few folks stopped by the house when you were napping. Annie, Ruth — they wanted to talk to you."

"Did Annie tell you what happened at the store today?"

Dat nodded.

"I didn't do it, Dat. I wasn't trying to sell their story to make a name for myself."

"I know, dear. I never would take that woman's word over yours, but that's not what everyone else is saying."

"I'm sure everyone knows . . . and believes the worst. I'm never going to fit in. I'm sure they're going to ask me to stop teaching school. Who would want their children taught by someone they think is exploiting them — their children? I don't know why I thought I could fit in. I'll never fit in. I was thinking . . . about leaving."

"I think that's a good idea," Dat said simply.

Lydia's head jerked up, and she narrowed her gaze on Dat. He was the last one who believed in her, cared for her — was he giving up on her too?

"When Annie came by I asked her to book you a train ticket. The train leaves tomorrow at seven a.m. out of Whitefish." He pushed a white envelope toward her.

With trembling hands Lydia pulled the computer printout from the envelope. The location read Pittsburg, Pennsylvania. "I — I don't understand."

"There is a small Amish community in a town called Meyersdale. My oldest sister lives there with her family. So does your mother."

"My mother?"

"Your birth mother."

The wind picked up, blowing a scattering of oak leaves and pine leaves against the front door screen. She tilted her head as she gazed at her father, realizing for the first time he looked like an old man, his beard more gray than black, deep furrows on his brow. He didn't seem sad mentioning the woman. In fact, as Lydia looked closer, hope lighted his gaze.

"But why?" Lydia's voice wobbled.

"I've told yer mem for years that you needed to go there — to meet Grace. I —"

"Do you know much about her?"

"I know plenty yet. And I think it's time fer you to know."

"Is — is Grace going to be sad . . . mad to see me?"

Dat's face softened. "Not at all. I'm sure she's been wondering all these years." He cleared his throat. "Like I *vas* saying, I thought you should have gone sooner. You should have known more. Grace wanted us to tell you her story, but Mem refused. She was afraid."

"Afraid that it would hurt me to know the truth?"

"Not at all. Afraid that you and Grace would have a special bond. I think Ada Mae was afraid that a closeness to Grace would draw you away, but I could see that not knowing caused you to run."

"Does she know I'm coming?"

Dat nodded. "At least I think she does. Annie contacted a driver to take you from Pittsburg to Meyersdale. He was going to tell her."

"But — how did you pay for this?" Lydia

stood and hurried to him, wrapping her arms around his neck. "I'm sure it cost a pretty penny."

Dat shrugged. "There's always a way. Besides, some things are worth more than money. The truth is worth far greater than that."

"I don't know. I'm still not sure if I can go."

"I heard a bishop preach once that the process for maturing as a Christian believer happens when we learn to replace lies with truth. It seems you've been making up your own story and the roots have gone deep. Think of truth as a garden hoe. Only truth can burrow down and dig out the bad. And more than that, truth will fill in all the empty spaces left by the hole. God's truth can do it."

Lydia nodded, understanding. "But after that? What then? I don't think anyone will ever believe me again. I don't think I can stay here. Their stories about what happened have already taken root in the community."

"Jest take the steps and do what God is asking you to do, Lydia. Trust Him to take care of the rest."

CHAPTER 35

Exhaustion caused Lydia to sink deeper into the passenger's seat of the *Englisch* driver's van. Her eyes had fluttered closed more than once on the drive from Pittsburg to Meyersdale. After three days on the train that was to be expected, but as soon as she saw the town's name written on a small white sign her eyes popped open. Was it possible that after all this time she'd finally get a chance to meet her birth mother?

Lydia squeezed her ribcage with both arms. Anger fought with excitement. Anger at who, though? At Mem for keeping her away from Grace, and Dat for letting her? At Grace for giving her to another couple, despite the circumstances? At the man who'd violated Grace, of course. Yet also the realization that if wasn't for that horrible act she never would have been born.

What did Grace look like? Did Lydia take after her in any way? What about her brothers? Did they live near? And what about extended family? She gazed out the window — fully awake now.

How can I be angry? Mem did what she thought was best. Grace too. And Dat. She hoped he was right, that this was what was best for her now. She didn't want to think about Gideon. She couldn't think about him. She didn't want to think about anyone in West Kootenai or what they thought of her. She'd cried enough tears on the train. She could only deal with one overwhelming problem at a time.

Lydia dropped her head back against the seat. Except for small talk, the driver had been silent most of the two-hour trip. "I should have asked you sooner, but do you know Grace, the woman I'm going to meet?" she asked the older man.

"Do you mean your mother?"

Lydia gasped. "How did you know she was my mother? Did the lady who hired you tell you that?"

"No, ma'am. I've lived here over ten years. I know all the Amish, including Grace. If you aren't her daughter I . . . Well, you just have to be, that's all."

Lydia nodded. She didn't want to ask any more questions. She wanted to see for herself. She wanted to hear the story — the truth — from Grace's mouth.

The van parked at a small, white farmhouse just beyond the Amish school. On the porch sat three men. All of them were thin, blond, and in their late twenties. All of them watched the van with eager anticipation. *My brothers.* She studied their faces as she exited the van, amazed they all looked so different. Although . . . each had something similar too — similar to the face she saw every day in the mirror.

Seeing their smiles she couldn't hide hers, even if she tried. She moved up the sidewalk and the tallest one opened the gate for her. He extended his hand.

"Lydia, I'm Isaac. I'm the youngest." He grinned. "Well, other than you." Isaac's eyes matched hers perfectly, as if they were cut out of the same mold.

"Isaac. It's a *gut* name — and the first time I've ever said the name of a sibling."

He smiled and then stepped back. The second man stepped forward. He was nearly as tall as Isaac, and his smile was lopsided, just as Mem claimed Lydia's smile was when she was excited about something.

"Lydia. I love that name. And I've prayed for you often."

"Thank you." She placed a hand over her

heart. "I know the prayers helped, even when I didn't know about you — about all of you." She lifted her eyes again. "And what was your name?"

"*Ja,* sorry. Abram."

"It's wonderful to meet you, Abram."

She looked past him to the man who stood on the top of the porch steps. Tears streamed down his cheeks and his shoulders shook. She hurried to him and offered him a hug. Her brother — her oldest brother — had a hard time letting go.

Finally, he released her and stepped back. "I'm Matthew, and I've never been considered a softy before . . . until now." Matthew wiped at his cheeks with the back of his hand. "It's just that I remember you most. I held you when you were jest a few hours old. I asked — I begged — Mem if we could keep you, but she said that you were a special gift . . . and the best gifts were the ones given away."

Tears moistened her cheeks. She nodded, not knowing what else to do, to say. "And where is Mem?"

Just then the screen door squeaked, and Matthew moved to the side. An older woman stood there, thin with blonde curly hair. Lydia gasped, understanding what the driver had meant. There was no denying she was this woman's daughter — no denying at all.

"Lydia." It was just one word, but it sounded like birdsong after a spring rain.

Lydia took two steps forward and the woman's arms were around her. Grace clung to her for a moment and then pulled back. "Won't — won't you come inside?"

Lydia nodded. The house was old, simple. It was clean and looked like a dozen other Amish homes she'd been in. Yet this one was different. This home belonged to her mother.

"I hope you don't mind," Grace said. "The guys are heading out for a spell. They wanted to stay, but I told them I wanted to spend time with you first. So they'll be gathering later with their families — well, the oldest two, at least. Matthew is married to Hannah and they have two boys. Abram's wife is Miriam, and they have twin girls. Isaac isn't married — not yet — but I know our *gut* God has a special woman out there somewhere."

Lydia nodded, and when Grace motioned to the sofa, she sat. The woman's smile was gentle, kind.

"Would you like a cup of tea?" Grace asked.

"*Ne.* Thank you."

"I'm so glad you're here," Grace said.

"*Ja,* me too . . . although this is different than I thought." Lydia looked around.

"What do you mean?"

"I don't know what to say. I expected tears. I thought it would be hard for you to see me."

"Hard? *Ne,* I could hardly sleep. I've thought about you so many times. Almost every day."

"But . . . after what happened. I'm sure those were bad memories. Mem — Ada Mae — told me the truth about how you became pregnant." Lydia sat back, not understanding why she was bringing this up. She knew she should ask Grace about her life, their community, but something inside couldn't talk about everyday things when the truth of the past hung so heavy on her heart.

"Bad memories . . . There were some." Grace lowered her head. "The rape, *ja.* It was horrible. I was so fearful, living on the farm alone with three boys. I blamed myself for so long. For months, I would replay in my mind what I could have done differently. Every noise kept me awake. I thought he'd come back. That he'd hurt the boys."

Grace shook her head. "But that was so long ago. Those fears are only distant memories. They have no place in my life anymore."

Lydia nodded, surprised in a way that Grace talked about the past without pain twisting her face. Lydia couldn't think about what had happened to her mother without pain filling her stomach. In a way she envied Grace for moving past it . . . for not clinging to the pain.

"It's *gut* to see you. You have my freckles," Grace said with a smile.

Lydia touched her nose. "*Ja,* I do. I never liked them . . . until now."

Grace told her a story about her freckles and how once she'd let her brother play dot-to-dot on her face. "I thought it was funny when he drew a tree jest like the one by the *dawdi* house out back, but Mem wasn't impressed." She then went on to tell Lydia about her aunts, uncles, and cousins. There was quite a number and Lydia knew she wouldn't be able to remember half of them — and who belonged to whom — even if she tried.

And then, when Grace paused in her story, Lydia scooted forward a bit on the edge of her seat. "So when you look at me . . . do you see him?" She placed a hand to her throat and fear coursed through her. The words were out. It was the question

she wanted to know more than any other —
and she couldn't believe she'd asked it.

"*Ne*. I see a beautiful young woman. An
unexpected gift that offered healing."

"Healing?"

"*Ja*. For when I wanted to hide in my
pain, to lock myself away, God forced me to
think beyond myself and my own fears. I
had you to think about. My boys."

Lydia wanted words to say, but none
came. She instead reached a hand out and
placed it on Grace's arm.

"I only wanted to protect you. Seeing how
beautiful you were — holding you —
brought healing. You were an expected gift.
A gift from God to help me overcome and
survive the experience."

"Is there a reason . . . why you didn't raise
me?"

"*Ja*. We lived in such a small community.
For weeks I didn't report the rape, but after
another young woman was violated I knew
I had to." Grace's hands quivered, and
Lydia reached over and held them, holding
them tight.

"I'm so sorry, Lydia. You'd think I'd be
over it by now, it's been so many years."

"Don't be sorry." Lydia's chin trembled.
"I expected it would be hard on you. That's
why I didn't want to come. I didn't want to

heap pain upon pain."

"Dear girl." Grace removed a hand from Lydia's grasp and placed it on her cheek. "Seeing you doesn't bring pain. Seeing you reminds me that God can turn even our darkest moments into something beautiful."

"It's easy to say," Lydia sighed, "but harder to believe, isn't it?"

"*Ja,* I spent many days crying. After Jacob and Ada Mae took you away I wasn't sure that I wanted to go on. My sister Betty came and stayed with me. She tells me now that I'd wander the house —" Grace's voice caught in her throat. "In my sleep I wandered the house looking for you."

"I'm so sorry." Lydia wished she had something better to say.

"I have to ask." Grace rose and moved to the window. "Why did you decide to come now?"

"There's a special man. He . . . he saw me as something beautiful. He convinced me that even though I was conceived in a horrible way God had a purpose and a plan for my life."

"I believe that too. In fact, it was your life that saved many from more pain."

"I don't understand."

"Even after I heard that another woman had been raped I didn't want to go forward

447

— even though I knew the man responsible. Everyone was talking about the other woman's rape around town, and I didn't want them to be speaking of me in such a way."

Grace turned back and looked at her. "Then I started feeling unwell. I thought it was the flu. I was knitting with a neighbor and I fainted. She called a driver and they took me to the hospital despite my protests. I was badly dehydrated. And . . ."

Lydia placed trembling fingers to her lips. "And they discovered you were expecting?"

Grace lowered her head and folded her hands in front of her. *"Ja."*

"So did you tell everyone then?"

"I told a few of the women from our church. I needed their prayers. Soon word spread. The police came and they spoke with me. I told them the truth."

Grace was silent then, as if she was lost in her thoughts.

"Did they ever catch *him*?" Lydia refused to use the word *father* to describe the man who'd done such a thing.

"Ja. I'd heard he'd gotten a job in town. He wasn't there, but his boss told them where he lived. As the police were driving there they saw movement at a house. They stopped to check and he was there, attempt-

ing to break into another Amish woman's home."

Lydia's mouth dropped open. "If you hadn't told . . ."

"If I had told the truth sooner, another woman would have been greatly hurt that night. Yet even as I told the police what happened I tried to convince myself that it was someone else I was talking about. I had no choice at that point but to tell the truth — otherwise other rumors would have started about my pregnancy."

"I can't imagine having a pregnancy under those conditions," Lydia said.

Grace returned to the sofa and sat down beside her. "The pregnancy became easier as I separated the act from the child, but there were so many people who didn't believe what I said was true."

"What? Really?"

"*Ja.* Some from the community — Amish and *Englisch* alike — thought I made up the story to hide a secret affair. That's when I made my decision about who should raise you."

"I don't understand."

"Our community is small, Lydia. I didn't want you to be raised being 'that child.' No matter what story those in the community believed there'd always be comments, looks, stares. No child should have to face that." Grace forced a smile. "I talked to my midwife one day. I thought she might know a couple. Joy bubbled over. You should have heard her speak of Jacob and Ada Mae. She said they'd been married nearly fifteen years with no children. She told of their love for each other and their love for God. I knew then that they were meant to be your parents."

"They were *gut* parents." Lydia pressed her lips together as memories scrolled through her mind. Times spent cuddled together telling stories. Times with Mem in the kitchen or with Dat in the barn. They hadn't been perfect parents, but they'd been *gut* and she couldn't imagine any couple loving her more. "You made a *gut* decision, Grace."

"Passing you into the arms of another was an act of love greater than I could do in my own strength. God was with me." Grace let out a sigh. "God is with me still."

Lydia nodded even as her heart filled to overflowing. How had she been chosen to receive such an amazing gift — not one but two mothers who loved the Lord and sought and followed Him?

"Darkness is a fact of life on this earth. I've had many emotions over the years; I won't tell you I haven't. I've been angry at God at times — first losing my husband and then losing you. I was mad at Him for not protecting me from that man. And I was mad at myself. I *vas* the one who approached that man, after all. Any way to blame myself, I did. I was innocent, but I didn't feel that way."

"Oh, Grace."

Grace held up a hand, and Lydia knew. Grace didn't want her sympathy. Grace wanted to be heard. "I didn't believe anything would be all right again. I felt so empty after you left. I wanted to keep you, to raise you, but I loved you too much for that. I couldn't have loved you more, daughter. I hope you see that."

Lydia nodded, realizing Gideon was right. "I do see that, Grace. I know the truth now . . . and I've never felt so whole."

The truth was like water seeping into parched ground. Lydia's soul soaked up Grace's words. How long had she been wanting to hear them?

"When we give God our problems and bitterness, He is faithful," Grace said. "God doesn't promise to keep us from all the troubles in this world, but when trouble comes He will be with us. My husband — God rest his soul — would remind me of that. When he knew he wasn't going to make it, and that the cancer would prevail, Sam told me he was going . . . but that God never would leave me. Sam told me to lean into God as I leaned into him all those years. It's something I've done, and it's the one thing that got me through —"

Grace's words were interrupted then by the sound of voices. "What's that?" Lydia asked, rising and moving to the window.

"It's a gathering for you, Lydia. An ice-cream social. There are so many from town — from our family — who wanted to welcome you home."

Is this where I belong, Lord? Me and my father?

CHAPTER 36

Lydia forgot how tired she was when she saw the gathering of people at her brother Matthew's house next door. She lost track of names beyond that of her mother and brothers. She received so many hugs that she had to readjust her *kapp* twice.

She lost a game of horseshoes to her two twin nieces, Emily and Katie — neither of whom she could tell apart. She also ate her fill of ice cream and tried to burn some of it off by pushing numerous children from their community on the tire swing.

She was just about to get off her feet and spend time sitting near Grace when Isaac approached.

"Lydia." Concern was on his face. "There is someone here to see you. Said he came a long way."

Gideon?

Her breath stilled, Lydia turned, following Isaac's gaze. She knew she should explain who Gideon was, but she couldn't think. Instead she hurried to the edge of the yard where he stood.

"Gideon? What are you doing here?"

"*Vell,* I came to deliver a message. Flew in a jet plane to get here too, if you can imagine that. The bishop said it seemed like the only right thing to do, considering the situation." He had a serious look on his face, but Lydia was happy to see that the anger was gone.

"I have to tell you, Gideon. I'm sorry I hid the truth. And you were right: my motives weren't completely pure. I did want the job, a book, and . . ." She let her words trailed off. "I wanted you."

She offered a sad grin. "But God used that in a way to bring me to Him. Even when I was thinking of me, soon He became the most important part. If I could do it over I would have told you everything. I would have admitted my desire for the teaching position sooner. I would have made you read every word the moment I wrote it."

"I know, Lydia. I shouldn't have focused so much on the 'why.' I should have concentrated on the woman you became. Sometimes people hide the truth because they're afraid of causing pain, but sometimes . . . well, what they set out for is different than what they get. Truth does that." Gideon's gaze narrowed. "Now, will you let me share my message?"

Worry rushed over her again at his words and the serious look on his face. What could be so important that he'd come all this way?

"A message? Is everyone all right? Is it Dat?"

"Your dat is fine, but I'm supposed to give you this." Gideon reached into his pocket and pulled out her cell phone, handing it to her. He attempted to hide a smile, but he wasn't doing a very good job.

"You forgot this," he said.

"*Ja,* I know." She frowned and looked down at the phone. It was turned on and the battery was fully charged. The notification said there was a voicemail. She shrugged and checked it.

Lydia, this is Bonnie, and I need to apologize. I messed up and I'm certain you believe I've ruined your life. I didn't understand your text. I thought you were sending your manuscript to be submitted to the publisher. I went to West Kootenai and explained everything. Your friends are great. Gideon's a keeper. But I'm getting ahead of myself. Because I need to ask your forgiveness too. Because I did something else you might not forgive me for. I

455

let the others read the manuscript. I only had one copy but they passed it around. Edgar said to tell you he smiles more than you said he did. I believe Gideon has a note from the others. Don't hate me.

Lydia hung up and looked up at Gideon. "Do you have a note too?" she dared to ask. He nodded and reached into his pocket to hand her a folded square of paper. She unfolded it and saw that it was written in a neat handwriting. Marianna's signature was first, but then dozens of others followed it. Annie, Susan, David, Julia, Edgar . . . and many more. Even Ellie's name was written in scribbly script at the bottom.

Laughter spilled from Lydia's lips, followed by tears of longing. "Ellie's practicing her letters." She glanced up at him. "What is this?"

Gideon smiled and nodded to the paper. "Jest read."

Dear Lydia,

We hope this letter finds you well. Yer dat told us where you'd gone and we're keeping you in our prayers. I filled in for school, and though I'm sure I'm doing fine all the children miss you and send you love. They can't wait for you to return. They'll probably be upset with me for saying this, but they talk about you like *Englisch* children speak of rock stars. After all, they've never known someone famous. But I'm getting ahead of myself.

I have to admit I was shocked and hurt by the arrival of that publisher. To hear that you'd been writing about us . . . We all felt betrayed. Mem later told me she went to confront you. Annie said the same. They both said they were glad you were sleeping at the time. They were thankful for the *gut* Lord for keeping their words where they belonged — in their mind, not on the tip of the tongue.

We heard you left Sunday morning. Your dat gave us your note apologizing on leaving without setting up a teacher first. We called a special meeting after church service. Many were mad, angry. We felt we'd been fooled. That's when an unexpected visitor showed up.

Bonnie caught a special flight from Mexico to Kalispell. I can't even imagine such a thing. She'd come to apologize to you . . . and to clear the air. She said you sounded distraught on your messages, and she felt horrible for the miscommunication. She also told us that from what she'd read she believed you truly had a change of heart and had returned to the Amish with pure motives. She let Gideon read a few parts first. Then we thought it would be wise to let our bishop read your words too.

His wife, Katie, sat beside him while he read, and when we noticed tears in their eyes we demanded we know what was there. Elton read us a few parts aloud — about the first time you read a note from the Promise Box and what God's promises meant to you. Not one cheek stayed dry that moment. All of us rejoiced at God's *gut* transformation.

One man didn't seem too happy about the pages being read. Micah rose and we thought he was leaving the room, but he walked to Gideon instead and offered an apology. After that Gideon stood and told us the story about Mose's death. He confessed to us that his words to you had been unkind right before you left, and he wept and questioned how he'd accused you when he'd been freed from so much. Only a few of those who'd been around awhile knew about the words on the tombstone, and all of us agreed that part of the story needed to be written too. So you have more work to do.

All that to say that we understand, Lydia, that you wrote the story in the notebook for yourself, Gideon, and your dat. But, dear friend, would you honor us by sharing your story with the world . . . and our part in it? The lady from New York said she is still interested. Edgar was the one who went to the guest cottage where she was staying and asked. He also asked if the book would make enough money for the publishing company to be able to donate enough to pay for an indoor bathroom and running water in the school. She said she believed it would.

Lydia reread Marianna's signature and all the others again too. She chuckled. She couldn't help it. Joy flooded over her. She looked to Gideon and thought for a moment that his smile was even larger than hers.

She turned the piece of paper over, expecting there would be more to the letter on the other side. Instead the page was blank.

Lydia's forehead wrinkled. "I don't understand."

"That's because I asked Marianna to stop

there. I told her I wanted to fill you in on the rest."

"*Ja,* what's that?"

"It's time to go back now, Lydia."

"To West Kootenai?"

"*Ja,* it's time to come home. There's something else too." Gideon sank to one knee.

Lydia gasped. "What are you doing?"

"Edgar told me this is how the *Englisch* do it. And since you like stories I thought I'd share one."

"A-all right."

Cheers rose up from behind her, and Lydia glanced back over her shoulder. The eyes of all the guests at the ice-cream social were fixed on her. It only seemed right that her family — *her family* — should be part of this.

Lydia turned back around and offered a smile to the man she loved with all her heart.

Gideon cleared his throat and peered up at her with emotion in his dark eyes. "You know, Lydia. I'm not from Montana. I went for hunting. I wanted to take home some antlers and have a *gut* story to tell."

Despite her nervous excitement, Lydia chuckled. "Well, you didn't get what you bargained for, did you?"

"*Ne,* I didn't get what I bargained for. I got better than that. For all my life I just wanted to be noticed. I wanted to belong. Now I realize where my true home is."

"Where's that?"

"Because of Jesus my eternal home is with my Father God. But on this earth, as far as I'm concerned, home is where you are."

"What are you saying?"

"I'm saying, if you still have the first Saturday in December free, I'd like to occupy your time that day by making you my wife."

Lydia tapped the side of her cheek. "Well, I'll have to check my schedule . . . but I think I'm free."

Free. The word echoed in her thoughts. What had that Scripture said: *"The truth will set you free"?* She hadn't understood that a few months ago. To her, freedom had been setting off on her own path, living by her own rules, plotting her own course. But true freedom was not only turning your life over to God and letting Him have control, but also looking back and seeing His path — seeing where He'd been and what He'd already done.

True freedom: it was something inside. Something beautiful.

What had Gideon said once? A free horse

461

wasn't one that roamed the hills. A free horse was one that submitted to his master in trust and understanding. She'd never felt freer than at that moment — not even when she'd packed a bag and headed into the *Englisch* world.

Lydia opened her arms. Gideon stood and swept her up in his embrace. He placed the softest kiss on her lips, and then he pulled back.

"Will you promise to love me . . . even when I mess up? Even when I don't always do the right things, say the right things?" he asked.

"*Ja.*" Lydia nodded. "Because I know it's in those hard times that God will use the pain to mold us into the people He's designed us to be. People who can love, who can forgive, and who can point others to freedom." Lydia sighed. "And . . . the truth is, Gideon, you are jest as handsome when you're angry as when you're happy with me."

Gideon chuckled. "And you're jest as beautiful when you're seeking an answer as when you've found one. And I have a feeling on this earth there will be plenty of both. And also enough of God's grace to lead the way."

"*Ja.*" Lydia smiled. "I agree. And to you,

Gideon, I make a promise: that I will always tell you the truth from now on. Unless you ask about who ate the last piece of pie — then there are no guarantees."

Gideon kissed her once again. "Is that a promise?"

"*Ja,* it's a promise . . . one I'll write down and slip inside Mem's Promise Box."

"Or write in a book?" Gideon cocked an eyebrow.

"Or write in a book." Lydia smiled. "If that's what the good Lord wants. But we'll just have to wait and see."

"Just as long as you write me as dashing and handsome." He smirked.

"I have no reservations about that." She snuggled her cheek into his neck. "Then everyone will know what a *gut* God we really have. One who brings hope out of pain and love. Well . . ." She looked up at him. "One who can introduce love on a beautiful summer day when two ordinary people least expect it. And One who can remind us that some things are worth living for."

"I like that, Lydia." Love radiated from his gaze. "I like that a lot."

Lydia pulled back and took his hand. "Now come and meet my mother. Oh yes, and my brothers too. I'm sure they'll put you to the test to see if you're the man for their little sister."

"I won't mind." Gideon chuckled and hurried forward, leading the way. "And for some reason I think the prayer of a young boy is being answered. A prayer he prayed as he gazed down at his baby sister."

Lydia glanced up and met Matthew's gaze. "*Ja,* Gideon. I think yer right." The tears in her eyes matched those of her brothers. "And you know it's a *gut* God to design something like that. A *gut* God indeed."

NOTE FROM EDGAR

I almost missed the wedding, but it's the publisher's fault. She arrived with an updated manuscript and asked me to be the first to review it. Lydia did a good job, but I do smile more than she said. I also like how she told the conversation between me and Gideon when I told him about Mose's death. It's a good writer who can do that — seeing as she wasn't there.

Back to the fact that I almost missed the wedding. I was still sitting at the store counter when I saw the buggy driving by. Lydia's dat was driving, with Lydia in the seat. I could see her front teeth from all the way in the store because her smile was so big. Blue did a fine job being hitched up too. Fine indeed. I always knew there was a good horse under all that wild.

I told the publisher that the only thing I'm worried about is that too many folks might come this way. We're real folks in this part, you know, and the girls in the kitchen — well, they can only make so many pies.

Oh, I made the publisher promise something else: that she'd keep the name for Lydia's book. *The Promise Box.* I like that. Much better than *An Amish Homecoming* — no offense. And I have a feeling Ada Mae would like that too.

Yes, Ada Mae, I can picture your smile too. Bigger than the Montana sky as you see what God did with your girl. He's good about keeping His promises like that. But of course, that's something you already knew.

Edgar

DISCUSSION QUESTIONS

1. Lydia Wyse returns to the Amish community of West Kootenai, Montana, after the death of her mother. How does Lydia look at the community differently when she returns this time?

2. Gideon Hooley is an Amish bachelor who has traveled to Montana to hunt in the fall. While he is there he starts working with a horse named Blue. How are Gideon and Blue similar?

3. *The Promise Box* is set in a small Amish community in Northwestern Montana. What did you like best about the setting?

4. Lydia is *Englisch* when she comes to town. Why did she leave the Amish? What did she gain by being part of the *Englisch* community? What did she lose when she

left the Amish?

5. Gideon returned to Montana to learn more of his past. Do you think his parents did the right thing by hiding the truth? Why or why not?

6. What new situations in her life made Lydia consider returning to the Amish?

7. How are Lydia's eyes opened once she starts reading notes and Scripture verses from Mem's Promise Box?

8. What did you learn about an Amish person's baptism into the church through Lydia's experience?

9. Gideon and Lydia had a quick attraction to each other. What character qualities drew the other?

10. Lydia became involved with the Amish community through interaction with the women and through teaching school. What do you like the most about Amish communities?

11. What do you think is the underlying theme of *The Promise Box*? How does this

theme play out in the lives of the main characters of the novel?

12. At the end of the novel Gideon discovers a truth in the graveyard. Why did this gift mean so much to him?

13. When the publisher arrived, the whole community believed the worst about Lydia. How did their rejection lead her to discovering ultimate truth?

14. At the end of the book Lydia meets the family she never knew. How do you think that meeting impacted her from that point on?

ACKNOWLEDGMENTS

Thank you to Amy Lathrop and the Litfuze Hens, Caitlin Wilson, Audra Jennings, and Christen Krumm for supporting me and helping me stay connected with my readers . . . and for the gazillion other things you do!

I wildly appreciate the Zondervan/HarperCollins Christian Publishing Team: Sue Brower, Daisy Hutton, Bridget Klein, Katie Bond, and Laura Dickerson. Also thank you, Leslie Peterson, for your great editing! I also send thanks to all the unsung heroes: the managers, designers, copy editors, sales people, financial folks, etc. who make a book possible. My name may be on the cover, but I couldn't do what I do without all of you!

Thank you to my friend Martha Artyomenko for reading through the manuscript and giving great input!

I'm also thankful for my agent, Janet

Grant. Your help, inspiration, and guidance are priceless.

And I'm thankful for my family:

John, I love that God brought us together and that I can share my life with such an amazing man! Thank you for believing in my dreams. Thank you for encouraging me and helping me every step of the way.

Cory, Katie, and Clayton what a beautiful family you are. You are proof that God answers prayers. I love you all, and I am in awe of how you love and serve God together.

Leslie, I couldn't be more proud of you, my beautiful daughter. I can't believe it's almost time for your college graduation. The years have flown by, but I love to see who you are growing in to be. I know you'll have an amazing story of your own. God has a beautiful plan unfolding for you.

Nathan, it seems in the last year you've come into your own. Keep doing great in college. Keep dreaming, and keep writing! Keep loving God with all your heart.

Alyssa, so many of my emotions of adopting you into our family have found their way into this book. You are one of the greatest gifts God has given me. Our family is blessed because of you. You are a joy and a delight!

Grandma Dolores, your love and laughter

brighten my day. I'm so glad to have you in our home. What a treasure.

Finally, to the love of my life. Thank you, God, for adopting me into Your family. The treasure of Your Word — Your Promises — has transformed my life.

The employees of Thorndike Press hope you have enjoyed this Large Print book. All our Thorndike, Wheeler, and Kennebec Large Print titles are designed for easy reading, and all our books are made to last. Other Thorndike Press Large Print books are available at your library, through selected bookstores, or directly from us.

For information about titles, please call:
(800) 223-1244

or visit our Web site at:
http://gale.cengage.com/thorndike

To share your comments, please write:
Publisher
Thorndike Press
10 Water St., Suite 310
Waterville, ME 04901